I0524834

PRESUMPTION

of

PATERNITY

A NOVEL

S.B. REDD

Presumption of Paternity is a work of fiction. Names, characters, places and incidents are either products of the authors' imagination or are used fictitiously. Any resemblance to actual persons, living or dead, business establishments, events or locales is entirely coincidental.

Copyright © 2012 by S. B. Redd

All rights reserved, including the right of reproduction, in whole or in part, in any form. No parts of this book may be reproduced in any form or by any means without the prior written consent of MavLit Publishing, LLC.

The quote used on the cover of this book appeared in the September 2011 *Midwest Book Review* for *Warped Intentions*.

ISBN-10: 0983115281
ISBN-13: 978-0-9831152-8-1
Also available in E-Book
ISBN-13: 978-0-9831152-9-8
Library of Congress Control Number: 2011921956

Printed in the United States of America

𝓜

MavLit Publishing, LLC
www.maverick-books.com
P. O. Box 1103
Irmo, S.C. 29063

Cover Design: Maverick Literary
Cover Photos: Getty Images

PRESUMPTION

of

PATERNITY

A NOVEL

S.B. REDD

Author's Note

Each year, thousands of married men face an unwelcomed and oft-times emotionally agonizing experience of learning that the child they presumed to be theirs is not. They learn either through the wife's admission, or through some other source.

Some define it as being cuckolded. Some are quick to cast judgment, declaring the man got exactly what he deserved. Some say it doesn't matter; the man should accept responsibility without asking any questions. I call it a shame and I emphatically don't apologize for my stance.

What makes paternity fraud such a hot-button item is how it is handled through our legal system. In the majority of states, the legal system elects not to deal with it. The legal system maintains decisions and actions must be made with consideration of a child's best interests; however, these decisions are not based on sound judgment. Rather, they are politically expedient and without any explanation.

When an explanation is offered, if any, many of these states say that there is a presumption of paternity once a child is born within a marriage. Therefore, it is more politically acceptable to ignore the truth even after it's been unequivocally proven and uphold a lie, extorting a man into paying child support for what isn't his.

Is it fair?

No.

Is it reality?

Very much so.

I am very much aware that there are men who choose not to acknowledge paternity or accept responsibility for their children. This is one of the reasons why the child support system has evolved into a multi-billion dollar enterprise that has the full backing of state and federal law.

Yet, I'm also aware of the many stories in which people whisper behind a husband's back. Sadly, he has no clue, and these hush-hush stories are more than likely to follow him all the way to his grave, the wife's grave, and to some extent the rest of the child's life.

With this book, you're going to see a different angle taken towards how paternity fraud is conceived, how it evolves, and how it is ultimately dealt with. In the end, there are often no winners in these nasty happenings, but such is life.

Make it happen, everyone!

S.B. Redd
s.b.redd@maverick-books.com
www.maverick-books.com
www.mavlitpublishing.blogspot.com

PRESUMPTION

of

PATERNITY
A NOVEL

S.B. REDD

Chapter 1

If there was ever somebody who could catch Garner Davis at the most opportune of moments it was Miriam Davis. He had long since accepted that she was just being herself. If he had any protests about her calling him, she'd remind him that she was the one who put him into this world, and she had the license to take him out of this world, no matter how tall or old he got.

This time, she caught Garner just as he passed exit No. 37 on I-20 eastbound. He was returning home from attending Divine Grace Fellowship in Pelion, a two-stoplight rural community in Lexington County just twenty minutes west of Columbia, South Carolina.

"Just what are you doing at 1:30 in the afternoon?" she inquired. "You know I should come down there to South Carolina and whip you for not calling me."

Garner rolled his eyes. He knew she had a legitimate argument. He was supposed to have apprised her of what came from Vernise Aikens' fake pregnancy ploy and other warped intentions. It was now late June, more than four months after that episode and her death, which occurred when she crashed into the side of a bookstore building trying to kill him and Tamira Lake.

"Don't tell me you've been busy at the station."

"I won't," Garner answered.

"So how have you been, little boy?"

"I've been getting along. I started going to church lately. I think I've found a place that I like."

"That's good. If there's one thing that I do regret with you, Norris, and Carla is I did not make church a priority in your lives. But I did the best that I could—"

"I know you did," Garner interrupted her. "And I have no complaints about that."

Garner figured that he would divulge about Vernise only if Miriam had asked. Not wanting the conversation to linger, he was quick to inquire about his eldest sibling, Norris, whose wedding to Shalinda was scheduled for October.

"I hadn't talked to him in a couple of weeks, but it looks like he's still dead serious about marrying her," Miriam answered.

"I guess that means I might have to take some time off and come up there."

"Probably," she said, sighing. "But you know what my feelings are about Shalinda. If it weren't for those three boys that they have between them, I'd have nothing to say good about her." She went on to volunteer to him that his sister, Carla, and his nephew, Corliss, had moved to a new apartment complex, and that meant Corliss would likely be starting the eighth grade at a new school. "I'll give you her new address whenever she gives it to me."

Miriam's voice was somber, and she was not her usual jovial with Garner.

"Are you all right?" Garner asked.

"I'm fine," she answered, sighing once more.

"So what's up; how's the court reporting business?"

"We're doing fine in spite of this economy. We might have to hold back on expanding into northern Virginia until after the election, but other than that I can't complain. We're still paying the bills and meeting payroll, and I'm able to pocket a little bit along the way."

Miriam's tone still had not changed. There was silence that lasted for several seconds.

"Mom, are you sure you're all right?" Garner asked.

Miriam took in a deep breath. "I'm sure I know how they got in contact with me, but Aaron's sister, Flora, called me this morning to say that he had a brain aneurysm last night."

Garner had not given any thought concerning Aaron in years. "What are you talking about?"

"I'm saying that Aaron was found dead with some woman, in of all places, here in Richmond. Flora said the woman ran out of her place naked and screaming that he died on top of her."

"No, you got to be kidding me?" Garner instinctively pulled off the freeway, exiting at No. 61; he continued the phone call from the parking lot of the newly constructed Wyndham Hotel.

"I wish that I was," Miriam said. "I just got off the phone with Flora We talked for about an hour, and you're the first one I've called."

He excused himself. He parked his Infiniti G35 Coupe and turned off the engine. "I barely remember Aunt Flora. Didn't she have a couple of kids?"

"A couple of kids?" Miriam reacted. "How about six of them." She also reminded Garner there were two uncles and another aunt on Aaron's side of the family tree, and among them there that had to be at least ten first cousins and countless other second and third cousins.

This was the first time there had been any interaction between Aaron's family and Miriam since before she served him a restraining order in August 1985, when Garner was ten. Aaron was escorted away by Richmond's police department, and Miriam's divorce became final a year after that incident. Aaron never bothered to contact Garner or his siblings, and they vowed amongst themselves never to have anything to do with Aaron or his relatives.

Miriam told Garner that Aaron found a new job at a major trucking company in Baltimore, Maryland, and he commuted regularly between there and Richmond. There was word that Aaron had fathered a daughter who should be at least high school age; Miriam said she was not aware whether the child's mother was the same woman whom Aaron died atop of while having sex.

"Are you thinking about going to his funeral?" Garner asked.

"I don't know. I mean, I was married to him for fourteen years out of my life. I might have been the only woman who ever stood up to him."

Garner admitted to Miriam that he might have felt even more emotional had it happened to ol' Spencer Watts' crazy ass.

"I know you're going to tell Norris and Carla about all of this, but do you think we all should go to the funeral?" he asked Miriam.

"Well, Flora's telling me that Aaron's funeral will be on Thursday here in Richmond. But I have something else to tell you." That was followed by a lengthy pause.

"What is it?"

"I've always been honest with you all your life, and I admit that sometimes I protected you a little more than your brother and sister," she said, biting her bottom lip afterward. "The truth is that he was not your father."

Garner straightened up in his seat. "Did I hear you right? You're saying that Aaron Davis was not my father?"

"That's what I said, little boy."

"I don't understand."

The derisive things that Aaron once said to Garner invaded his mind along with the things he remembered Miriam saying in an attempt to soothe the sting of those comments. Then he considered the obvious differences between himself and his siblings—they were dark skinned as opposed to his fair complexion and light-colored eyes much like Miriam. Now it had made sense to him.

"Then who is my father?"

Miriam hesitated. "The day I gave birth to you it was both a time of joy and sorrow. Joy that I had you. Sorrow because I could never share that day with the person whom I know would be proud of you."

Garner became impatient. "Just give me a straight answer."

Tears began welling in Miriam's eyes. She excused herself and returned turned with some tissues.

Okay," she said, composing herself. "Your real father was a hell of a man. He was smart, well spoken, and focused. I met him when things weren't going well with Aaron. Obviously, we had an affair. But it was not the typical affair. We really were in love, and I was going to take both you and Norris and leave Aaron. Then I got pregnant with Carla, and our plans changed. I don't regret anything. But I guess I am sorry for myself that I never had a chance to start a new life much sooner."

"You said 'was' while you described this man. So what was, or is, his name?"

"His name was Garrett Chaney. He was a military officer, a lieutenant colonel."

"Why do you keep saying was?"

"This is tough, little boy," she answered; it was obvious that she started choking back tears. "You father died of a rare muscle disease while you were in high school. Remember when you were in tenth grade, I told you I had to leave town for a week, and I had your aunt Leah to watch over y'all?"

"Barely."

"The hardest thing was visiting him in that hospital room. I don't know how I got over it, knowing that it would be the last time I'd ever get to see him. I guess because I had you, I was able to make it without having to be committed to some mental ward."

"What did he have to say?"

Miriam's face beamed with pride. "A lot of our last conversation was about you. He would have been so proud of you—I know that I am."

"Whoa, it's a good thing that I got off the freeway when I did," Garner reacted. "This is a lot to handle."

"If there's anyone who could handle this kind of news it's you, Garner," Miriam said. "That was why I never petitioned for child support from Aaron because I did not think it was fair that he should pay for another man's child; he'd already paid enough by helping to provide a place to stay and put food on the table while we were together."

Numbness began creeping in. He struggled to say the right words to his mother. "You still didn't answer my question. Should I go to his funeral?"

Miriam pursed her lips. "I don't know, Garner. I just don't know. Personally, I'm not even sure if I want to go because my heart was never with that man even before Carla was born. I've never said this, but Carla is the result of him forcing himself on me one night when I begged him not to—I guess you understand why."

Garner nodded. "That you wanted to make a clean break, if you could."

"Yes, something like that."

Both Garner and Miriam tried speaking at the same time.

"I'm sorry if I've disappointed you," she said. "I'm sorry if it appears that I've lied to you after all these years. But I promised myself that I would never tell you anything about it unless Aaron died before me. And if I had died before him that was something I was willing to take to my grave."

Chapter 2

Each night over the next couple of days, Garner called Miriam with more questions about Garrett Chaney. That was the only way he could manage any sleep.

"How could you have lived all these years without telling me?" he asked.

"Am I being put on trial?" Miriam retorted. "I told you that I'm sorry you had to learn about it this way."

This was the first time that Garner had ever felt any sense of betrayal by Miriam. All these years, he saw a nurturing, loving side to her; it still did not register with him that she was capable of withholding truth from him.

"You know, I never saw myself any different from Norris and Carla. Maybe because you instilled in us that we were family, and we had to stick together. You always said you loved us and treated us all the same. Now I'm beginning to wonder about that."

"I worked very hard not to show any preference among all three of you just for that reason," Miriam said, feeling discomfort with the tenor of Garner's questions. "Did any of you ever lack for any major thing when you were growing up? I worked two jobs to make sure all of you had what you needed, in case you forgot."

"No, I haven't forgotten. What I have a problem with is that you had an affair with another man, and I'm the result of it. Now I see why Aaron used to say things the used to say to me."

Yeah, you have those light-colored eyes and that high yellow skin just like your mama. You must think you're more than everyone. I'm here to tell you that you ain't shit, just like your mama—shit makes me fuckin' wonder if you're really my child.

All those years, Miriam felt she managed to disprove any of Aaron's assertions that Garner was not his child. In her defense back then, she used to remind Aaron about his infidelities. But all that did was create more animosity.

Sighing, Miriam tried to smooth it over once more, although it was the first time in more than two decades.

"Garner, sometimes a woman can only stand so much of being mistreated. I was in love with Aaron in the beginning, but then I saw he was not the man whom I first met when I was twenty-one years old. Maybe I wasn't the woman that he first met, too. I think you can understand that, don't you?"

"Yeah, I understand that much."

"I went through a lot in that marriage. I dealt with his drinking, his beating on Norris and Carla, his talking to you the way he did, and then him raping me," she said, cringing. "I did not look for Garrett. Sometimes, I think maybe God saw my tears and gave me new hope."

"So, how did you two meet?"

That memory brought a smile to her face. She recalled his sparkling gray eyes, angular face, and his insignias on his light green military officer's shirt that suggested he'd accomplished much. He definitely would have been a more plausible choice among her family members.

"Of all places, the store I used to work at."

"I don't believe it. A checkout line at Ukrop's?"

Miriam adjusted herself to an upright position on her bed, brushing back her hair. "I remember giving him his change. But it was the way he took the change out of my hand that just did something to me. I think he knew it because he came back to the store an hour later and made sure that he got in my line."

She recalled that he gave her his telephone number, but she kept it unlike other men who attempted the same thing. Several days passed before she considered calling him. When she did contact Garrett, he seemed genuinely glad that she called him. That was hardly the way Aaron treated her.

She went on to tell Garner that early on she would meet with Garrett whenever she'd visit family members who lived near the military base in Fayetteville, North Carolina. She believed that Garner was conceived during the Fourth of July weekend in 1974. Those visits continued even after Garner was born.

"So, you mean to tell me those times when you had to go out somewhere you were with him?"

"Something like that, not always. We knew we didn't have a lot of time, but we sure made the best of it. You know, that was before cell phones and the Internet. So we wrote a lot of letters, and he was very careful to call me only when I was at my other job on Grace Street."

Miriam went on to say Garrett was older than her—eleven years—but at that point in her life she never gave any thought about their age difference. He was far more mature than Aaron, in her opinion. She suspected having already served ten years in the military before they met coupled with two-and-a-half tours in Vietnam had a lot to do with it.

"I should be able to find something out about him through the Army," Garner wondered aloud.

"I do know that Garrett was from Hutchinson, Kansas. He had a white father and black mother, and he had a brother, Preston, who I think still lives in Wichita, Kansas. We've talked on a couple of occasions. He's the one who told me where Garrett was buried at Arlington National Cemetery. I've gone up there to visit his grave every year since all of you left home."

Garner wondered whether his biological father experienced some of the same things that he experienced because of his complexion.

Miriam had once told him about some of the same petty jealousies that she experienced during her childhood and throughout her adult years.

Then he mused, "You know what? You used to say if God intended for me to look more like Aaron it would have already happened. Looking back, I guess there was no way possible."

"There was also no way possible I could have told you anything about it back then. I think it would have confused you even more. Do you understand now why I said some of the things that I said?"

"I do, but all of this is going to force me to look at Norris and Carla all too differently."

Miriam sighed, recognizing the predicament that she created. "All I can ever ask of you, Garner, is to treat your brother and sister like I've always taught you to treat them. You're now thirty-three years old. It's not like you're thirteen."

Eyelids becoming heavy, Garner finally acknowledged that he needed to end the conversation and get some rest. He planned on driving up to Richmond in the morning rather than flying.

Chapter 3

The greeting between Miriam and Garner was awkward at best. Garner showed no willingness to hug his mother and give her a peck on her cheek.

"Are you staying long this time, or are you going back to South Carolina after the funeral?" she inquired, walking towards the kitchen.

"I hadn't decided," he said. "Ever since I left here for college, I can't say there's been much incentive for me to come back here."

Miriam had bought a new five-piece natural wood kitchenette since his last visit to her home in Chesterfield County. Taking a seat with her back to the window, she reminded Garner that she was still his mother despite what he might think of her.

"I don't expect you to understand everything that happened between me and your real father," she said. "But one thing I do expect of you is to be mature about this—"

"Mature? I think I have been mature about this," Garner interrupted, leaning against the counter adjacent to Miriam. "I'm here for some man's funeral who isn't really my father's, and I'm here talking to you, aren't I?"

Garner stared at Miriam longer than usual just to convince himself that he was still talking to the same woman he had known to be his mother. Although now five months shy of her sixtieth birthday, she still was a stunning sight. She still was on the slender side, although her hips had widened two sizes since she met Garrett nearly thirty-five years earlier; her naturally auburn colored hair still was not dependent on Ms. Clairol; her skin was vibrant, void of age spots as common with lighter skinned people; she showed subtle signs of aging around the creases of her green eyes.

Shaking his head and sighing, Garner said, "If there's any consolation, I'm not ashamed of you. I'm just disappointed to find out when I'm thirty-three years old."

Miriam invited Garner to sit at the table; her eyes began to mist. "I can't tell you how proud I am of you, little boy. I know Norris and Carla are finally doing all right for themselves. But out of all my children, you're the one that I always believed who could do big things in life."

She reflected on the countless times she used to tell Garner that, yes, he was different from the rest. "There are some things you just can't teach . . . you always wanted to succeed in life. I think it was naturally in you."

He stood up with his arms opened, beckoning his mother. She was eager to get that customary hug and peck on the cheek from him.

"Did you bring much with you?" she asked, relieved in countenance. "I have your room all ready for you, and I planned on making your favorite cubed steak, rice and gravy, and cornbread for you."

When Garner returned with his clothes, Miriam informed him that she had already contacted both Norris and Carla about Aaron's funeral. He thought he might be able to sway their opinions since he made the drive up from Columbia.

Garner had not spoken to Carla since Mother's Day—he last spoken to Corliss back on his birthday in March.

"Is this my youngest and only sister?"

"Is this my knucklehead younger brother?"

They both shared a laugh. Carla updated him on the transition she'd undergone since her promotion at First Principal. Her diction and voice was much like Miriam's.

"I never thought I'd be the one talking like Miriam when she says that some times she feels like she's an adult baby sitter."

"You mean they're that bad?"

"Lawd, yes!" she said, nodding emphatically. "It makes you wonder who their parents were. Things that you would think are common sense: Telling a customer thank you, understanding that the customer's doing you the favor by calling; if it weren't for the customers, they wouldn't have a job."

"Sounds like you have a department full of black people."

"Humph, more like a department full of niggers. The bad thing about it is that you're trying to help them keep their jobs."

Garner cleared his throat and explained his reason for calling her. "It's not like I'm hell-bent on going to this man's funeral. I just thought it would be respectful—even if he didn't deserve it."

There was a prolonged silence between them. Carla had closed her eyes, calming herself down. To this day, the memories of Aaron's beatings remained vivid with her.

"You know he'd be in jail today for some of the things he did to us, Garner." She admitted that's why she's been a little soft on Corliss because of what happened during her childhood.

"I perceive that means you won't be going at all?"

"That's right, Garner. I won't. I have nothing else to say on it. Corliss knows he had a grandfather named Aaron Davis; that's all he needs to know about that man."

"I understand," Garner said.

Miriam, who plopped down in her recliner, joked that Garner should have taken her cue that Carla was uninterested in attending Aaron's funeral. But Garner had to convince himself—a trait she said he inherited from his biological father.

"As much as I admit that I was attracted to him, I really tried to resist him. But Garrett was a persistent man," she recalled. "Once he wanted something, or he decided that was what he was going to do, that was the end of conversation."

"If this man was such a great guy, why didn't you just divorce Aaron and get on with your life?" Garner reacted.

"It's never as easy as you would think," she answered, staring off to her left. She let out a sigh. "There's so much you have to think about when there are kids involved."

She excused herself to go to another part of her house, returning with a small photo album. She sat next to Garner and pointed at a picture of her wearing a white dress and Aaron, who sported a short afro, a thin mustache, sideburns, and wearing a dark suit. They were an attractive, young couple that appeared to have the future at their beckoning.

This was the first time that Garner had seen Miriam and Aaron's 1971 wedding picture since childhood. She offered Garner a chance to browse through the photo album. There were several baby pictures of Garner and his siblings along with some old black and white pictures of herself. Stuck between a picture of Carla and Garner's great-aunt Doris Brazelle was one taken of Aaron on Christmas Day: he was in a drunken stupor, collapsed in his living room chair, and managing a weak wave towards the camera.

Tapping at the picture with his index finger, Garner erupted into a hearty chortle. "Remember that picture?"

"Who can ever forget it?" Miriam replied. "He stayed out all night and staggered back in the house that morning. Didn't you take that picture, Garner?"

"Was that a Polaroid picture, or one from the Kodak camera? You know if Aaron ever found out somebody took a picture of him like that, it would have been an ass beating."

That was among the few mild memories either Miriam or Garner had of Aaron. Glancing at the picture once more, Garner felt compelled to question whether Miriam was really in love with Aaron.

She replied, "I thought I was in love with Aaron, and I went along with whatever he said and wanted." But she also admitted that pride motivated her to remain in her marriage. She wanted to prove her family wrong about Aaron not being the type of man she should have married.

"When did you know things were not right?" Garner asked.

She reclined back in her chair. "It wasn't long after we married that I found out that he was not all that attentive, and I wondered whether he really wanted to accept any responsibilities. [And] when he started staying out at night drinking—the typical bull that some wives go through with their husbands—I had to have been about six months pregnant with Norris [in 1972]. I complained about it, but it didn't make things any better. I'd call home to my family; they didn't want to have anything to do with it."

Miriam motioned for Garner to answer the phone since it was closest to him. He was not familiar with the older lady's voice on the other line. Flora introduced herself to Garner as his aunt, prompting him to grimace. She was among the least favorite of Aaron's relatives among Garner and his siblings.

"It's been so long since I last talked to you, Garner. You had to have been eight years old, or something like that," Flora said. "Is Miriam around?"

Flora, four years older than Aaron, was the only one among Aaron's siblings and first cousins whom Miriam could stand. The rest of his relatives that she was familiar with were itinerant, boisterous party goers and carousers who incorporated every four-letter word possible into their vocabulary.

Whenever the Davis clan hosted large family gatherings, they were usually held at Flora's house just off North Laburnum. Miriam was comfortable with bringing her children around Flora because she and her husband, Lonnie, appeared to have lived a responsible lifestyle.

Another reason for Miriam holding Flora in moderate esteem was because she was the one who volunteered to give her something borrowed for their wedding as a token of accepting her into the Davis family.

"Miriam, I just wanted to remind you the wake is at seven o'clock at the Singleton Funeral Home on Hull Street," Flora said. "I know it's probably been at least twenty years since I've last seen you; it would be nice to see you again."

"Yes, that would be nice."

Garner figured that he would also contact Norris about attending Aaron's wake just to settle the burning thought within him.

"Big bro' what's up?"

"You got it, little bro'."

Norris had a soft tone about his voice, giving the impression that he was always too cool for his own good. It definitely made good for the Mack Daddy side to him. But Norris was also the moody one among his siblings. Some days he was a great conversation. Most days, he was worst than talking to a steel door.

Testing Norris's mood, Garner inquired about the tickets to three Richmond minor league baseball games that he gave for Christmas. Norris snickered, "Man, nobody wanted to go, and I wasn't going unless they wanted to go."

"I thought y'all were into baseball?"

"They were. I guess they're more into basketball now. They saw KG [Kevin Garnett] and the [Boston] Celtics in the playoffs, and now that's all they're talkin' about." Norris volunteered that he sold the tickets to a friend of his on the job, making a small profit.

All Garner saw was that he spent two hundred dollars for nothing.

"So I bought something for Shalinda with the money. Gotta keep her happy, you know—"

"I don't know," Garner reacted, rolling his eyes. He immediately suspected that Shalinda, his brother's long-time live-in, bought another of her notorious hoochie outfits and the latest human hair. "Are you and Shalinda still planning to get married October?"

Norris yawned into the phone and stretched. "We tallkin' about just doing it at City Hall and gettin' it over with." He yawned again. "It ain't like I don't know her. I've known her for, what, fifteen years?"

Sensing his conversation was getting nowhere, Garner decided to divulge his reason for calling. "Mom said she told you and Carla about our father dying, and his funeral is tomorrow. The wake is later this evening."

There was a lengthy pause. Norris drifted off in thought, closing his eyes.

"Man, you know we all agreed a long time ago that we wouldn't have anything to do with him or his family," he said. "All he was to me was my mama's sperm donor."

Garner mentioned in passing the only reason why he came up to Richmond was out of respect for Aaron. "He was our father, you know—"

"Maybe he was *your* father," Norris snapped.

If you only knew, Garner said to himself. He suggested it would be good for Norris's sons to at least know who their grandfather was, as well as any relatives he chose to introduce them to at the funeral.

"I'll have to talk to Shalinda about that," Norris answered. "Good talkin' to you lil' bro, but I gotta pull a two-day shift starting tomorrow."

Chapter 4

*C*an I explain something quick to you, little boy? Miriam queried Garner. He nodded.

"I'm not surprised at all your brother and sister chose not to go. Aaron wanted no part with his children. He never contacted me. He actually thought he got back at me for that restraining order and all he did was hurt himself. And the sad thing about it is that he'll always be remembered for the way he died, which is worse than the way he lived."

Garner mused to himself one of the first sermons he heard Pastor Brian Lanier preach. Using an example from the Old Testament, Lanier read from a passage that contemplated after an individual's greatness diminished some die, even without wisdom.

"What do you want people to remember you for? What do you want people to remember you by?" Garner remembered Lanier asking the congregation. *"Do some of us live our lives so carelessly that, for all of our book sense, we don't have an ounce of common sense?*

"It's a shame that some of us live sixty, seventy, even eighty years before that realization is made. And for some of us, it's still too late."

Garner gave thought to his own shortcomings, and then Aaron's most glaring failure.

"I actually feel sorry for my father, uh, I mean Aaron," he said. "I wonder what went through his mind before he died. I mean, did he even have a chance to ask God to forgive him? It makes you even wonder did he go to heaven or hell."

Miriam bit on her bottom lip before she replied. "I hate to tell you, that's not your concern. Aaron was sixty-two years old. I talked to him about his drinking and disrespecting me, and Lord knows other women probably talked to him about the same thing."

Glancing over at the grandfather clock, Garner noticed it was almost 5:15 p.m. His stomach growled; he had a serious taste for Miriam's meal that she prepared for him.

"I heard that," Miriam said. "Come on over to the kitchen."

Aaron's death and his siblings' unwillingness to attend his wake did not have any effect on the way he gobbled two plates of cubed steak, rice and gravy, plus two slices of cornbread. Watching Garner eat so heartily was one of the pleasures Miriam always drew from his visiting her.

Joining him at the table, Miriam volunteered that she would be attending Aaron's wake but not his funeral. She felt that was the least that she could do being his ex-wife and the mother of two of his children.

"Do you really feel like going?" he asked.

Miriam gave him a slight nod before sighing heavily. "All I can say is that there are things we do in life that have nothing to do with us." She tapped lightly on the kitchenette before continuing. "I gave birth to all three of you. I think about some of the sacrifices that I made—the lack of sleep, the lack of money at times, the lack of guidance sometimes—but I knew I had to do it. I had to forget about myself a lot of times and think about providing a decent life for you, your brother, and sister."

"I don't get it," Garner replied, still chomping on his cube steak.

"You won't understand until you're a parent, let alone a spouse. Maybe it's good that he's dead instead of me . . ."

A wave of somberness and a sense of surreal overcame him. He never imagined that death would visit him so closely and so relatively early in life. Although he did not have any fond memories of Aaron, he realized that was still the man who provided for him and his siblings while he was married to Miriam. That could never be underestimated, he reasoned.

He recalled that Miriam always taught him that he needed to be the better man in most life situations. Drawing upon what moral foundation he'd developed, Garner recalled it also meant being the one who was willing to forgive and forget.

"Mom, I was wrong for talking to you the way I had all week," he later told Miriam in the parking lot of Singleton Funeral Home.

Miriam leaned over and kissed Garner on his cheek. "It's all right, little boy. I always said that I taught you better. You're just proving it."

Both Garner and Miriam appeared reserved, yet solemn when they entered the mortuary. It had been a decade since he last attended a funeral, and that was for Doris, his maternal great-aunt. He was a pall bearer for that service in Wilmington, North Carolina.

A taller, serious looking man with a voice that reminded Garner of Lurch's character from the *Addams Family* greeted them and directed them to Room "A" where there was on the miniature sign board that read DAVIS.

"Do you recognize any of these people in here?" he whispered over to Miriam.

"Barely," she answered. "But how do you think I look?"

"You look fine, mom. Just help me out with some of these people, if you know them."

At the front of the parlor was Aaron's casket. There were sparse floral arrangements nearby. A few people sat near the front. Garner locked elbows with Miriam as they walked past Aaron's casket: he wore a black suit with a red rose on his left lapel. He bore a serious look, which hardly complemented his aged and hardened features.

Miriam tightened her grip of Garner's hand, which signaled him to move on.

"Are you all right, mom?" Garner whispered to Miriam.

She closed her eyes, trying her best to block out the negative memories. She chose to surmise that Aaron's death offered a cruel reminder of what time and circumstance could do to individuals.

"I'm fine," she answered. "I'm actually glad that we came. Now I can close that door once and for all."

They took a seat about three rows off to their right, giving them an unobstructed view of Aaron's casket. They both scanned the obituary that was provided. It noted that he was born in Hopewell, a town located about thirty minutes southeast of Richmond, where he attended the former and all-black W.E.B. DuBois High School. It also noted that he worked in the Richmond-Petersburg area until he moved to Baltimore, where he worked at Dinkins Transport until his death. He was survived by two brothers, a sister, four children, grandchildren, and a host of nieces, nephews, and cousins.

Miriam pointed out to Garner that Aaron's family probably took the easy way out by being non-descriptive in listing his survivors.

"It doesn't matter now," she said. "Such is life—"

Chapter 5

Garner insisted that he and Miriam take a trip up to northern Virginia and visit Garrett Chaney's grave. That was a welcomed suggestion, Miriam thought, because it showed that maybe Garner had accepted his parentage.

Emotionally, the trips to Arlington National never got any easier for Miriam because no other man ever held a special place in her heart like Garner's biological father. He was the first man who truly romanced her, enabling her to feel like she was the special woman in a man's life. He was also the first one who ever gave her cause to express herself sexually with a man.

Garner noticed the apprehension on Miriam's face once they approached I-395 freeway exit No. 8 that led them to Arlington National Cemetery.

"Are you uncomfortable with me asking you to show me my father's grave?" he queried.

Miriam took in a deep breath, letting it out slowly. Looking out the passenger window, she also managed a wistful smile. "I guess I'm not sure what to expect. I never thought I'd be visiting Garrett's grave site along with you."

Grasping Miriam's hand, Garner conveyed his support. "I need to do this just as much as you have done this by yourself." Crossing the Potomac River via the Memorial Bridge, Miriam then pointed out one of the subtleties of driving to Arlington National, specifically on Memorial Drive, at the posted speed limit.

She also quipped how she got lost the first time she ever came to Washington, D.C. "I ended up over by the Department of Treasury before I realized that I made the wrong turn as soon as I got off the freeway. To be honest, I'm still prone to getting lost in this place."

There were three cars ahead of Garner as he approached what some might considered one of the country's most hallowed grounds. As he kept his foot on the clutch and hand on gearshift, he felt he could no longer hold back the other questions he had within him.

"How many other people know that this man Garrett Chaney is my father? I know his name isn't on my birth certificate but—"

"I've not even told my own family about this," she answered. "I told you that I was prepared to go to my grave with this."

"Do you know if he had any other children?"

"Garrett never mentioned anything about other kids." Miriam's eyes began misting. "You should have seen the look on his face when he saw you the first time. He had the biggest smile when he held you over his head and cradled you in his arms. You had to be no more than two months old." She reached into her purse and retrieved some tissues to dab at her eyes.

"I didn't realize you really liked this man."

"It was more than that . . ."

Garner was not sure how to react to what Miriam had just said, but he knew by her mannerisms that it was no act. He confessed, "Mom, you know, I don't think I've ever been in love with any woman like the way it sounds you were in love with my father." He was moved to somberness, realizing he was not the product of a careless fling. "I hope one day I can say that I've been in love with someone like you two were."

The traffic started to move at the main gate. They eventually drove about a half-mile inside the grounds before they reached a familiar sea of white gravestones all perfectly aligned and equidistant from each other.

"You can stop right about here," Miriam instructed him. She brought with her on this balmy July afternoon another red rose with its stem clipped short, which she planned to tie to the American flag. Inwardly, she prayed that she might be able to keep her emotions in check around Garner.

In the immediate area was a sea of lush greenery and aura of tranquility with birds finding refuge in the nearby trees. They walked a moderate distance from the roadside before reaching Garrett's grave.

Atop of the headstone it read,

GARRETT FLOYD CHANEY
LT. COLONEL
April 29, 1938 – April 5, 1991.

The moment unexpectedly hit Garner—he had to compose himself by blinking his eyes several times.

Softly spoken, he observed, "I was not quite sixteen when he died . . ."

Miriam knelt before Garrett's gravestone and replaced the rose. Garner helped her back up. She reciprocated by giving him a peck on his cheek. Hand-in-hand, they both stared down at Garrett's grave marker.

"All I have is you and the memories of Garrett. I can only believe that your father would have been a great father to you and even a great husband to me; it just didn't work out that way," she said, gripping Garner's hand. "I guess that's why I have been very picky all these years when it comes to male friends. I don't think I've met too many men that have measured up to Garrett's standard."

"Oddly enough, mom, I'm not even worried whether he made it to heaven or not." Rather, Garner believed for the best, and he hoped whenever his time does come that God would prove it to him.

Chapter 6

The station allowed Garner to take off an extra week in lieu of his family emergency. When he returned the Tuesday following the Fourth of July holiday, there was an office plant on his desk. Also waiting for him was a small stack of sympathy cards, including one envelope that had three hundred dollars in it.

His first order of business was to send out an e-mail to the entire newsroom thanking his colleagues for their thoughtfulness. Next, he purposed to sift through seventy-four e-mails that filled his inbox. An e-mail with "Mr. Garner Davis" in its subject field was among the first he opened.

Hi Garner, I was thinking about you and I decided to e-mail you. I hope you're doing well...Kadrece.

Garner planted his chin into the palm of his left hand, brooding. He snorted at Kadrece's audacity to locate him after walking out on him during their dinner date at The High Cotton in Stone Mountain, Georgia. His last image of her was excusing herself from the table, and then her telling him that she no longer had time for non-committal men.

Fuck her, he thought.

He immediately sent the e-mail into the trash bin. But just as he was poised to permanently delete it, he decided to open it again.

Shit, after all these years, Garner realized that he still was hooked on some Kadrece Kendricks. Staring at his computer screen, he reasoned that he'd done dumber things in his life than what he was about to do. He clicked the SEND icon atop the response that he just written:

> **Kadrece, it's nice to hear from you. Are you still in Tallahassee or Atlanta? I think I still have your numbers, but to be on the safe side e-mail them to me again . . . Garner.**

Chapter 7

Taking his mark at the end of the set's news desk, Garner nodded and thanked news anchor Steve Crider, saying it was great to be back. He spoke about the Chanticleers football program opening its fall practice session on the first Tuesday in August as their coach, Larry Fritzer, expected to welcome twenty-three first-year players.

No sooner than the all clear was given at the end of the six o'clock broadcast, Garner mouthed, "I got through that one. Now I'm really back!" and gestured to have wiped off a heavy accumulation of sweat from his brow.

He ventured over to his newsroom desk and checked his e-mails once more. There, he noticed one that had "Call Me" in the subject field. He felt something grip his stomach—that one had to belong to Kadrece.

He clicked it open. She had given him both her cell and home numbers. He checked his cell phone for both entries. There were no changes. More than six months had passed since he last spoken to her. He thought that he might be able to resist for at least another six months. Or could he?

"I had prayed that you would call me," she greeted him. "I asked that if it was really within His will that you would call me."

Garner was surprised. "Uh, I can't say that I prayed about talking to you—"

Realizing that might offend her, he continued, "But I guess it's nice that we are talking. Are you going to tell me that you're also married like Sabryan told me last Christmas?"

"Now why would I tell you something like that?"

"Are you?" Garner insisted. "You haven't answered my question."

"Your Honor, let the record reflect that I am not engaged to anyone, and I've not gotten married," she joked. "Will there be any other cross-examining today?"

Now that was the Kadrece he'd always known being good for a smart-ass response. There was a time when their conversation would eventually turn to sex, and they would seduce themselves into stealing away time together for one of their known romps—the sweetness in Kadrece's voice was always intoxicating to Garner's ears.

"You really do sound well," Garner said. "I know you probably look even better."

"I definitely feel that way. If you remember Nedra Mayfield, my best friend from college, we've been going to the gym a couple of times a week and I've lost almost thirty pounds since I've last seen you. I've probably not been this way since before I went to college."

Garner could not fathom a slimmer Kadrece showing even more curves. He closed his eyes and tried imagining how Kadrece might look minus those pounds.

There was silence among them. Searching for a new topic to converse over, Garner said, "I still find it hard to believe that you would pray for me. I thought after what happened in Atlanta that you would be just like the rest of them who have cursed me." He did not bother to mention that one of them might be doing just that from wherever she was in eternity.

Kadrece sucked her teeth. "Now why would I do that, Garner? If you stop to think about it, you're not the most faithful and committed man I've ever known. And if any woman should know that about you, I do."

Not to be controversial with him, Kadrece explained to Garner that she simply had been thinking about him lately and she still considered him a good friend, even special. She reminded him how she often expressed her fears of failure.

"You always told me if I didn't believe in myself, nobody would believe in me. I always liked that about you, Garner. You were never threatened by my being a confident woman. Some of the men you know I've been with were. Maybe that's why I never lasted long with them."

Since deciding to attend church on a regular basis, Kadrece said she's tried living life from a different perspective. She apologized for not explaining herself to him when she last saw him in Atlanta.

"I'm not going to sit here and say that I didn't notice that," Garner said. "I just figured that whatever changes you've been going through were maybe for the good."

"Thanks for understanding—I think," she replied.

"It's not a problem, Kadrece. I still think you're a beautiful woman inside out, even if I don't completely understand you."

"Why haven't you ever tried finding out?"

Garner openly pondered Kadrece's comment. He reasoned that one person had to be willing to be transparent, and the other person had to be receptive, and vice versa. Besides, for years, both of them knew about many of each other's sex partners. They even went as far as offering suggestions to each other. The problem with that was that it sometimes resulted in them sneaking off to explore some of those suggestions on each other.

"So you're going to say you know me better than I know you?" he quizzed her.

"I probably do," Kadrece said. "Women are like that. We pay attention to things that you guys always overlook."

"Give me one good answer."

"I'll give you two: I know that you, Garner Davis, have always been your happiest around me. You may have liked Sabryan, for example, but you weren't happy around her. That's why you kept coming back around me."

"So why is it you allowed me to keep coming around you?" he countered. "And don't say anything about a man can only do what a woman lets him."

Kadrece did not immediately answer. All Garner heard was her breathing. After several seconds, he broke the silence between them. He volunteered, "I can probably answer that one for you, but that's the very thing you've been trying to avoid the past two times you've seen me."

"Garner, do you think it's always been about sex? Why can't it be that I liked your company? You're an articulate and intelligent man. Or have you ever stopped to realize that about yourself?"

"I'll say this much, I've probably surprised myself a time or two. I know I've never been some dumb jock because my mother would never allow that." He did not elaborate any further.

"Garner, can I ask you something serious?"

"Sure."

"What have you thought about doing with your life in the next few years? And this isn't an interview."

He repeated the question once before responding. "I think about that all the time, Kadrece. You know better than anybody that I would like to be farther along in my profession."

"What about in a relationship?" Kadrece asked. "Do you plan to live your life going from woman to woman, from pussy to pussy, and from bedroom to bedroom? There can't be any satisfaction out of that."

Garner had wandered off in thought about his recent visit to Virginia.

"Are you still there?"

"I'm still here—"

"Have you ever thought about settling down with a special someone in your life?" Kadrece asked.

She thought about Nedra and her husband, Crennell Winslow, and the seemingly happily-ever-after life that they've enjoyed. She also thought about her sister, Kamryn, and her husband, Mitchell Kevin Fauntleroy; her brother, Wesley, and his wife, Chandra. All of those women had openly spoken of how they were the center of their spouse's universe.

"I hope some day I'll be able to say that I have someone special," Garner answered. "Still, I wonder sometimes if I'm cursed."

Kadrece felt melancholy for both of them. "It doesn't have to be that way, Garner." More so, she was surprised that Garner had not picked up on that she had always liked him.

"You know what, Garner?"

"What?"

"I really miss you."

"Why did it take us so long to realize that?"

Kadrece had no explanation, nor did Garner. A wave of giddiness overcame him, causing him to grin, while Kadrece felt relieved that a burden was lifted off her shoulders. It made it easier for her to apprise him about her immediate plans: job interviews first in Greenville, South Carolina on Tuesday; and later in Charlotte on Thursday. Both places were about ninety minutes away from Columbia.

She said, "If you're not busy, I'd really like to see you."

"Do you know yet where you are staying in both places?"

"They haven't told me."

"Just give me a call when you get into Greenville."

Chapter 8

Kadrece began as a law clerk with Marshall Shaeffer and Kline Bradley after she was admitted to the bar in 1996, and she had been there ever since. She became a partner at Schaeffer, Bradley and Kendricks in February 2007 after winning a state supreme court case in which a $3.857 million wrongful death award was reversed for their client, Seminole Cable. It later ruled the company was not even liable to pay for another $425,000 in benefits that were due to the deceased employee, Thomas Barker, citing loopholes in the federal government's Employee Retirement Income Security Act (ERISA).

She decided to interview at Duggans and Chattell Law Firm in Greenville for the purpose of having some kind of leverage for the job she really wanted, a position at the prestigious Wytheman & Pepper law firm in Charlotte; its list of corporate clients included financial giant First Interstate Commerce Bank.

Duggans and Chattell was an aggressive firm that specialized in litigation on behalf of corporate clients. They offered her a $25,000-a-year raise and a $25,000 bonus—the latter half up front and the other half payable after she passed South Carolina's bar exam—on top of paying for her moving expenses to the Greenville area.

"Ms. Kendricks, we find your tenacity in the way your cases are litigated to be exceptional," Stephen Duggans told Kadrece during dinner that Tuesday night. "We think you would be more than a valuable asset at our firm. We would like to see you get squared away with your bar admission as soon as possible—"

Kadrece took Duggans' comments in stride. "I'm looking forward to broadening my career horizons. I've read about your firm's reputation from afar. I'm sure that my philosophy about law and doing business fits very much in your corporate mission."

Inwardly, Kadrece's mind was elsewhere. All she thought about was meeting up with Garner. She excused herself.

"Have you been thinking about me lately?" she inquired, calling Garner from the ladies' lounge.

Garner was at the station browsing the Internet for material for the eleven o'clock show. "That's an understatement."

"Is it something that can be measured?"

Chortling, Garner replied, "Depends on what you were thinking of." He glanced over both shoulders before he leaned back in his office chair, tugging at his dick.

"All right, let's keep our minds renewed," Kadrece said. "I just want to let you know that I'm here in Greenville having dinner with one of the law partners, but I should be coming through there late tomorrow afternoon."

"I'm glad you called me. I really have been thinking about you all day. I've been wondering how you've been since we last talked—you know, if you made it safely."

"Well, I'm standing here in one piece. Hopefully, I'll be seeing you about this time tomorrow, okay?" She glanced at her watch, realizing she'd been away for more than five minutes; that's not the kind of impression that she wanted make on a job interview. "I better get back to this dinner."

"Think you might take the job, if offered?"

"It depends on what the other people in Charlotte are talking about. Talk to you later."

Kadrece left Greenville that Wednesday afternoon with an offer from Duggans and Chattell. What clinched it for her was the way she impressed the other partner, Milton Chattell, by explaining the Seminole Cable case.

"First of all, I proved that [Thomas] Barker's death by electrocution was the result of him coming to work already impaired, having taken an over-the-counter medication that caused him to become drowsy, which was negligence on his part. It wasn't until we brought people in for testimony under oath that we found out that Barker confided in a couple of his co-workers that he'd taken the medication," she explained to him.

Taking command of the conversation, Kadrece asked to chart out the remaining major points to the case on Chattell's dry erase paneling beyond the right of his cherry oak desk.

As she drew out the flowchart, she went on to say, "I then simply played the law against Barker's widow by using legal precedents set forth since 1993 that have sided with companies and ruled they were not liable for paying large awards or damages under ERISA.

"Instead, we proved that the company could only be liable for a negligible $1,260—or Barker's share of premiums paid under the company's current health insurance policy at the time of his death."

She then strode confidently back to the plush leather chair in front of Chattell, who by that point was sold on her.

Chattell said, "We're more than confident, Ms. Kendricks, that you'll meet the state's criteria and will be fully on board with us before the end of the summer."

On her drive from Greenville on I-385 southbound towards I-26, Kadrece smirked at the idea that Chattell, a white man in his mid-fifties with salt-and-pepper hair, was just as engrossed by her mocha chocolate legs and bodily attributes that filled out her navy blue business skirt.

"Hi, how's your day going for you?" Garner easily recognized the jovial tone in Kadrece's voice. "I've just passed an exit No. 54 here on I-26. How far is that from where you are?"

"Uh, have you passed any signs that had Clinton on them? he responded.

"I think so."

"Oh, you're about forty-five minutes to an hour away."

"Good, because I've been under these white people's scrutiny for the past twenty-four hours and all I want to see now is a friendly face. Can you provide that for me?"

This was not something Garner could have imagined a month ago. He checked his office desk clock. It was 4:45 p.m., and he was in the process of completing his script for the six o'clock broadcast.

"You know I won't be able to see you when you first reach town?" he said.

"Of course," she answered. "If anybody should know what your job schedule is like, it's me."

"I keep forgetting that."

"I don't expect you to do that once I get there, or I'll have to discipline you for that."

Garner reminded himself about the disappointment he experienced in Houston after similar banter. "How did the interview go for you?"

She glanced into the rear-view mirror, brushing her bang back to her right temple. "They offered me a position right on the spot; one down, one to go—"

"I knew they would offer it to you. All it took was for them to listen to you talk all that legal jargon like you used to try on me."

"Something like that," she said, chuckling. "Listen, I know you've got a show to get ready for. You know how much of an independent woman that I am. So just tell me a place where I can freshen up and hang out."

Kadrece took down Garner's directions to the Green Leaf Suites about three miles east of the station on Garners Ferry Road. She arrived there a little more than an hour after hanging up. There, she tipped into the bathroom and changed out of a light blue blouse and her one-inch heel business shoes into a white blouse with a plunging neckline and her black stilettos. After freshening up her make-up, she hung out at the hotel's bar where she happened to catch the evening news.

A sense of pride overcame Kadrece while she noticed Garner delivering the sports. As she watched intently, she wandered off into mischievous thoughts of undressing him, and more. She also squirmed in the plush lounge chair in an attempt to divert the increased tension between her thighs.

One last tidbit of information," Garner mentioned, "the Milwaukee major league franchise, which is the parent club to Columbia's Gamecocks, announced it got reigning Cy Young Award winner J.J. Klaussen in a deal that sent four players to Cleveland . . . Milwaukee said it has every intention to signing Klaussen to a long-term deal after his contract expires at the end of the 2008 season . . . Back to you, Steve—"

She waited about fifteen minutes after the broadcast before she contacted him from the hotel.

"You looked so handsome in front of that camera," she greeted him. "But you've always looked that way."

There was a tinge of sensuality to her voice. Garner nearly blushed at Kadrece's comment. Still mindful of her professed transformation, he offered, "I'll see you in about five minutes. There's a decent seafood place that just opened on the other side of town on Broad River Road."

"I love seafood," she exclaimed. "You've always known what I like!"

"Are you going to be waiting inside in the lobby, or outside of the hotel?"

"You just make it here."

Stopping off at the bathroom on his way out, Garner readjusted his gray jacket and re-tucked his white business shirt into his matching gray slacks. He also adjusted the erection that began forming inside his pants so others would not recognize his business. He ran a comb through his dark, wavy hair, and he wiped off the light application of make-up that he used occasionally for the camera.

The rush-hour traffic was cooperative heading eastbound on Garners Ferry Road, leading commuters to Columbia's outlying areas like Eastover, Hopkins, and for some all the way out into neighboring Sumter County.

When he dashed into the hotel's parking lot, his heart sank to his stomach because he recognized just how succulent Kadrece looked—and that was from the immediate distance. He maintained a speed just above idling in the parking lot until he stopped in front of her. She still wore her hair short and wavy with the side-swept bangs. Her inviting smile reminded him just how much of an ebony goddess she really was.

He rushed to exit his vehicle and open the door for her. She chided him: "Garner, you know I can do that myself."

Rejoining her in the car, Garner replied, "Can't you appreciate me being a gentleman for you?"

She glanced over her left shoulder, smiling. "Of course I can. But right now, I'm looking forward to some seafood!"

The Deep Blue restaurant was just as good as Garner had described to Kadrece. She ordered a seafood sampler plate that included scallops, jumbo shrimp, and fried grouper; she also had a baked potato, house salad with honey mustard dressing, hush puppies, and sweet tea. Garner went with a smaller serving of whiting and fries along with hush puppies. He also had water with lemon.

"I guess you were hungry, hmmm?" Garner teased.

Kadrece gave him a sideways, yet seductive glare. She crossed her legs beneath the table. "You know all I need now is a bottle of some sparking wine and I'd be no good." She also allowed her mind to wander off about listening to some Isley Brothers, a prerequisite of hers before lying next to somebody between the sheets.

"I thought that was a thing of the past since you've been going to church," replied Garner, with raised eyebrows.

"Some things are," she answered; she then leaned back into the booth cushion with her arms folded.

Garner paused. "Have you ever been to Columbia?"

"Probably back when I was in high school. I can tell the city's grown a lot since then. When I drove in on I-26, I can remember when they had only two lanes. Now they have three."

"Had you checked into a hotel room?"

"Not yet."

"Good. I was thinking about putting you up in a room closer to where I stay. They just renovated a Green Leaf hotel right at the Two Notch Road and I-77 interchange. You'll be less than ten minutes away."

Kadrece leaned forward upon her forearms and teased Garner with a view of her cleavage, smiling. Then she reached for her purse, sliding out from the booth.

When they reached the Green Leaf Suites, Garner parked his car at the hotel's foyer, expecting Kadrece to park behind him. She chose to find a parking space just beyond. No problem, Garner thought. He figured that he would just offer to take her luggage.

Kadrece let down her window just as Garner drew nigh to her car door. She had already hiked up her business skirt so that it revealed her legs and a hint of her black thong piece. She had also unbuttoned another blouse loop, revealing more of her cleavage that he had delighted himself upon so many times in the past.

Searching for the proper words, Garner slowly suggested, "Are you going to pop your trunk for me?"

"No, I'm not."

Garner then cast a hard glare at her; his grayish eyes narrowed. "What are you talking about?"

"You never asked me if I wanted to stay here," she answered.

He straightened up, folding his arms. "All right, would you like to stay here at this hotel, or would you prefer another place a little farther up the road?"

"I would prefer not—"

Leaning against the side of her car, Garner looked away before re-establishing eye contact with her. "I don't understand?"

"Do you have a problem if I stayed at your place?" replied Kadrece, who glided her tongue across her top lip, waggling it back and forth. Then she glanced into the rear-view mirror, checking her bangs.

"Stay . . . at . . . my . . . place . . . This has to be some test, right?"

"It's not some test, or even a joke. You never even offered me to stay at your place, which is where I want to stay for the night."

Inhaling deeply, Garner closed his eyes and shook his head.

Women, he lamented. *They are the most beautiful species on the earth and sometimes the hardest to understand.* "Isn't that contrary to what you'd been espousing to me the past couple of times we've seen each other?"

Kadrece turned on her engine. "Didn't you say you lived not far from here?" She allowed her right hand to trail down from her neck to her cleavage.

"I did—"

"Well, what's taking you so long?" she answered. "I think we've got a lot of catching up to do."

Chapter 9

They got no farther than Garner's privacy patio when Kadrece ordered him to put down her bags. Garner briefly stared at Kadrece, but he had a good idea what was on her mind. He extended his arms to her; their bodies converged in a tight embrace and sensual kiss.

First, it was slow, a meshing of their lips together. Then she opened her mouth and offered him her tongue to suck, which he eagerly received. Almost instantly, Kadrece's nipples hardened and she felt the wetness flowing from her pussy. Only her thong piece kept her juices from trailing down her inner thighs. Garner rested his hands on her ass, stroking and kneading it softly through the fabric.

Damn, he was almost in dreamland as he felt its fullness and firmness. She pressed her body against his while they continued in a series of wet, passionate kisses.

Garner was so caught up in the moment that he slipped his hands under her skirt. It had been roughly three years since he last felt her flesh in that manner. He lifted Kadrece from her feet, and she coiled her legs around his waist—he felt heat emitting from between her thighs.

If he could have unzipped his pants, he would have pushed it between her soft folds, giving her the kind of fuck that she once was accustomed to with him. Withdrawing slightly, Garner glanced over his shoulder at the door before making eye contact with Kadrece again..

He suggested, "We don't need other people knowing our business." He hugged her and inhaled her fragrance. He closed his eyes. The moment reminded him of the good old lustful days with her.

"It's been a long time . . . a long, long time," he said softly to her.

Kadrece kissed Garner lightly on his lips before uncoiling her legs from around him. She stared admiringly into his eyes. "I know the feeling."

For a moment, she contemplated her newfound commitment to church. She dared not to consider the devil had made her do any of it. No, this was something she badly wanted, and she was willing to deal with her conscience in her own time.

After Garner led her inside his condominium, Kadrece took a seat on his king sofa, and she struck an inviting pose for him with her legs crossed. "I didn't tell you that you looked so handsome and sexy today on TV that I had to ask the Lord to forgive me for what I was thinking."

"After what we just did outside," replied Garner, who sat opposite of her on the sofa, "I know the Lord is expecting at least that much from you."

"So we're full of jokes, aren't we?"

"I don't think 'jokes' is the operative word right now."

When it came to women, Garner's instincts always told him never to get into any guessing game. Besides, all the chemistry that had been transmitted between them strongly hinted at Kadrece wanted him as much as he wanted her.

Convinced of that assumption, he beckoned Kadrece to nuzzle up against him. Resting his hands across her breasts, Garner spoke in a low, mesmerizing tone.

"I've always been turned on by you, and I'll always will, Kadrece," he said. "It's been that way for me ever since the first time I saw you that afternoon in the Humanities building."

Kadrece placed her hand on his, closing her eyes to reminisce about that meeting from nearly a half of a lifetime ago. "So you're admitting that you've never been able to resist me?"

"I can't, because I know you're not someone that I can find every day."

"I'm glad you realize that."

Garner adjusted his position on the sofa, allowing for Kadrece's body to recline against his. She let out a soft moan when he ran his hands across her breasts again, stopping to caress and squeeze them. Much to his surprise—and perhaps relief—she offered no resistance when he unbuttoned her blouse another loop. He slid his hands inside and lifted her breasts from within her bra. He then proceeded to play with her nipples between his thumb and forefingers.

"Garner, baby," Kadrece reacted. His eyes widened and he froze, expecting the inevitable let down.

"Don't stop—"

"Don't stop?"

She wiggled her ass against him; her voice became sultry. "Don't stop."

Garner resumed massaging and kneading her breasts, as well as toying with her nipples. She reached back and stroked his face. She went on to confess, "I guess I'm the one who couldn't resist, too."

"Hold on," Garner said, maneuvering himself in front of her.

Kadrece quickly sat up and undid the other buttons on her blouse. After he helped her out of her top garment, she twisted her bra around to the front, unhooking it. All along, Garner's eyes were riveted on her flesh.

Once she leaned back, he proceeded to apply his lips and tongue to her, and his breath against her nipples gave her chill bumps all over. She sucked air and balled her fists, pounding them lightly on his back. "Oooh shit, Garner," she exclaimed. "You're making me forget that I actually go to church—"

Garner mumbled something unintelligible to her, but mentally he relished in being the one responsible for her breaking her vow. He paused to slide her skirt down past her ankles, and he followed that up with a quick motion to remove her thong piece. He revealed a wide grin once she was exposed to him.

"Aren't you a little over dressed?" she queried.

He nodded. "I guess I also need to look the part—"

Without commenting, Kadrece knelt in front of Garner and helped him out of his slacks. She was more preoccupied with freeing his dick from inside his black bikini briefs than with helping him unbutton his shirt. He was left with taking care of that amid her loud slurping and gurgling. Once he shed his final stitch of clothing, he immediately closed his eyes and placed his hands on her shoulders, pushing his dick farther inside her mouth.

"Damn, Kadrece . . ."

He repeated it several times as he felt her head bob back and forth into his groin. "You're the only one who's ever sucked my dick like that."

She paused to steal a glance at him. "I am? Are you sure that I'm the only one?" She resumed her affections by stroking his dick with her right hand and teasing his mushroom-shaped tip with her tongue.

Garner tensed. "Mmmm, I can't lie; you're the only one."

Satisfied with his honesty, Kadrece squeezed his ass cheeks, inducing him into fucking her mouth. Although it had been quite a while, her instincts took over as she relaxed her throat muscles to accommodate his length and thickness. Garner groaned when she stopped to stroke his dick again, but he smiled once he realized she also began licking the underside of his dick. He also let out a few obscenities when she positioned herself under him to lick and suck his balls.

Pausing this time to catch a quick breath, Kadrece queried, "Am I the only one who can take care of you the way you want and need to be taken care of?" She gave his dick a couple of sensual tugs, adding, "Why don't you move back on that sofa, and I'll show you."

Garner helped Kadrece up from her knees, and he led her to lay back on the king sofa. He ran his hands along her legs and thighs before parting them. Then he lunged forward, causing her to gasp.

"Damn, baby—"

It was all over at that point. Kadrece melted in his grasp and she purred at first to his gentle flicks upon her clit.

"Dang, Garner," she moaned, as he pushed his tongue inside her pussy. She held her legs apart for him as he alternated his attention between her pussy and clit.

"That's right, baby, suck this sweet chocolate pussy . . . suck it, baby—"

Thoroughly aroused, Kadrece's body tensed and she pressed his head into her mound. Her breathing became halted and she arched her back. "Oh baby, that's it . . . that's it, baby . . . that's it!"

"No, turn around."

Dutifully, Kadrece positioned herself on all fours on his sofa. Her apple-shaped ass cheeks naturally separated before Garner, exposing both her pussy and asshole. "That's what I'm talking about," he grunted, as his dick disappeared between her soft, turgid flesh.

Kadrece's self-imposed celibacy was officially over. Even more telling was their sexual reunion, which Garner told Kadrece that each stroke that he intended to give her was to reinforce his desire for her. Meanwhile, she felt validated that she was a man's desire even if it meant fucking again before she married.

Bracing herself on the sofa arm, Kadrece pushed her ass forcefully into Garner's flesh, and she made deep gyrations with her hips.

"Oh baby . . . oh baby . . . now you're getting it!"

"Just what I'm getting?" he inquired.

"My sweet pussy—"

Garner reacted by grabbing her ass cheeks and increasing his thrusts for a sustained run of about two minutes. He delighted in the way she threw her head back and screamed obscenities at him. Aggressively, he leaned forward against her and clutched her breasts for leverage while he maintained his intense strokes.

"Why did you have to be a bitch to me all this time?"

Kadrece pushed her ass hard against Garner's flesh to elicit deeper strokes from him. Looking over her shoulder, she inquired, "Am I making it up to you now?"

He decided to use her shoulders as leverage for his thrusts. His breathing had changed from hard to panting. "You cheated both of us out of times like this."

"I won't any more, baby . . ."

"How do I know that?"

SMACK!

"I'm sorry that I've been such a bitch to you!"

"Why didn't you want this dick?"

SMACK!

"Because I was scared of falling in love with your sweet dick—"

"So why you need it now?"

SMACK!

"I know there's no other dick as good as yours, baby!"

"You're goddamned right."

SMACK!

"Oh shit, I wanna cum so bad!"

Garner knew any variation of the cowgirl position was Kadrece's favorite to reach an orgasm. It also afforded him a visual treat of her breasts bouncing and bobbling, as well as a treat of watching her ass bounce and jiggle when she rode him.

Taking their action to the living room carpet, Kadrece mounted Garner without any hesitation or hindrance. She placed her hands on his chest to balance herself while she squeezed her pussy muscles for a wet, tight feeling against Garner's dick. His eyes widened and he tensed. Kadrece knew she had him at her mercy.

"Any woman ever fucked you as good as this?" she teased him.

He shook his head and hoped like hell that he would not ejaculate.

"Tell me," she demanded of him, riding his dick even more convincingly.

"No."

She bent slightly forward and dug her fingernails into his chest, but Garner retaliated by grabbing on to her hips and pumping furiously inside her. It was not long before she had closed her eyes tight and gritted her teeth.

"Shhhiiit, Garner!" Kadrece groped for anything behind her to keep her balance as her body tensed and shuddered. "Why do you always do this to me?"

Smirking, Garner mischievously replied, "So was this an exception or the rule?"

Kadrece, still breathing heavily, slumped forward onto Garner, allowing his still rock-hard dick to slip out of her pussy. She kissed him softly on his cheek, then lips. Placing his hand behind her head, he then pushed his tongue inside her mouth.

She paused from sucking his tongue to reply, "Baby, you've always been the exception *and* the rule in my life."

Kadrece's satisfied countenance made Garner feel extremely giddy. It was more than tempting for him to consider returning to work with her scent mixed with his cologne and the smell of sex wafting from him. He mused why be ashamed of letting others know what he had done. Hell, in Tallahassee, he'd gone back to work on several occasions with a few passion marks that she'd given on his chest.

"What's got you staring off into space?" Kadrece said, wiggling her hips against him. "You've forgotten what it's like to have the real thing?"

Garner, lying on his back, still had Kadrece in his arms as she lay nuzzled up against him. He turned on his side and gazed into her eyes. He also managed a mischievous grin. "I wished we could have done this sooner."

Kadrece had now turned on her side. "Why sooner?" She placed her arm around his waist.

"I don't know," he answered.

"Well, I'm a lawyer, not a mind reader."

Garner inhaled deeply, letting the air out slowly through his pursed lips. Meanwhile, Kadrece had now shifted positions, rolling on top of him. She squirmed until she was comfortable.

"Are you scared of saying you missed me?" she inquired

"No."

"Then say it."

There was a faint sound of Garner's hand rubbing Kadrece's backside. He then pressed his pelvis up against hers. She reacted, "That just says you like my stuff."

Arching his neck, Garner finally replied, "Kadrece, I miss you."

"Why couldn't you just tell me that?"

"I should have."

Kadrece reared up, supporting her weight with her elbows. She studied Garner's expression: she knew he was in some form of contemplation. She lowered her head and lightly kissed his chest before nibbling on his nipples—his dick immediately responded to her tongue and lips.

"I know you, Garner Davis," she said. "You can fool the rest of them, but you can't fool me."

"Do you really think you know me?"

"Wanna find out?"

Shaking his head, Garner conceded to her debating prowess. "I don't need my head to be any more fucked up before I get back to the station."

Chapter 10

A few hours later

Typical of a summer night in the Columbia area were crickets chirping in the distance. Garner had other things on his mind as he tossed and caught his car keys in the parking lot of his condominium.

"Shit, E-9," he mumbled, referring to a baseball terminology after he dropped them.

Sighing, he picked them up and continued towards his patio gate. A familiar female's voice greeted him, causing him to flinch.

"What took you so long?"

Kadrece awaited his arrival sitting in a white plastic lounge chair with her legs crossed and arms folded, but now she began pulling her Jacksonville football tank top over her head. Her naked body was like a silhouette before him. He made a quick survey of the area for any neighbors outside.

"I just couldn't wait for you to come inside." She made sure that she spoke loud enough that only he could have heard her exchange.

Immediately, Garner thought about that nut he wanted badly to bust since he grudgingly went to work nearly four hours ago. He took a couple of steps in her direction, but she closed the distance. His wide grin was inviting; they entered into a tight embrace. His hands slid down along her back and settled on her ass cheeks; he rubbed his erection against her mound as they entered into a wet, passionate kiss.

As she came up for air, Garner slid his tongue between her modestly full lips. She was eager to suck hard on his tongue. Now it was his turn to come up for air, separating himself from her.

"I never expected this," he said. "I'm not really sure what I should do."

She chortled, casting a seductive stare at him. "Garner, you've never passed up on this mocha chocolate that melts in your mouth and cums on your hands and dick." She then inserted her middle finger between her slippery folds and offered him a taste—he licked off her nectar with the tip of his tongue.

"You like that, don't you baby?"

"Always," he answered, smacking his lips for emphasis.

Kadrece rested her forearms on Garner's broad shoulders, and she rubbed her breasts against his chest. She mentioned, "I think it might be a good idea not to get your clothes all sweaty out here." She had a point: the humidity was at sixty-five percent and his shirt and slacks would be soaked in a matter of minutes. She also hastened his compliance by tracing a trail with her right index finger from his stomach down to his zipper.

He reacted, "Aren't you concerned about somebody seeing us?"

"I don't recall you ever being worried about that before. Remember that afternoon in Daytona Beach when you brought me on that media golf outing?"

"Please don't."

They both shared a muffled laugh recalling how they, being the only blacks at the event, had sneaked off for a quickie somewhere between the fourteenth tee and green at the Deland-O-Links Country Club.

Garner kicked off his loafers, unbuckled his belt, and slid down his slacks. He also mentioned, "I thought about sucking your toes tonight."

"You did?" she replied, helping him to unbutton his shirt.

"Uh-huh."

"You should have told me. Well, you can lick my ankles and suck more of my juice off my finger."

"I'll remember that."

Though their bodies were a sharp contrast in hue, they otherwise had complementary preferences. She preferred men over six feet tall, and taller women were what he fancied. He also liked the way her pussy seemed to naturally accommodate him no matter what position they fucked. She had expressed to him in the past that she was even more turned on whenever he bottomed out inside her.

"Garner, I'm sorry for tripping out on you the way that I had," she said. "I really mean that."

Extending his hand out to her, he led her back over to the same chair from where she greeted him. A moment like this had been something he'd fantasized about: With the right woman, he would spend part of the night naked on the backyard deck of his semi-secluded residence.

He guided her to sit on his lap. He also kissed her on her neck. "Apology accepted. I'm sorry for being so selfish. I should have respected your desire to answer up to a higher responsibility."

Returning the kiss, Kadrece replied, "Apology accepted." She adjusted herself on him so that her breasts were at eye level with him. Wiggling her upper body, she went on to say, "You know the Bible talks about men allowing a [woman's] breasts to satisfy him—"

She sucked in some air and arched her neck as Garner's tongue and thin lips touched her skin. A muffled moan was his acknowledgement.

"You like sucking these big titties, don't you Garner?"

He nodded. He then placed his left hand on her right breast, caressing and kneading it. "Suck my titties like you really want to please me," she urged him, slipping her left hand down to squeeze his rock-hard dick. He responded by lightly nibbling her nipples and fluttering his tongue on them.

Kadrece felt as though her clit would explode. Sucking in more air, she cradled Garner's head. "Baby, you're so good to me . . . you've always been."

Maybe Kadrece's words were prophetic, for it seemed that her breasts did satisfy Garner's initial lust. Now he wanted more. Straightening himself in the chair, he ordered her to stand up. He looked Kadrece up and down, nodding in approval.

"Turn around," he said.

She was slow to comply, thinking that perhaps Garner would perhaps penetrate her from a standing position. But she noticed that Garner had stood up and slid the other chair in front of her.

Then he sat back down behind her.

"Bend over," he said.

With her ass cheeks naturally separating for him, Garner leaned forward and pushed his tongue inside her soaking wet pussy. He also reached up and squeezed her cheeks. She immediately sucked in air and moaned out his name—she also tensed after his tongue brushed against her swollen clit.

"Shit, baby. That's it. Suck it!"

Kadrece began rotating her hips and pushing her ass back into Garner's face. She arched her back and shut her eyes tighter, even moaning louder, once he began teasing her with playful licks around her puckered entry.

He paused to question her, "Tell me you like your asshole licked and eaten."

"I do, baby. I love you licking my asshole!"

"Beg me to do it again."

Slipping her hand between her thighs, Kadrece rubbed her clit and moaned. "I want you to lick my pussy and asshole, Garner." He responded with a playful smack on her cheeks.

"Beg me again!"

"Mmmm, baby, please lick my pussy and asshole—"

Working in concert, she allowed him to insert his finger inside her pussy and massage her g-spot region while she rubbed her clit. In a matter of seconds, her face contorted and her body shuddered.

"Oh god, baby," she said, still bent over struggling to catch her breath. She placed her hand on her forehead, shaking her head. "That was so intense. I thought I was going to pass out."

Garner stood up behind Kadrece, his arms wrapped around her and rubbing his erection against her ass. She rested her head against his chest. He mentioned, "You know, it's been so long since we've—"

"I know. But I don't want to talk about that. At least right now."

He led Kadrece back inside his condominium and all the way to his bedroom. Without another word spoken, she sprawled herself out on his bed, offering him an inviting pose. Then she reclined back, extended her arms out to him, and he knelt onto the bed and joined her.

As their bodies meshed and worked in unison, Garner experienced a *déjà vu* moment. There was something in the way that Kadrece had cast a sultry gaze back at him and offered him an inviting smile that reminded him of their first time together at her off-campus apartment nearly thirteen years earlier.

Back then, though, Kadrece was only the second woman Garner had ever gone to bed with. But as it was then, and as it was on this mid-July night in the Columbia area, their chemistry was inexplicably sensual.

"I really miss you, Garner. I really do," she whispered into his ear. "You don't know how bad that I've wanted you."

At that moment, Garner damned near allowed the most feared four letters for a man to utter during sex to slip off his tongue, but he caught himself just as he did as a twenty-year old.

"Kadrece, I . . ."

She finished the thought for him. "I know you do, too, baby." Her body still tingled from his pussy eating, and no matter where Garner's strokes reached their destination she was like a volcano ready to erupt. They fucked briefly from the spooning position. Then facing each other, he delivered hard, deep thrusts with her right leg straddling his shoulder.

"Do you still need other women to satisfy you?" she questioned him

He shook his head.

"Tell me, Garner, do you need to fuck any other women?"

Slightly annoyed, he grabbed both her ankles and pushed her legs back, slamming his dick furiously inside her slit. Breathing heavily he retorted, "Do you need to fuck other men?"

"No baby—"

"Say it again, damn it!"

"You've always satisfied me, baby. I don't need another man."

His ego massaged by her pussy, he finally acknowledged, "I'm not looking for another woman. I just want your pussy to satisfy me."

"Oh shit," Kadrece gasped, as she arched her back and tensed beneath him. "I'm cumming!"

For once Garner did not feel he was obligated to prove just how skillful he was in bed. Kadrece's pussy felt too good to hold back— they had been at it for less than ten minutes.

Garner reared his head back; Kadrece felt his dick getting thicker even as his strokes changed from rapid to slow, deep searching ones. He opened his mouth, but did not utter anything. Thirteen years of off-and-on fucking gave Kadrece an innate understanding of him.

"Are you ready to give it to me, baby?" She ran her hands up and down his sweaty back and along his ass.

He lowered his head and kissed her. "Just a little more . . . damn, this pussy feels soooo good!"

"When you do, I want it in my mouth."

That was all that Garner could handle. He ceased fucking and immediately withdrew, and Kadrece got on her knees in anticipation of her reward for having provided him a much-desired sanctuary between her thighs.

"Here it is, baby . . . here it is . . . oooooooohh!"

Kadrece took hold of Garner's dick, stroking it and coaxing it to fruition. After a loud grunt and expletive from Garner, she eagerly sucked and swallowed his very essence.

Chapter 11

Damn, it was nice to have some dick, Kadrece thought. But that giddiness quickly changed into a moment of sobriety. She pulled down the toilet seat in Garner's bathroom and silently prayed that her soul would be kept and forgiven. She reminded herself of a verse that spoke of her having an advocate who prayed continuously for her. How ironic that she would pursue profession that the Savior of her soul was described as somebody whose role's been to argue or prosecute on someone's behalf.

Oh well. Sinner tonight, saint tomorrow.

Shifting her thoughts back to Garner, she felt a sweet throb between her thighs again. She cracked open the bathroom door. "Think you'll be up before eight? I have an appointment in Charlotte at eleven o'clock," she yelled. "You know how I'm not much of a morning person."

Garner knew it was more than likely he'd be the one up ahead of her. He reached across his bed and set his alarm clock for 8 a.m., although he was usually up just before seven.

"Do you think you have a good chance of getting the job in Charlotte?" he asked.

She reappeared from the bathroom. "I think so. I know I've got at least the offer in Greenville." Sliding under the covers, she leaned forward and kissed him fully on the lips, pushing her tongue inside his mouth. He was eager to suck it and fondle her breasts simultaneously.

She tried diverting his attention by tapping him on his hip. "Mmmm, haven't you had enough?"

"You're the one who started it," he answered, lunging towards her left breast.

She nudged him away before turning her back to him. He settled in by spooning up against her and with his hands covering her breasts. But then he withdrew, lying on his back.

"Why did you do that? I was just getting comfortable," Kadrece reacted. "It's nice lying next to a man once again."

"I . . . uh, well, it is what it is."

Kadrece did not like that response. She turned over and faced him. "Are you having a problem with this?"

"I like this. I, uh, was thinking about something else."

"I told you, Garner, I'm an attorney, not a mind reader."

Rolling his eyes, Garner inhaled before he posed his question. He prefaced it by telling Kadrece about how glad he was that they had reunited. He followed that, saying, "I just never asked you why have you come to South Carolina looking for work?"

"Is that all?" She rolled off him and onto her back, staring at the ceiling and sucking her teeth. "You should know that answer."

"I know you have a sister (Kanitra) and a brother (Wesley) who is an attorney, and you have that brother-in-law (Kevin Fauntleroy) in Atlanta who's one."

"That's right. I could easily get on with them. But that's never been me."

"It still doesn't answer why you're here in my bed?"

"Do you have a problem with me finding work here in the Carolinas?" She still had managed to remain sweet and calm in her voice, although her patience was about to go tilt.

"No. But I think you would be curious if I were to tell you that I was interviewing for jobs in the Jacksonville and Tampa markets."

"True, I might."

Kadrece explained that she had worked with attorneys Shaeffer and Bradley for eleven years. And while she had become a partner in the firm, she said she was not happy with the direction of her career.

"Have you thought about starting your own firm?" he inquired.

She sucked her teeth. "Have you been checking out the economy lately?"

"I know you've built up a long client list."

"Yeah, but when you ask to be bought out of a partnership, you lose access to all those names. I'd have to start over. So if I'm going to start over, I might as well go somewhere else."

"Okay, do you think you have a good chance of getting the job in Charlotte?"

"I think so. I know I've got a good job offer in Greenville. An of-fer from Wytheman & Pepper would be a stronger one."

She went on to explain that she was inclined to accept the job in Charlotte if it were offered because North Carolina had easier bar admission requirements than South Carolina for practicing out-of-state attorneys. "It may be a slightly more expensive route in North Carolina," she said. "Attorneys are allowed to apply without having to take the written bar exam that South Carolina requires all attor-neys to pass. They then pay a non-refundable $1,500 application fee along with providing an extensive amount of paperwork and back-ground information."

She also told him that Wytheman & Pepper was a plush job that could further her career.

"It's nice to be in demand like that," Garner said.

"True enough," she answered. "It's also nice to be wanted." And with that, Kadrece turned over again on her side and wiggled her ass against Garner. The sticky cum that she felt upon her flesh brought a smile to her.

Chapter 12

Since their college days, Kadrece valued Nedra Mayfield-Winslow's opinion more than her mother's and sisters' opinions.

"It's not like you've told me where you were staying," Nedra said after they greeted each other. "You couldn't have been that busy—"

Kadrece often mused to Nedra, thirty-eight, that she felt bad for her sons, Brandon and Cosby, if they ever attempted to lie to her because nothing ever got past her.

It's like talking to God, Jesus, and the Holy Spirit!

"Yes, I have been that busy. Matter of fact, Duggans and Chattell, the law firm in Greenville, gave me a formal offer—close to a $20,000 raise plus a $25,000 bonus," Kadrece said. "Now I'm driving up to Charlotte for this other interview."

"Hold on, Kadrece—"

In Nedra's supervisory capacity as an ombudsman manager, she was besieged by a constant flow of traffic in and out of her office.

"I'm back," Nedra said, sighing. "I wonder if I'm a mother to sixty-five people around here."

Kadrece chuckled. "You do have those maternal traits."

There was the faint sound of fingers pecking away on a keyboard. "Now, tell me, did you pray about any of this before you left?" Nedra inquired. "Are you sure all of this might be in His will?" There was the sound of someone knocking on her office door in the background.

"Come in!"

"There you go again, always preaching to me," Kadrece reacted. "Why don't you just start your own church? I'm sure you'd scare the hell out of a lot of people."

"I'm going to act like I didn't hear that. Hold on—"

Several seconds passed before they resumed their conversation. "I'm back. Now what did you just say?"

Kadrece remained silent.

"I thought so," Nedra said in an authoritative voice. "You know not to mess with the anointing."

They both shared a laugh. Unexpectedly, Kadrece yawned into the phone.

"What's wrong? Stayed up all night?" Nedra inquired.

"I had to be out before 9:30 so that I can get there for this eleven o'clock interview, but that meant for me getting up around eight. You know how I am about getting up early."

"Lord, do I . . . I can't believe that you've actually made it to church on Sundays."

"Do we just have to go there? You and Gar—"

"What did you just say?"

"I said do we just have to go there."

"And after that you said what sounded like a man's name."

Busted again.

This time, Kadrece had done it to herself. Sighing, she braced herself for Nedra's interrogation. Maybe it might be for the good after all, she thought. "Yeah, that slipped, didn't it?"

"It all depends."

"Well, I recently got back in contact with Garner Davis. You do remember him? He lives in Columbia, South Carolina."

"Who can forget?" Nedra replied. "You two just never seem to stay away from each other."

"That's not nice. Garner's a friend. Probably the best male friend

I've ever had. I think you're jealous of me knowing him."

Nedra had stopped her multitasking and leaned forward upon her forearm. She shifted her feet under her desk. "Kadrece, why would I be jealous of some man who thinks he's God's greatest gift to women? At least that's what I remembered of him when he was here in Tallahassee." She leaned back in her chair, staring out of her office window. The weather there was sunny, humid, with a slight breeze and a chance of afternoon showers.

"Garner never acted like that around me," Kadrece snapped back at Nedra, exhaling in disgust.

"You know how I am, K-girl. I'm all about doing things the right way."

Nedra had been a big reason why Kadrece had started attending church. Kadrece thought that perhaps if she cleaned up her act that she might attract the right people in her life like Nedra.

"I think Garner's been misunderstood. And after dealing with others in my past, I'd rather deal with a man who has faults that everyone knows about than someone who goes around deceiving people."

"Hmmm, you really like Garner—I don't know why you do. But why is that you two never tried having a real relationship?"

"We've kinda talked about it. But I don't want to be so pushy about it this time around . . . Hold on, Nedra, somebody's on the other line—hello?"

Garner had cleared his throat just before Kadrece answered. "I was just thinking about you."

That brought a smile to Kadrece's face—she thought his timing could not be any better. "I was just talking about you."

"I hope that's a good thing."

"Oh, it is. Can I call you back later?"

"Okay."

Kadrece clicked back over to the other line. "Nedra?"

"I'm still here." She had resumed her multitasking on the computer and sifting through the stacks of papers on her desk.

"Speaking of the devil . . . that was Garner just calling me to say he was thinking about me. Now does that sound like someone who thinks he's God's greatest gift to women?"

"Is that right?" Nedra reacted before pausing. "Are you leaving out any details that I should know about, or do I need to use my prophetic gifting?"

"We've talked about a few things. In fact, we've talked about a lot of things."

"Well, that's nice," Nedra said, rolling her eyes. She had always believed that Garner was not the kind of man that Kadrece should ever involve herself with even on a casual basis.

"I thought you were my friend," Kadrece said.

"I am your friend. We're like sisters."

"Then why aren't you happy that we've gotten back in contact with each other?"

"Because I know eventually you two are going to—if you've not already done it— start having sex. That's going to go against everything I thought you were now trying to stand for."

"Nedra, you're always preaching to me."

"If I don't, who will?"

"Well, let the pastor do it, or God Himself, please—"

"Okay, but you know when you sow according to the flesh, you reap according to the flesh. And that's never good."

Kadrece knew it was time to end this conversation before she revealed more than what she should. She confided in Nedra that she would like to use either opportunity in Greenville or Charlotte as a stepping stone to other career options.

"Are you really serious about leaving Tallahassee?" Nedra inquired.

"I just might be, and I wouldn't be far from my parents and the rest of my brothers and sisters if I took a job in the Carolinas."

"I forget you're not from Florida. I better get going. I've got a couple of my chil'uns in my office."

Chapter 13

Three days later

Never in Kadrece's wildest imagination did she ever think that she would be lying next to Garner looking back to this time a year ago.

Changing thoughts and position in the bed, she nestled against him and pondered her immediate future. The picture still seemed incomplete, and she desired a clearer one.

Kadrece then sat up in the bed, leaning back against her elbows. She glanced to her left, smiled, and gave Garner a light peck on his neck. She reasoned for all of Garner's faults as a womanizer, a highly sexed man and irresponsible when it came to relationships, his wit, intelligence, and suave were worth desiring. It was equally worth seeking God's forgiveness since she reneged on her self-imposed celibacy.

She pulled back the covers on him and enveloped his dick in her mouth—it might be the only time that she'd be able to take it all at once. Within seconds, she had repositioned herself so that her head bobbed freely and at a slow pace. Once she felt his length and thickness fill her mouth, she withdrew and began hand stroking his shaft.

She was unaware that Garner's senses and consciousness were heightened. He thought that he was having one of those enviable sex dreams—the ones that felt so damned real—but ultimately ended just when it seemed the sex began. He began moving his hips to the tugging and pulling on his dick. Kadrece replaced the handwork with her lips. She darted out her tongue, allowing the tip to make contact with his flesh, and licked away the bead of pre-cum that he produced. Then she went back to making subtle suction sounds with her warm, soft lips.

Kadrece heard Garner moan for the first time. They soon achieved a fluid rhythm between her sucking and his thrusts. Determined to tantalize him to submission, she withdrew and left enough moisture on his dick so that she went back to giving him a hand job.

Garner opened his eyes, beckoning, "Come on, get on top."

"No, baby," she responded. "This one is all about you."

Garner knew experientially that Kadrece often reminded him about her love for sucking dick and swallowing his semen. But in male terms, he was not a fool to pass up on a good blow job, either.

He spoke barely above a whisper. "I love it when you take all of my dick inside your mouth."

"So, do you appreciate a good woman?"

"Definitely!"

That response was the kind that turned on Kadrece. Her nipples hardened and her clit throbbed—she could not make a move without hearing her soaking pussy. She was tempted to multi-task by sucking him and manipulating her clit, but she suppressed the urgency in favor of making a definitive statement with him.

She withdrew and cast a seductive gaze at him, stroking him by hand once again. "Is this something that you can get used to every morning?"

Garner, lips parted, nodded. Kadrece reacted with a serious look. Not to ruin the moment, he went on to reply, "Are you willing to do this for me every morning?"

She smiled. "As long as you treat me right."

He sensed a slight tingle starting in his balls—the feelings of an ejaculation he hoped to delay. "That shouldn't be a problem because I'll do whatever it takes to make that happen." He writhed to her soft touch. "Come on; let me feel my dick inside your pussy—"

"You can always have me any way you want. But can't you just enjoy what I'm doing now for you?"

Kadrece paused and slipped her left middle finger in her mouth. Then she ran it along his asshole and sensitive area between his balls.

"Damn, Kadrece, what you're doing to me?"

She returned a mischievous stare at him. Adding to the seduction, she opened her mouth and gave his dick a broad swipe with her tongue.

He remarked, "You've never sucked my dick like this before."

"Maybe because we never got to a place where I felt comfortable doing all this," she responded, stroking him by hand. She then resumed sucking his member.

Garner groaned, "Oh, fuck!"

Kadrece's head bobbed at a faster pace—she made him feel as though he fucked her tonsils.

"Damn, I'm about to lose it, Kadrece!"

Sensing his urgency, Kadrece opened wider. She knew one of the tricks to giving a great blow job was making sure the man of her desire felt only flesh and no teeth.

Garner clutched the bed sheet and tensed. He even curled his toes. "I don't want any other woman sucking my dick except for you . . . Oh shit!"

Kadrece felt the initial spurt hit the back of her mouth. She then enveloped as much of his dick as possible—not a trickle of his cum escaped.

"Only a woman who loves her man sucks dick like that," Garner said, trying in vain to keep his composure. He then shook his head in admiration. "Only a man who's into his woman can appreciate what she just done for him."

Licking her lips and then smacking them, Kadrece beamed in reaction to what she thought was the most sincere thing she'd ever heard from Garner.

"Damn, what you're trying to do, Kadrece? Get me to marry you?"

She managed only a seductive smile. "I just want you to experience something as good as you've given me this week. Can I fix you something to eat?"

Garner could not resist the swelling of emotion within. He got out of his bed, put on some athletic bottoms, and followed Kadrece into the kitchen. He shadowed her every move.

"I'm not going anywhere until tomorrow," she said, looking back at him. "And when I do leave, you'll always be in my heart."

"That's good to know because I don't want to let go of you this time, Kadrece."

She placed the container of apple juice on the counter. She also lowered the heat on the hash browns and sausages that she started preparing for them. "And what do you mean by that, Mr. Garner Davis?" she queried.

He leaned forward and kissed her on her left cheek. "It means that I really want a serious relationship with you. No more of these booty calls that we've had in the past. You deserve much more than that."

He drew her closer, giving her a tight hug.

Kadrece was incredulous. "Garner—"

"I can't explain it," he went on to say, "but I've never been this happy before."

"Now I'm the one who's happy," she said, eyes beginning to mist. "I knew I made the right decision taking the trip up here."

Garner motioned for Kadrece to sit on his lap at the table. "Does that mean you're saying yes to me?"

She kissed him fully on his lips; he understood what that meant. He also realized this was the first time that he formally asked a woman to be his.

On Sunday morning, Garner broached whether Kadrece might be interested in visiting his church before she returned to Tallahassee via I-20 westbound and later Atlanta's Hartsfield-Jackson Airport.

"I need to be back in Atlanta before 12:30, baby, otherwise I'd love to come with you," she told him.

Garner did his best to hide his disappointment. "I understand. I forgot that it takes three hours, if not more, from here to Atlanta's airport." He mentioned that he wished she had more time to have gone to church with him.

Kadrece moved with diligence to pack. "I'm sure that I would, if it's a place you're happy with."

A half-hour later, Garner helped Kadrece with her luggage out to her rental car. It was a somber moment for him. They gave each other a tight hug and a long, passionate kiss.

"Thanks for visiting me," he whispered to Kadrece. "I'm really happy that you're my lady. I—"

Her eyes began to mist. "I better leave now, or I'll start crying."

No sooner than Kadrece left Garner's condominium complex, she sobered up and pumped her fist like she had tugged hard on a slot machine and had hit jackpot. Two out of three wasn't bad, and there still was a fifty-fifty chance that she might go perfect in the Carolinas.

She was so elated with how her plan worked almost to perfection that she called Nedra despite it being close to the time she knew that her family would be heading out to church. Her heart pounded in nervous anticipation of Nedra picking up.

"Praise the Lord, sista!"

Nedra was the least amused. "Praise Him for what?"

"Praise Him because He is good."

"I bet he was good—"

Kadrece sucked her teeth. "Nedra, you sure know how to steal somebody's joy. I'm beginning to have regrets that I called you. Besides, I just wanted to let you know that I'm heading back to Atlanta, and I should be back in town late this afternoon."

There were shouts from Nedra's sons in the background. She asked Kadrece to hold on. There was a faint one-way conversation that transpired. "Now you two know better than to act like that, especially on Sunday morning. I'll deal with you two when I get off the phone."

She huffed, returning to the phone. "All right, I'm back . . . I take it that you and what's his name spent at least some of your time above the bed sheets."

For years, Kadrece had wanted to tell Nedra that she finally gotten a man of her own and to rub it in by telling her to take that, Ms. Goody Goodie.

"We spent time clothed and in our right minds," Kadrece answered. "We even had a righteous conversation about church. There's a lot more to Garner than you've ever given him credit for."

"Well, I guess, then, that I'm glad for you. I just hope that you two understand the importance of commitment and respect."

Kadrece rolled her eyes. "We did talk about commitment and respect. We know that we've played on other people, but that's in the past. Garner's one-hundred percent committed to me; I know it in my heart." She went on to tell Nedra that things did seem to happen in their own time, and she was more than ready for it.

Nedra inhaled through her nose. "Okay, if he's one-hundred percent committed to you, are you just as committed to him?"

There was a pause.

"I told Garner that as I gave of myself to him that he was receiving all of me. So yeah, I'm totally committed to him."

"That's not what I asked you. I said, are you committed to him?"

Kadrece became annoyed. "Yes, Nedra, I am committed to Garner. One–hundred percent. Are you satisfied now?"

There was more noise in the background. Nedra knew that she might have to become a referee and the enforcer. Her youngest son, Cosby, was crying and the other one, Brandon, had run to Crennell.

"Listen, I've got to go. But I'll be praying for you, Kadrece. Call me when you get back in town, okay?"

Chapter 14

Two weeks later

Kadrece had three court briefings all in succession over at the Leon County court facility, and she had two meetings scheduled that afternoon back at the law office. Admittedly, she thrived on days like this especially once she broke through her usual morning stupor. She was more than capable of multi-tasking clients, shuttling between the law office and court, and managing phone calls throughout her workday.

A call from the 864 area code broke her attention during her mad scramble back to the law office between her morning and afternoon schedule. A wide smile graced her face.

I knew he would be begging me for some soon, she remarked.

"Attorney Kendricks—"

"Uh, Ms. Kendricks, this is Steve Duggans. How are you today?"

There was no immediate reaction.

"Hello, Ms. Kendricks—"

"Oh, I'm sorry, Mr. Duggans," she finally answered. "I'm doing fine."

"Great. I wanted to call and see where you were with our offer to join us here in Greenville."

"Your staff was very gracious to me," she said. "I've just not want-ed to make any rushed decisions."

"It's not often that I meet talented people like you," Duggans said. "I really believe you'll be able to go a lot farther in your career by joining us. We want to make it worth your while."

She nodded. "Mmmm, how much would you assign a value to that, Mr. Duggans?" She spoke with raised eye brows. She recalled to herself that Duggans sneaked a couple of glances at her chest.

He cleared his throat. "Kadrece, we're prepared to improve our offer by another $5,000 in salary. That, of course, is pending you being admitted to the South Carolina bar, which we fully expect you will."

"That's right, I would have to be admitted to your state's bar," she answered. "Does your state allow me to practice temporarily?"

"Normally, we don't seek out-of-state talent. All of our talent is homegrown. But we feel you're that exception. We would like to move on this very soon."

Kadrece clenched her fist and teeth. Although she had a good idea on what direction she wanted to take, she had not even discussed her considering options in the Carolinas with neither of her partners, Marshall Schaeffer or Kline Bradley.

She requested, "Mr. Duggans, may I get back with you on my deci-sion later this afternoon?"

"That would be fair enough. I'll look for your call."

From the parking lot of her law office, Kadrece's next phone call was with Stan Mancini at Wytheman & Pepper. She convinced her-self that two weeks had been damned long enough to decide on whether they wanted her. An office assistant transferred her to Man-cini's office, but all she got was his voice mail. Being the detailed person that she was, she made it a point to get his cell phone number during her visit.

"Stan Mancini," he answered hurriedly.

"Yes, this is Kadrece Kendricks."

"Ah, yes, Kadrece. Great to hear from you. How's the weather down in Florida?"

Humph.

Kadrece sensed a disconnection from Mancini. It was similar to what she experienced during her visit.

"You need to come down here. You might like it," she answered. "If you're into golf, I can show you a few nice courses over near Fort Walton Beach."

"Sounds like something I might have to take you up on."

After mimicking Mancini with a male's masturbation gesture with her left hand, Kadrece cleared her throat and spoke in a more serious tone. "All invitations aside, I'm sure you know that I'm calling you about any decision that Wytheman & Pepper's reached."

"Uh, Kadrece, we're still in the process of evaluating everyone. I do want to let you know that our principal partners were highly impressed with your career highlights and the dimension you might bring to our firm."

"Thank you." She shifted in her car seat, leaning against her door cushion. "Well, if I had not already mentioned this, there is another firm that holds me in similar regard. I'm sure you understand that I must also make sure that I'm not closing the door to any opportunities that may be out there—"

"I understand, Kadrece. But I'm in no position to hurry the process. Like most companies, we want to feel comfortable with knowing that we've attracted the best of the best."

A sense of calm prevailed upon Kadrece. "I see, Stan. Well, the invitation is still out there for you if you're into golf. It's been great talking to you."

"Thank you. We'll be in contact."

Bastards!

Two out of three still was not bad, Kadrece surmised, and maybe it was better to make a decision based on an option in which she was wanted. In her next move, she contacted Duggans, informing him that she would accept the firm's offer.

"That's outstanding," Duggans reacted. "Milton had to appear in court unexpectedly, but he told me that we should expect a call from you today. We didn't think it would be this soon."

"I was more than impressed by your firm's interest in me. It really meant a lot."

"Well, great. I'll let Milton know that you'll be coming aboard. Over the next couple of days Sharon, my assistant, will be helping you out with anything involving your move to South Carolina. Once you're here, we'll also work out some kind of schedule for you to prepare for your bar exam."

Kadrece pursed her lips, exhaling loudly. The reality of her decision had sunk in: she was about to navigate a new course in her life. She leaned back in her car seat, closing her eyes. This time she inhaled deeply through her nose, letting it out slowly. She wondered would life show any semblance of being the same with this decision.

Seconds later, she let out another sigh. She knew this meant sharing her decision with Marshall and Bradley, who had become her friends in addition to law partners. She checked her watch. It was 1:15 p.m., and she had fifteen minutes before her scheduled meeting with representatives from Reedy Dynamics, a military contractor near Pensacola.

Meanwhile, her next phone call answered on the second ring.

"Nedra—"

She spoke in her most professional of business voices. "Hold on, please—" The phone receiver rattled. "Okay, I'm back."

"Are you sitting down?" Kadrece blared.

"Of course, each day I come here they chain me to my seat," she answered. "I think the only time they let me up from here is to use the bathroom, and I'm not even sure about that."

"Sorry that you're so busy. But so am I today."

There was knocking on Nedra's door in the background. "Come in!" One of her subordinates came rushing in to give her details to a report that she requested. "Can you give me a couple of minutes?" The employee consented. There was the sound of the door closing.

"All right I'm back, but you better make this fast, K-girl."

Taking a deep breath, Kadrece divulged, "I've decided on moving to South Carolina."

Nedra straightened up in her office chair. "You've decided to go where?"

Kadrece smiled. "South Carolina."

"This has nothing to do with what's his face?"

"It might and it might not. I'll be getting a $25,000 raise, and I know the cost of living is much less there in South Carolina than it is here in Florida."

"Are you sure about that, and have you prayed about this?"

"Yes, I have. I've felt a lot of peace about my decision."

"Look, we'll have to talk about this later. I better handle this employee. She can act so helpless if I don't act in a motherly way with her."

Kadrece's hoped that her next call would be less suspicious. That call picked up on the fourth ring.

"Mother dear . . ."

"I'll always be she."

After glancing into the mirror to brush her hair away on the sides, Kadrece returned her attention to Johnette Kendricks. "I don't have a lot of time, mom, but I wanted to let you know that I'll be moving to Greenville soon."

Johnette searched for a place to sit in the family's home in Norcross, Georgia, a suburb of Atlanta. "Can you repeat that?" She leaned back in a comforter chair in the great den.

"I said I just accepted a job at a firm in Greenville, South Carolina. I'll be giving up my partnership stake here in Tallahassee."

"My lawd . . . Have ya thought about what you'll tell ya father? What about your brothers and sisters?"

"Mom, I just called Mr. Duggans not long before calling you." She leaned back into her car seat, exercising her neck.

Johnette began mulling Kadrece's announcement. "How long have you been in Florida?"

"Mom, since I came here for college. That's been since 1990."

"I see . . . and now you want to move to South Carolina?" Johnette paused for several seconds. "And you didn't come by here when you went to Charlotte not long ago—"

Kadrece became impatient. "What are you getting at, mother dear?"

"Um, Reecie, I was just trying to understand what you just told me."

"What is there to understand? I've accepted a job in South Carolina."

"Well, tell me this: is it somebody there that I don't know about?"

Kadrece rubbed her forehead and she shifted in her seat. "I'm not going to beat around the bush. I have a male friend in South Carolina. Is there anything else you want to know?"

Johnette was moved to laughter. "Well, that explains why you didn't come to visit us when you were in Charlotte."

"See, mom," Kadrece reacted, exhaling in disgust, "there you go again."

Johnette shook her head. "Lawd, help this girl." Meanwhile, she ran through her own mental checklist of men whom Kadrece have come to pick her up at the family home. The most likely one that came to mind was Furnell Toliver, who worked at Combes and Spivey architectural firm in nearby Marietta, Georgia.

She then queried, "Is it male or female, and how long you've known this person?"

Kadrece decided to keep Johnette in suspense. "Hey, I've got only a couple of minutes to get inside. I've got a couple of briefings back-to-back this afternoon. And I've got to start on my plans moving to Greenville."

"I guess that's not a bad move," Johnette remarked. "You'll be much closer to home, and at least you didn't forget about ya family."

Kadrece decided early on to share her news with Garner at the end of his workday. She anticipated he would be back from the station around 12:15 a.m. When she called, she wore a thin see-through and was laying across her bed on her back, caressing and kneading her breasts.

He picked up within a couple of rings. "Hey, sexy, handsome, freaky man" was the way that she greeted him.

"Huh?"

"Don't ruin the mood for me, baby."

Garner grimaced as though he had made a major blunder by not recognizing Kadrece's voice. "I'm sorry. It's been a long day for me today."

"It has?"

"Yeah, there's been a lot of politicking lately. I was warned that I had to cut back on how much I criticize those sorry ass Chanticleers. The station's scared that they might lose money if I tell too much of the damned truth."

Kadrece bent her legs and shifted her self-pleasuring downward. "I'm sorry to hear that, but I know you'll handle it like you always do." She let out a soft sigh as she felt her clit swell to her touch. "Baby, I just want to let you know that I'm taking the job in Greenville."

"Really? You're taking a job there?"

"Uh-huh. I feel I need a change. I mean, I'm a partner in a firm that gave me a chance after I graduated. But I felt that I was only going to go so far before I hit that glass ceiling with them."

Garner had started shedding his clothes, not caring where they dropped in his bedroom. He retrieved a pair of light workout pants out of his dresser. Then he made his way back into the living room where he plopped on his sofa. "Why don't you just say you took the job only to be closer to me?"

"Being closer to you would be only one of the benefits of my decision," she answered. "I want to advance my career, but now I've made this decision I also want to give our relationship the chance it deserves."

She then spoke in a more seductive tone. "Have you been thinking about us?"

"I've missed you every day that we've been apart. I told you that I really didn't want a long-distance relationship."

"Well, I've made my decision. So now that won't be an issue. I plan on finding a place and everything by the first of October."

"That's a little over a month from now," observed Garner.

"Aren't you excited? I know that I am," she said, pausing to manipulate her pussy and clit. She spread her legs wider and thrust her hips to the rhythm that she had now achieved between mind and body. "This will be the first time that we'll really have a chance to support each other in a way other than us creeping."

He chortled. "We don't have to do that any more." As devious as the thought was, he was more than mindful that some of their most spontaneous and erotic encounters occurred while they cheated on the other person—both while he was in Florida and later in Texas—just to maintain their sexual relationship.

Feeling equally as mischievous, he slipped his hand inside his athletic pants and gripped his now semi-erect dick. He went on to query, "Kadrece, do you think that we're capable of being faithful to each other?"

She closed her eyes while she inserted two fingers inside her soaking wet pussy. "I think we're able to because I think we know what we want at this stage in our lives." She maintained reasonable silence while her body tensed and she experienced a tingling orgasm. It was just as much of a plausible completion to her day.

"Hold on, baby," she requested of him.

He sat up and clicked on the television. There was a political show on the MSNBC channel.

She placed the phone near her pussy. She then asked, "Can you hear this?"

Garner muted the television. "Sounds like you were doing something that I wish I was there to see."

"Can't you tell that I miss you? See how you're bringing out the old Kadrece?"

"I like that old Kadrece. And I like the new Kadrece," he said, pausing to chuckle. "You're making it real tough on me."

"Don't worry, baby, I'll make it much easier for us real soon."

Chapter 15

Several weeks later

In most years, the major league baseball postseason would be one of Garner's areas of intense interest. Even he noticed a lack of enthusiasm in his voice when he reminded viewers during the 6 p.m. broadcast that the World Series was being contested by Tampa Bay and Philadelphia, and it had nothing to do with either team not being a marketer's dream match-up. He had a deep longing to be elsewhere on game day and any other sports-related function, but he really did not understand it.

On this particular day, he was more than eager between broadcasts to head for the sanctity of his car—and a comfortable distance away from the curious minds and ears that pervaded in the newsroom. Easing back in the driver's seat, he dialed home to Richmond, where he hoped to be the recipient of a voice of reasoning.

Miriam's greeting actually produced a relieved smile. "It's about time you called. I know you didn't want me to get in my car and show up at your front door." They shared a quick laugh. "How you've been taking care of yourself?"

There was a pause from Garner. Usually, he'd tell Miriam about what was going on at the station and whom he'd pissed off while interviewing.

He finally said, "I-I . . . was just thinking—"

"Thinking about what?"

"How have you been since we went up to Arlington National?"

"Humph, you're just now asking me that?"

"Well, I wasn't sure if I should have asked you," he said. "I know I had a lot of things to think about. You know, finding out that the man who died wasn't your father is a lot, but then finding out that my real father had been dead half a lifetime ago was even more."

Miriam breathed a noticeable sigh of relief. She reminded Garner about her keeping the secret about her relationship with Garrett had been a gut-wrenching and agonizing ordeal for more than three decades.

"I hope you understand that I've always done everything I could possible do to be a good mother to you," she offered; there was somberness in her voice.

Garner nodded before he replied. "Mom, I can never bring myself to think anything negative about you. I'm just glad to know who I really am, however little that might be." There was little emotion in his voice. He went on to say, "Did I tell you that I've been going to church lately?"

"I don't recall, but that sounds nice," Miriam said. "I've been a little slack lately, myself."

"Yeah, I found a church in a place called Pelion. The pastor's a good guy. It's the first time I felt like I've been a part of a place that was sincere. Nothing like some of the clowns I've told you about in the past."

"Is he on television?"

"Not yet."

There was another pause. The next sound was the warning chime in Garner's car and the engine responding to his light tap on the accelerator.

"Where are you right now?" asked Miriam.

"I'm in the parking lot at work, and I'm about to take off from here. I still have the eleven o'clock show to do."

Garner began brooding to himself about the last time he felt a similar impulse to confide in Miriam. That conversation was necessitated out of exasperation and desperation because he had put himself in an unwanted situation with Vernise.

Carefully, Garner cleared his throat and reminded himself to speak in a clear, unstressed tone. "Can I ask you this question?" He sensed Miriam's silence was a green light to continue. "What were some of the things you dealt with emotionally when you felt the way you did for my father?"

Uneasiness and shame consumed Miriam. She braced herself for another foray of interrogation. No matter what, she had long since resolved that she would never let go of any good memory she beheld of Garrett.

"Everyone's situation is different," she began explaining to him. "I think sometimes Garrett was an outlet and an escape from reality in dealing with Aaron. So I was not sure for a long time about my feelings. But I miss Garrett a whole lot. I really do."

"Do you think if things were different that you two could have gotten married?"

She smiled and closed her eyes. "Garrett wanted so badly to slip a ring on my finger. He said he was always happy to be around me, and I think that would have made him the happiest man on earth. He was willing to pay for my divorce; I wouldn't let him because I was concerned something might get out and cause problems for his career."

Garner had taken the surface streets to Blythewood. Not even the driver of a powder blue Hyundai Elantra who did not seem to know whether she would turn right into any of the driveways near the Richland Fashion Mall on Beltline Boulevard failed to faze him.

"I see," he commented, down shifting. "I asked you that question because I think I've got some serious feelings for somebody."

"Is it someone I know?"

"You might . . . Her name is Kadrece."

Miriam placed a hand on her forehead and later scratched her scalp. She moved from her bar stool near the kitchen to one of her living room chairs. "I don't recall you mentioning her name."

She had now clicked on the television, catching an update on the presidential election. She had been following it with great interest because media reports had suggested Democrat presidential nominee Barack Obama might be pulling ahead of Republican John McCain in Virginia.

"Mom, I've known her since college. I know I've said her name around you at least a couple of times—"

"It must not have been too loud."

"Well, I'm telling you loud and clear: I think I have some serious feelings for a lady named Kadrece."

"Now I remember that girl Sabryan," Miriam interrupted him.

He grimaced at the mentioning of her name. Inhaling deeply, and then letting the air out slowly through his nostrils, Garner now wondered if he should have just taken the freeway back to his place because his impatience for the red lights had surfaced.

"What's so special about this Ka-drece?" Miriam queried. "I hope you're using better judgment this time."

Beads of perspiration began forming on Garner's brow. "Kadrece and I go way back. She's smart. She's a lawyer. And she just moved from Tallahassee to South Carolina."

"Well that's nice, but tell me more." She then reacted to her comment by snapping her finger. "Hey, whatever happened to that woman who sent you that fake pregnancy test?"

Garner, bristling at the memory of Vernise, grabbed his gearshift lever and power shifted into fourth.

"Damn," he mumbled, reacting to the slight grinding of gears.

"What was that?"

"What happened to what?"

"You heard what I said."

"Oh, she's dead."

Miriam's heart sank to the pit of her stomach. "What happened?"

"She drove into the side of a building. Suffered severe head trauma. She died on impact, if not shortly after that." He leaned back hard in his seat.

"That's sad," Miriam responded. "You know God don't like ugly."

"I wish I could say that—"

Garner had managed to block out much of his recollection of that fateful night just eight months earlier. Some of it had to do with the immediate implosion of his acquaintance with Tamira.

For the next month or so, she hounded him with hateful phone calls blaming him for the drama and trauma that she experienced after witnessing Vernise's death. Then she contacted him one afternoon at the station apologizing for her immaturity. Garner mindlessly asked her if she wanted to make an effort at reconciling. They agreed upon a meeting in Orangeburg; they ended up spending a night at her place. They drifted back apart in a span of three weeks.

By that time, Garner had discovered Pastor Lanier's church, and he began immersing himself into a renewed commitment. His time at Divine Grace helped him to better deal with his past.

Despite the bad news about Vernise, Miriam still was curious about Kadrece. "That's fine this one is an attorney and she's smart. What do you really know about her since it was obvious that you didn't know much about that other one?"

Sighing heavily, Garner attempted to buy time by glancing at his rear-view mirror. "What do I know about Kadrece? Where do I begin?"

"I'm listening—"

"She's talked a lot about church in the past year."

"That's fine she goes to church. Now what else do you know?"

"Umm, she's the youngest of five in her family."

"So she's a spoiled brat."

"Well, uh, she's never been married and she has no children that I know of."

"Now we're getting somewhere."

"Uh, we've kinda become serious since last month."

"Last month?" Miriam's voice went up a couple of octaves, and her maternal antenna became more sensitive. "I thought you said you've known her since college."

"I have. I mean, we've, uh, kinda had a really casual relationship until last month—"

"Oh, you mean, the two of you used to see each other for sex only? You know, back in the day we used to call that kind of thing friends with benefits."

Sighing again, Garner shook his head, realizing that he'd never outlive his mother's scrutiny. "Mom, Kadrece and I decided to be serious after all these years. And I think we might have something going on."

"All right," she replied with a hint of resignation in her voice. "Make sure that your eyes are open and you guard your heart."

Chapter 16

Kadrece did receive some good news on Thursday that she passed the state's bar exam with an overall score of eighty-eight. She took time out to contact Nedra and her parents, respectively.

All three parties initially shared in the good news before digressing to something that placed Kadrece on the defensive.

"Well, not everyone can be like a Billy Graham telling everyone the only woman that he ever knew was Rose Graham," she snapped at Nedra, who commented that she often prayed for Garner's deliverance and salvation.

Nedra was taken aback by Kadrece's sharp retort, and she knew Kadrece was revving up to say more.

"I know when my time's up," she told Kadrece. "Would you please tell Garner that I asked about him?"

Kadrece's father, Hilton Sr., digressed to chiding her about the lack of contact she's maintained with them in recent months.

"I think it's the least you can do after your mother and I worked as hard as we did to put you and your brothers and sisters through college," he said. "That's all I'm asking in return from you."

She always knew how to pierce through her father's rough exterior. "And I love you too, daddy."

Hilton, a retired senior urban planner, was quick to regroup. Johnette had whispered to him about Kadrece's involvement with Garner.

"Hey, what's this I hear about you dating that yellabone named Garner?" he inquired. "I thought he was just a flash in the pan like the rest of them."

"Daddy, we just really got started."

"I don't know about his kind," Hilton lamented.

"What is there not to know about him?" Kadrece replied. "He's fine as you know what. He's good at what he does. He's respectful, thoughtful, and I'm glad that he's now in my life."

"Humph, I done told you about them pretty boys. They think they're something having that bright yella skin, maybe some straight and nappy hair, and those light-colored eyes. They ain't about nothing."

Kadrece knew where this conversation was headed.

"Daddy, there will never be as good a man as you," she said. "But I do think you might like Garner if you can ever look past your prejudice."

"Girl, who you're calling prejudiced?"

"Daddy, I've gotta go. Love 'ya!"

Kadrece's workweek was dulled by an uncomfortable Friday morning interaction with Duggans. It was just her good fortune that Duggans was the lone obstacle between Kadrece making it to her office without any interaction. She rued her decision that she had stopped off in the break room to create a cup of tea.

Duggans had placed his two glazed donuts and coffee on the table once he noticed Kadrece, folding his arms like and instructor. He'd already been at the law office since 7:30 a.m.—his red power tie was loosened at the collar and he'd already rolled his white sleeves up to his elbow.

"Mornin' Kadrece," he greeted her with a broad smile.

Kadrece did not immediately return the smile. "Good morning, Mr. Duggans." She lowered her head and stirred in two teaspoons of sugar into her orange flavored tea bag.

"Kadrece, how many times I have to tell you that you can call me Steve?"

She took a small sip from the tea. It was not sweet enough, but it would have to do. She figured maybe another time she'd get it right.

"I guess I'm still new . . . sorry."

"Now let's say it together . . . It's *Steve*," Duggans said, making a gesture with both hands.

Kadrece finally managed a smile. "I get it . . . Steve . . . good mooorning!"

Duggans beamed with pride and he nodded in approval. "Good morning, Ms. Kendricks." He then strutted off to his office like he had more than his just his ego stroked. The interaction left her wondering what had she gotten herself into.

When Kadrece returned home late that afternoon, she received a certified letter from her former law partners in Florida asking that she repay them $20,000 for breaking her partnership agreement. This came as a surprise because she'd already given them her book of clients along with the promise that she would not solicit nor accept any work from them for at least five years from the date that she left Florida.

Kadrece felt as though she'd just been robbed at gunpoint after leaving a lottery redemption center. Just when it seemed she had secured the remainder of her bonus, she just had amplification on what it was like to have a word sown in her life only to have it stolen by the enemy. So far, she spent only a fraction of the initial $10,000 that she received after she signed on at Duggans and Chattell, but she was more ambitious in her ideas about the other $10,000.

"I can't believe it," she mumbled to herself at the mailbox. "I hadn't even seen the damned money—"

"I never thought they would be so backstabbing," Kadrece wondered aloud while she made somber procession from her SUV to her condominium. This was not about an employee who left her former employer high and dry. "All that talk about how they'd miss me," she hissed. "The only thing they missed was the damned money that I brought in for them."

She was tempted to call both of her former partners and curse them out. But her father's preaching came to mind. Hilton, a long-time deacon at the family's church in Atlanta, often told his children that they would learn of their true worth by the words, sentiments, and actions expressed behind their backs by their critics and friends.

The kitchen was a sore sight. Kadrece had neglected it to the extent that there was a stack each of plates, glasses, and silverware in the sink. She also left a pot and skillet atop the stove. Just off to her right, and next to the refrigerator, she winced at realizing that she had not taken out the trash. TGIF was not in order.

Walking past the kitchen, her guest bedroom was just to her left. Her work desk was cluttered. There was only a clearing for her printer and where she hooked up her laptop. She hung her purse on the closet doorknob, and she placed her attaché case on the floor just off to the right of her desk. She was determined to ignore the mess and her bad news long enough to check her personal e-mail account on Hotnet.com.

Seventy-two e-mails filled her inbox dating back to the previous Sunday. About one-third of the way through her e-mails one with "My Chocolate Ecstasy" in the subject field piqued her attention. Raised eyebrows transformed into a wide grin once she read the brief message that was sent at 5:47 p.m.—about forty minutes before she had arrived home.

> I never realized the value of a good woman until you reappeared in my life. You've given me new meaning to what living is all about.
> It's been a wild week for me. I can't wait to see you when it's all over.

Surely, this had to have been something pre-ordained. There was no other way to explain it, she thought. She searched over her shoulder for a phone, but she figured that could wait just a little longer after she took time out to straighten up her place and relax with a clear mind.

The first thing she did was take out the trash. She figured that was the least she could do since the trash bin was just around the back of her building. When she returned, she noticed a red, gold, and white delivery envelope just to the right of her door. She realized that she was too caught up in the letter from her former partners in Florida to have even recognized it.

Browsing the paperwork, she noticed that it had a Columbia origin. She thought that it must have been something from the South Carolina Bar—a formal welcome letter or invitation to some event for newly admitted attorneys. She was slow to open the parcel, considering the last thing she wanted to think about was anything having to do with her profession.

The contents in the parcel changed her attitude as six live red rose petals fell to her living room carpet, and she recognized the familiar handwriting with "Kadrece" on the violet birthday card-shaped envelope. She made haste to put the delivery envelop on the counter and she took a seat on one of the kitchen chairs.

"God, I don't deserve this," she whispered to herself. "But you know my heart."

Chapter 17

A hot bath, candle-lit bathroom, and spending time exploring her body for pleasure had rapidly become an appealing thought. Only that Kadrece longed to share her moment of sensuality with the man who was responsible for this good feeling: Garner.

She rushed to stuff her dishwasher, sweep the kitchen floor, and clean the stove top. She also made a quick pass through the rest of her place: she got rid of unnecessary paperwork in her workroom; she replaced the towels in her bathroom; she also straightened up her bed covers in the bedroom.

Because she was visiting him, she did not worry about taking a shower because she could always do that at his place. She packed enough clothes to last her through Tuesday, including an outfit for church. She also brought her Bible, a couple of law books to prepare for her case work during the week and a few of her favorite intimate play items— her digital camera, a brand new seven-inch rabbit vibrator, a Mardi Gras mask, nipple nooses, and some berry scented arousal cream—along with a couple of silk chemise gowns.

Kadrece left her place around 7:45 p.m. If there was any doubt that she might be affected by fatigue while driving eastbound on I-26, that all dissipated by the time she reached exit No. 66, putting her about halfway to Blythewood.

"Hey handsome," she greeted Garner, placing him on her loudspeaker. "Whatcha doin'?"

"Missing you."

"Really?"

"Really."

"Well, that's nice to hear because I really think what you did today for me was really, really sweet. I think the roses and the card is something that I'll never forget."

Garner, who was between evening shows, had stopped by the grocery store at the time of Kadrece's phone call.

"You don't know what this relationship has done for me," he commented.

"That's good to know." She thought about her cadre of Garner critics. She wished that she had recorded their conversation just to prove to them that there was substance to their relationship. "I'm on my way to Columbia to spend the weekend with you."

"You know I've got a noon game to cover tomorrow. This one's between the Chanticleers and their rival from across the state in Clemson. I'll damned near have to be there at nine o'clock just to make sure that I get a parking spot for our truck."

"Oh, so that's why I see so many cars with orange tails and paws driving towards Columbia?"

"Uh-huh."

"Well, that has nothing to do with me and you. I don't want to sleep alone tonight, tomorrow night, and the next night," she said. "Can you handle that?"

Garner looked around before he considered his response. He had been walking along the main aisle next to the meat department. He tried keeping his mind off Kadrece's thought-provoking dare.

"Oh, I can handle that and anything else you might throw at me," he said. "You forgot that I was a pretty good baseball player?"

"Player, yes," she chortled. "I know the same man that I'm talking to once had three women in the same day—one of them was me."

"I don't know who your sources were, but I think they're a little off or misleading."

"Garner, do you know who you're talking to? Remember, this is

Kadrece. The same woman you're now calling your Chocolate Ecstasy?"

"I know who I'm talking to."

"All right now." She could not resist rubbing her left breast with her right hand. "I like the way you realize who I am in your life." Her tone had become sultry.

"How far are you from Columbia?" he inquired.

"I think I just passed exit No. 74."

"Okay, that's the last Newberry exit. You still have about forty-five minutes before you're here," he said. "I might be back at the station by the time you get here. I've got to prepare for a live shoot in front of the stadium."

"So I'll get a chance to see my man on television?" she moaned into the phone, stroking her pussy through her sweats. "I might break out with one of my toys while I'm watching you. That'll be better than watching a movie that I probably shouldn't be watching."

"Bye, Chocolate Ecstasy."

"Bye, baby."

Knowing that Kadrece would be in town for the weekend made it easier for Garner to tolerate covering the Chanticleers-Bengals football game at Winnetka-Benson Stadium. He could readily assume the mentality of a media mercenary, touching on all the happenings that would be important to his viewing audience yet at the end of the day he could care less. All that mattered was him getting paid.

What was more important was Kadrece had become his sexual and emotional rescue. He was willing to do whatever it took to ensure that she would continue to avail herself to him.

The benefits were that Garner saw himself in an enviable situation. He knew there were many other individuals' life situations desiring to have someone significant. It seemed like lyrics to a song, but he began to understand there was some truth to wanting someone to hold on to. Just like there was something about wanting someone to confide in with his most important thoughts and aspirations.

And, yes, even someone to fuck and who would love fucking him in return.

As it had become their habit, Kadrece left his porch light on to denote that she was inside. He let out a light chuckle when he glanced off to his right and recognized that she was not outside waiting for him. That was a definite possibility had it been during the summer.

"Where's my sexy Chocolate Ecstasy?" Garner said as he stepped inside his condominium.

"Waiting right here for you, baby." Kadrece, reclined on the sofa, had been teasing her clit and tasting her pussy nectar for the past ten minutes or so. She immediately sprung up to greet him. "I miss you."

Garner's eyes widened once he recognized she was wearing a black silk chemise and her breasts bobbled freely under the garment—his dick also responded to her body making contact with his.

They engaged in a tight hug and a long, wet kiss before separating.

"I just had to be with my man tonight."

"I'm glad you're here."

"Guess what, baby?"

"Why don't you just tell me," Garner answered.

Kadrece pranced over to the dining room counter and unfolded a letter. She announced, "This says that I passed the South Carolina bar exam. I thought I might surprise you with that."

Nodding his head, Garner flashed a smile and extended his arms out to her. "Come here, sexy woman—"

He slipped his hands under Kadrece's chemise, cupped her ass cheeks, and kissed her. He also pushed his tongue inside her willing mouth. Both of them felt a hormonal surge. Kadrece was the one who separated them this time.

"Is that all you have on your mind?" she asked.

"I am a man, what do you expect?"

"Point understood."

"I'm sorry, what was your score?"

"An eighty-eight."

"Wasn't that better than what you scored in Florida?"

"I made an eighty-three on that. All that matters is you pass. And for me, I'll also get paid."

"That's right. You have a bonus coming?"

Kadrece led Garner by the hand over to the sofa. She sat down first, with him joining her. "I hope so—"

Raising his shoulders, Garner inquired, "What do you mean, hope so?"

"My ex-partners are claiming that I owe $20,000 for breaking my agreement with them. Humph, they don't know who they're messing with."

"Well, they might not. But I know who I'm crazy about."

Kadrece leaned back and nuzzled her back into Garner's chest. He responded by wrapping his arms around her, running his hands over her breasts. "And who might that be?"

"You," he answered. "Now you have me wondering if life been any easier without as many women in my past."

"Garner, you keep saying all the right things, I'm going to be attacking you right here in this living room."

As Garner drove to Winnetka-Benson Stadium, he went into deep reflection from transpired the night before with Kadrece. Their kisses, touches, caressing, and hugs were only trumped by their working in sensual tandem, producing a magical and kinetic chemistry that he only once dreamed of.

Moments like this had never hit so close to home with him. The only way he could relate to it and capture what he felt was through his vast selection of music. He chose selections from the group Hiroshima with off-title cuts "I've Been Here Before" and "Once Before I Sleep".

Of the two, "Once Before I Sleep" was a poignant reminder of finding calm and optimism amid a turbulent situation. He was so moved by the song that he damned near wanted to turn around on I-77 southbound and return to his place just to spend more time with Kadrece. He wondered to himself if these were the same feelings that his father, Garrett, experienced whenever he thought of Miriam.

By the time he reached the media's parking area at the state fair grounds, the working professional in Garner had re-emerged. It was a matter of simple deduction: these were once-in-a-lifetime emotions that he could not squander. It just so happened, too, that he received a text message from Kadrece.

I woke up with the sweet taste of your cum on my tongue :)

Garner returned a fast response.

There's more where that came from.

I know. I want more :)

Kadrece continued sending a steady stream of text messages throughout the day. It was equally fun and arousing to her. She mused whether her pious friend, Nedra, ever considered doing anything like that with her husband. Hell, she also mused whether Kamryn or Kanitra did the same thing at all with their husbands.

Even if they did, she suspected none of them had the sex life as she had and still be able to balance it with a sense of morality and consciousness of church.

She sent Garner a text message around 1:25 p.m., having no clue that the Chanticleers and Bengals were midway through the second quarter.

I just love the way your tongue felt up my asshole ~~

A surge of pride came over Garner once he read the text. For a selfish moment, he saw himself among a scant minority in the media that had it going in his sex life. He replied,

Would you like my dick there next time?

Did you have something planned for tonight?

About forty-five minutes later Kadrece created another buzz in Garner's jacket pocket.

> I liked the way you had me on the table licking
> my clit ~~

Garner almost missed what proved to be one of the more pivotal plays during the Chanticleers-Bengals game while reading Kadrece's text message. He caught the tail end of an electrifying eighteen-yard scramble at the start of the fourth quarter by Bengals quarterback Brice Simon, which put his team in field goal range. The Bengals went on to upset the favored Chanticleers, 31-16, enabling them to become bowl eligible just like their intrastate rival.

More than ninety minutes passed before Garner managed to respond to Kadrece's last text message. By then, he was taking one of his shortcuts from Winnetka-Benson Stadium back over to the station.

"Hey, my Chocolate Ecstasy," he began telling her, "how did you like my table manners?"

He reminded her that she was the one who suggested that she lay on the kitchen table while he sucked her pussy to a scintillating orgasm. He also incorporated the use of her rabbit toy.

"Mmmm, who taught you?"

"Maybe I was just so into you that I kinda knew how you'd want it."

Kadrece smiled. "I've been bragging about you being so attentive to me."

Garner could not react exactly as he wanted. He had to maintain his attention on the road. "Why would you be telling others about our business?"

"Baby, don't worry. Haters will be haters," she said. "I was just trying to send a little message out to them."

The mood in the air always seemed subdued in the Columbia area whenever the Chanticleers lost in football. It was partly amusing to

Garner because the garnet and black clad shoppers at the Village at Sandhill wore mostly shocked and dumbfounded expressions. Whereas, those who wore orange and white strode with a bit of measured glee.

The only thing Garner concerned himself with was a confrontation by some poor sap of a Chanticleers fan who blamed him for them losing against the Bengals now for the tenth time out of the past twelve years—a simplified way of saying why fan's the abbreviated term for fanatic.

A more welcomed sight came in the form of Garner spotting ol' man Spencer Watts and his wife, Shirley, entering Books-A-Plenty bookstore. He picked up his gait to catch up with them.

"What brings you on this side of town, ol' man?" Garner yelled from behind.

Spencer, sporting a leather jacket, dark hat and slacks, was the first to react by pivoting in mid-step to put a face with the voice.

"None of your, uh, business!"

They both shared a laugh, butted shoulders, and they embraced each other.

"Hello, Ms. Shirley. Long time no see—"

"It has been, Garner. You've been taking care of yourself?" she said, flashing a bright smile; she wore a gray cardigan, black velour slacks and a matching buttoned V-neck blouse, as well as black shoe boots.

"Young buck, the wife and I are over here because I just had to get me a couple of books on our new president. Can you believe it, my president's a black man?" Spencer said, stopping to chuckle; he also added a wink and a nod. "Oh, I forgot. You're just like him."

Garner threw his head back and smirked. Meanwhile, Spencer extended his hand out to him once more. This time, it was more fraternal.

"Man, where you been? I call you at the station, and you're always busy. We were supposed to do lunch."

"I know. I've had a lot of things going on," Garner replied. "And then just when I thought things would slow down, I saw an opportunity to help out with the election. I thought that might help me down the road for my career."

"I gotta tell ya', I couldn't believe they had you doing that. I thought you were out of sight that night. You had those white people scared of you. Shit, I even had Shirley watching you."

Garner explained to Spencer that the 2008 presidential election was too important not to offer a black perspective. "I just wanted to keep them honest."

"See, that's why I prayed for someone like you. I knew if the right person ever came to that station it would bring about some change." Spencer stooped to pick up a special *Life* magazine edition and a copy of Obama's biography sequel, *The Audacity of Hope*.

"You know what? Obama's a smart man," Garner said, pointing at Spencer's copy of *The Audacity of Hope*. "I suspect he wrote that book, in part, to help market himself with an eye towards running for president some day."

"You know what?" as Spencer stopped to puff out his chest. "You gotta hand it to me. I told everyone about Obama being the fulfillment of Dr. King's 'I Have a Dream' speech long before it was popular to make that comparison."

Nodding his head, Garner said, "You still have it, ol' man."

"Shiiiiiit, you damned right I do," he reacted. "Look here, I see Ms. Shirley's ready to leave. You call me some time next week." She soon joined him holding a cup of coffee in her right hand and a copy of *Husbands, Listen to Your Wives* tucked under her left arm.

Chapter 18

If the purpose of Pastor Lanier's messages were intended to bring introspection and repentance into the lives of his parishioners, he reminded his growing congregation of now more than fifty that no matter how much one's life appeared to be in upheaval God's thoughts for His people have always been of peace and optimism.

Lanier used the example of God's elect in the Old Testament that faced imminent wrath and judgment for their rebellious ways. Despite the multitude of warnings, they chose to worship false idols and indulge in questionable lifestyles that provoked God's anger. Few people stood for righteousness, which he alluded to in a prior passage that exalts a nation. And those who truly had a heart for God, he said, bitterly mourned for their fellow people.

"We should be like the prophet who wrote the passage that I'm referring to," Lanier said, "who managed to have some presence of mind of giving credit to God's grace, which renews daily for an undeserving people like ourselves.

"That, y'all, was an example of someone who had a serious relationship with God. That was someone who lived with a deep assurance that his God would always look out for his good—even in the midst of a perilous situation. How many of us can say that today during these uncertain times?'"

Lanier then closed his Bible and zipped its cover. He stepped to his right and away from the pulpit, inviting everyone to stand while he introduced an altar call for anyone who desired prayer. He went on to say, "For the right of privacy, I'm asking that everyone bow their heads."

Garner bowed his head and gave serious reflection upon the message. He recalled silently the many days that passed after he lost his job in Houston wondering if God really cared whether he ever found a job in his profession once again, or that he would forever be penalized for his womanizing behavior.

"Would everyone grab the person's hand that you're standing next to?" Lanier requested.

Garner extended his right hand and clasped Kadrece's left hand. For all the times he'd gone to church on Sunday, having sinned the night before, he felt it a rarity that he did not feel any weight of condemnation.

Meanwhile, Kadrece could only think of how strange it felt that she would be standing at a non-denominational church in South Carolina as opposed to the Baptist church she attended back in Florida.

Before she bowed her head again, Kadrece took a small side step to her left and nudged against Garner's shoulder. She had just recognized one of the female members cutting a jealous stare in their direction.

"How did you like church?" Garner asked, as they headed westbound on Route 178 towards the I-20 interchange.

Kadrece was slow to respond. "How long have you been going there?" The relative smallness of Divine Grace Fellowship reminded her of a children's Sunday school classroom at the Kendricks' family church in the Atlanta area

"Since the spring."

"I see—"

At least there was reason to offer a much sharper rebuttal to the next Nedra snipe at Garner, Kadrece thought. Now it was a matter of becoming comfortable with the idea that he might invite her again to his church.

"Hey, I've been checking out a few places in Greenville," she offered. "One of them is a big place, and they have a mixed congregation."

"And this is in Greenville?"

"Uh-huh. The pastor's white, but I've been told that about forty to forty-five percent of the members are black. They have about six to seven thousand members at the church, and they hold two services on Sundays."

Garner shook his head. He could not fathom a place like that. His church was all black despite Pastor Lanier's vision of a multicultural congregation.

"There's another place that I'm interested in," she said. "It's a predominately black church with a black pastor. I think I might be more comfortable there, but I hadn't decided on a place."

"Hey, let's talk about church later. The stores in Lexington County aren't open until 1:30 p.m., but there are stores open right now in Richland County. There's a place I want to stop by." And with that, Garner pressed the accelerator and shifted into fifth gear as he merged onto I-20 eastbound.

Garner thought the moment was right to ask Kadrece if she would assist him with some additional holiday shopping before they approached the Village at Sandhill shopping area.

"You've never ask me anything like that before. I'm flattered," she responded.

He shrugged. "You've come to church with me. You are my lady. Why not help me out?"

The first stop they made was at a linen and bath shop that was going out of business, as had so many other retail stores because of the country's economic downturn. He explained to her that he was looking for gifts for both his mother and sister.

The linen shop had little selection. It had been ravaged since store discounts reached fifty percent. So they proceeded to a bath and body works shop. There, Kadrece helped him choose a lavender fragrance bath set for Carla.

"That was easy, wasn't it?" Garner asked.

"If you say so—"

They walked hand-in-hand to some other stores along the driveway. The final store was the one that Garner really had in mind. "I've wanted to do something really nice for my mother, but I always worried about how she'd react to it."

"Why would you be worried?"

Garner peered over at Kadrece, waiting to make eye contact with her. "I think you know that I've been her favorite. She's proud of all of us, but she talks about what I've done more than my brother and sister."

"If I were your mom," Kadrece answered, squeezing his hand, "I wouldn't be ashamed of that."

Both looked at each other and smiled. Garner then gestured with his head that they walked towards the jewelry shop that was just to their right.

Inside, the salesperson, Naomi Cason, was the same one that he interacted with just the night before. She was thinly built, but with model features and in her mid-twenties. She wore an ivory colored pantsuit.

"Hi, may I help you?"

"Yeah, I told you the next time I came here that I'd bring some help," Garner answered.

"I see that you have." Naomi replied. "Have you decided on what you wanted?"

Kadrece joined Garner by his side, reaching to hold his hand. He went on to say, "I want to see something nice for my mother. Can you show the bracelets again?"

"Sure, over here—"

After spending roughly ten minutes over the selections, Garner asked Kadrece what she thought about a fourteen-carat gold diamond cluster ring for Miriam.

"Are you sure you want something like that for her?"

Garner gave a pained look. "I know I came here looking for a bracelet, and now I'm over here at the rings. I don't know—"

"I've got another customer," Naomi said. "Let me know when you've decided on something."

Leaning against the counter, Garner waited once more to make eye contact with Kadrece. He extended his hand out to her, smiling.

"You know, I actually came here to buy you an engagement ring," he said. "The one that I had in mind was right here."

Kadrece's mouth was agape and her eyes began welling with tears while Garner gave her a tug to come closer.

"I asked Naomi if she would be working today, which she said she was. I'm surprised that she remembered what to talk about."

"Garner, uh, I'm . . . shocked. I, uh, don't know what to say—"

He motioned for Naomi to return. Kadrece was giddy and beaming.

"So you've decided what you're going to do?" she asked.

"Yeah, show her the one that I picked out."

Naomi placed on the counter a three-quarter carat, fourteen-carat gold solitaire. Kadrece wiped a tear that streamed down her left cheek.

"Does that mean you like it?" he asked. "I guess if you try it on, that also means you're saying yes."

"Damn you, Garner Davis," she mumbled, shaking her head. "You really surprised me today. I'll never forget this."

She slipped on the ring and held it up to the light; her grin got wider. "Yes, baby." She jumped up and down in the same spot.

He stood with his arms folded, admiring her. "Yes to what?"

Hand trembling, she held the ring up again. "Yes to you. Yes to this ring, and it fits!" She also felt her heart pounding through her blouse. "That's what I'm telling you." She began processing thoughts of how incredulous things had turned out for her.

With a nod of his head, Garner told Naomi that she could put it on his card, and she'd wear it out of the store.

Kadrece accepted the tissues from Naomi. "How did you know my size?" She dabbed the corner of both eyes, choking back more tears of joy.

"Remember, I'm a reporter. I was taught to be observant."

Moments later, Garner and Kadrece held hands tightly as they walked out of the jewelry store. When they approached his car, she clenched his hand tighter, signaling that they stopped.

"Before you say anything, I know we had not talked about love, or even being in love," he said. "I just want you to know that I've been in love with you a long time. I did know that it would come back to me this way."

"Baby," she said, smiling. "I've felt the same way. I love you, too."

They entered into a tight embrace and they gave each other a passionate, wet kiss before agreeing that they had better take their business back to his place.

Chapter 19

Divine Grace Fellowship had arguably the only other action going on in Pelion on New Year's Eve beyond the spate of firecrackers and gunshots being fired around town. The church's membership had increased to nearly one hundred people, and the converted two-story home's sanctuary was crowded. Pastor Lanier had already begun discussing among his church's leadership council about the possibility of moving to a larger facility.

The New Year's Eve program consisted of testimonies, praise and worship, and Lanier's message before midnight. Kadrece seemed comfortable with the church's order of service while Garner often mentally ignored all the segments except for when Lanier preached.

Lanier spoke on the true meaning of being a believer. He articulated that Christians, spiritually speaking, are the Hebrews of today. And if one traced the meaning to Hebrew, he said, it meant to cross over in the original language.

"Amen," he added. "Abraham, who lived in what's modern day Iraq, was regarded as the one who crossed over the River [Euphrates] and into a place where God said He wanted His covenant with him.

"I believe this is a time—a God-appointed time— that we must be like Abraham and cross over as well. There are things in our lives that we need to leave behind and trust and follow God. I challenge all of you to be like Abram in these troubled times and economy."

Shortly after midnight, Lanier beckoned some individuals up near the pulpit. The first person was Shenara Ferguson, a divorcée in her early forties with two children. Just as she closed her eyes and raised her hands, Lanier bowed his head and began speaking in tongues. His wife, Turquoise, who stood next to him, gave her the interpretation.

"Sister, I know you've visited us here a few times. So you know this is not something we do for games. We take the Lord's work very seriously," she told Shenara. "I feel in my spirit the Lord's telling you that you have been in few good relationships, but many bad ones.

"I believe the Lord is telling you that you have to become like Joseph and confess what was meant for bad, God had meant it all for good—"

Shenara, who wore a navy blue pants suit, began to double over, sobbing. She then gazed up at the lights and ceiling and gave thanks. "Lord, only you know," she finally said, bowing her head and shaking it; the congregation offered a mild applause.

Lanier continued, "Sister, be strong in the Lord and in the power His might . . . God bless you—"

Meanwhile, Garner was ready to elude this part of the service.

"Brother," Lanier said, pointing in Garner's direction.

Garner looked around, and then at Kadrece.

"Yes, brother . . . you; please come up here," Lanier said, stopping to remove his brown suit jacket.

Though slightly shorter than him, Lanier placed his hand on Garner's shoulder, smiling at him. Meanwhile, Garner recounted his feelings of distrust for pastors, particularly those that exploit members by self-promotion, deception, and manipulation of weaker minds.

After brief silence, Lanier went on to say, "Brother, God's going use you. You'll see that promotion does not come from the east or west, but promotion comes from God . . . Bless you, my brother; go in peace—"

Garner reacted stunned. First, because there was no traditional Pentecostal theatrics from a pastor yelling and calling fire down from heaven. Secondly, he thought Lanier would have gone as far as telling him that he lived in lust, considering that Kadrece was present with him. Finally, he felt an unusual peace after the Lanier had prayed for him.

Just as Garner reached his seat next to Kadrece, Lanier had also motioned with his right hand for Kadrece. She initially nodded in his direction for clarification.

"Yes, sister . . . you; come up here, please," he answered, stopping to wipe his brow with a white handkerchief monogrammed with his "BL" initials.

She gave Garner a concerned and somewhat embarrassed look at him. He returned a slight shrug of his shoulders. She was reluctant to walk up near the laminated glass pulpit where Lanier and his wife stood. Her heart pounded hard because of her apprehension.

Trying to put her at ease, Lanier's wife positioned herself besides Kadrece, draping her arm across her shoulders.

"Sister, God says I know your thoughts. And your thoughts, says the Lord of Hosts, are not My thoughts neither your ways are My ways. But know that I am God, who is the author and finisher of your faith," the pastor said.

"I speak words that come to pass, for so shall it be the words that come forth from My mouth . . . Amen. God bless you, sister."

Lanier's words pierced Kadrece conscience. Inwardly, it was as though she'd been placed on trial herself, appearing before the Supreme Judge, Defense and Prosecuting Attorneys, all in one. After a brief prayer given by Lanier's wife, she returned to her seat next to Garner showing no emotion.

On their way back from the service, it took all of Kadrece not to share her indignation about Divine Grace with Garner. In the most tactful way that she knew, she was careful to say, "Baby, I don't know any other way than to tell you that I would prefer not visiting your church again."

"Did somebody approach you and tried slipping their phone number in your hand?"

"No, baby."

"Did some lady give you the evil eye, and you felt that it was not best to make a scene?"

"Baby, I'm not worried about some other woman and you. They have nothing on me."

"That is true."

"I'm just not comfortable in a place like that. I love God, and I can tell that you love God, too. It's just that I don't connect in a place like that."

"Okay, can we talk about that another time?"

"Fine with me."

Unexpectedly, Kadrece unhooked her seat belt, leaned over, and searched for his pants zipper. She looked up and gave him a seductive glare. "I did have a taste for something while I was in church. I hope nobody was trying to figure out what it was."

Garner did not resist when she slipped his dick free. He eased up on the accelerator and leaned back slightly in his seat so that he could better enjoy Kadrece's sensual lips and dazzling tongue teasing his shaft.

She paused once more, making eye contact with him. "I've been without this for almost a week. A healthy girl like me needs a steady diet of dick to stay happy and less bitchy."

When she resumed, she brought Garner to ejaculation while he drove at sixty-five miles per hour on I-20 eastbound. Meanwhile, she masterfully did not allow for a single cum spurt to miss coating the back of her mouth. Then she sat up in the passenger's seat smacking and licking her lips.

"I needed my protein, too, baby," she quipped. "And that's just for starters."

Chapter 20

Mission Grove Community Church was a place that Kadrece happened upon during the holiday season. She discovered it while she attempted to bully her way into one of the turning lanes over near the Westgate Mall on Blackstock Road.

The traffic, however, never allowed her over. Before she knew it, she'd driven past the railroad tracks and just off to her right was a beige stucco exterior church complex. She took that as a sign from above that maybe this was a place that she needed to visit—it became a part of her New Year's resolution to find a place of worship.

On that first Sunday, she wore something that was conservative— a Dana Buchman black pantsuit with a white Liz Claiborne cashmere pullover and pearl earrings—which she hoped would not draw any attention to her.

When she turned into the church's driveway, she paid particular attention to the substantial representation of shiny, well-kept Mercedes, Cadillac, Lexus, Infiniti, and Acura models more so than the contingent of older Ford, Honda, Hyundai, Kia, and Chevy models that also filled the lot. That told her Mission Grove had to be somewhat popular because smaller, lesser affluent churches usually had members driving the unappealing vehicles—the pastors included—

like at Garner's church.

Upon her entry into the church's foyer, Kadrece felt an immediate connection with Missionary Grove.

"Sister, praise the Lord," a lady in her early forties greeted her with a smile and a pleasant hug. "I'm Carnette Flemming."

"Good morning."

"I didn't get your name," Carnette said, still grasping her hand.

"It's Kadrece."

"Well, we hope you like it here. There is always liberty wherever the spirit of the Lord is." Carnette had now released Kadrece's hand.

"Thank you."

Kadrece veered left towards the sanctuary. Two reasonably tall men greeted her. The one to her left, Wade Dye, handed her a program. He had a pecan tan hue; he was distinguished by a medium-length, reddish brown 'fro with speckles of graying. His voice was rather formal and reminiscent of the late Roscoe Lee Brown.

"Feel free to sit anywhere you like," he said, nodding at her.

The other one to her right, Levi Harriston, had already noticed her while she was with Carnette Flemming. He was more than eager to catch her attention by clearing his throat.

"Praise 'um, sister," he said, allowing her flesh to meld in his grasp; the inflection of his words had a more churchy tone to them. "I've never seen you among us. Is this your first time here?"

She turned to him with her black leather Coach bag draped over her left shoulder and her left hand in plain view, hoping that he recognized her engagement ring. "I'm sorry. I didn't notice you. But, yes, it is."

"Well, we hope you enjoy it here. We'll be giving you a visitor's packet during the service."

"Thank you."

Kadrece went about mid-depth into the sanctuary before she chose an aisle seat in the section of pews to her right. Based on her timing, she arrived just as the praise and worship segment began. The praise leader went through a selection of three songs before giving way to a relatively short, barrel-chested man who appeared to be in his early fifties. He placed two books on the lectern part of the pulpit.

In a partly raspy tone, he requested that everyone "greet somebody who you didn't come here today." That was followed by a hoarse "God bless you."

Kadrece elected only to stand and shake hands with a couple that had turned around and smiled. Another lady whom Kadrece guessed to be in her early sixties approached her in the aisle with a hug.

"Sister, it's nice to have you here," she spoke into her ear. "We hope you enjoy yourself."

Before Kadrece had managed to sit down, a male's voice had arrested her attention from behind; he spoke just loud enough that only she recognized it: "Sista, glad to have you here—"

Kadrece slowly turned to her left. It was Harriston, a dark-skinned church brother grinning as they made eye contact. She noticed that he was rather robust in stature. He wore a navy blue Mario Vicci suit. He had thinning eyebrows and a significantly receding hairline.

Had this been her church in Tallahassee, there were ways to avoid people like Harriston. But she resigned herself to remaining cordial, accepting the handshake offer.

"Thank you, nice to be here." She decided if he approached her again during or after the service that it was fair game to ignore him.

Within a minute or so, the same man who asked everyone to greet someone now asked everyone to take a seat. Kadrece figured that this man had to be the pastor. Her suspicion was correct after another brother of the church, Deaton Phillips, prayed over the offering and made reference to him as Pastor Sherwin T. McBride III, which he acknowledged with a head nod. There was additional talk regarding the church's fund-raising campaign to equip the church with the latest high-definition technology.

McBride, now having turned on his remote microphone, interrupted Phillips. "That's right y'all. Some of you have seen on TV that everything's goin' digital in a few weeks. That means we need to keep up with the times. And I know the economy's bad, but we're dealin' with God's economy . . . Amen?"

Most of the congregation joined in response.

"Amen . . . So do as the Lord lays on your heart. Because you can't beat God givin'," McBride went on to add.

Kadrece found herself captivated by McBride's message, which he spoke on the example of a prophet who approached a widow who was broke and soon to be without food for both she and her child.

"Some of y'all thinking right now there's no way I'm givin' to this preacher and I can barely pay my light bill," McBride said. "That's especially the time that you need to give.

"Some of you don't realize that you could be missing your blessing by holding on to your little bit of nothin'. Like I said during the offering, if we're God's people, we operate in a different economy. And that economy is fueled by what?"

He cupped his hand over his left ear, but nobody from the congregation spoke up with the answer.

"Now who's church am I preachin' to this morning?" So he posed the question again. "What's God's economy fueled by?"

He was slow to form the word "faith" with his lips. Then he stopped in mid phrase to say, "Come on y'all, say it's faith. Now look around and tell someone, 'God's economy is fueled by faith!' "

By the end of the McBride's sermon on faith, Kadrece felt more than convinced that she had visited the right place. She reasoned that McBride simply confirmed the word that Pastor Lanier had spoken to her during the New Year's Eve service. Life could not get any better, she thought, and damn those who expressed skepticism about her decision to move to South Carolina.

Chapter 21

The bonus money that Kadrece received from Chattell and Duggans was now in the clear. Her former partners in Florida inexplicably dropped their threat to sue her. She promptly celebrated her $10,000 cash infusion by trading in her Ford Escape for a 2009 charcoal BMW 328i model.

One of the first places that she proudly displayed her car was at Mission Grove. It was also an opportunity to do the same thing with Garner, whom she asked to drive her there. She knew it would give her great satisfaction to observe some of the gawking and evil eyes by some of the women of the church.

"Baby, thank you for coming to church with me," she told him while they sat in the parking lot. "This really means a lot."

He leaned over and kissed her on the cheek. "You really look nice today," he said, admiring her black and red V-neck dress.

When Pastor McBride asked the church to stand up and greet another person, Levi Harriston went out of his way to work through the small cluster of members who assembled near Kadrece's aisle seat.

Garner, who sat uncomfortably next to Kadrece, had already entertained thoughts of just waiting out the service back in her car.

"Excuse me brother, good morning," Harriston said, extending his hand out in front of Garner. "I'm Brother Levi, and you are?"

"Garner," he muttered; he was visibly reluctant to shake Levi's hand.

Harriston lunged in back of Garner to interact with Kadrece. His face lit up as he extended his hand out towards her. "How you're doing, sister?" he inquired. "Is this somebody whom you invited from your job?"

"Oh, no," she replied in a demure tone. "He's my fiancé."

Harriston turned his attention back to Garner. "W-w-well, you certainly are a lucky man there, brother. We hope you enjoy your visit with us today." Then he walked to the back of the church.

McBride spoke on the popular principle that there is power in agreement and in the power of the spoken word. He based his sermon on a passage that declared whatever was loosed on earth will be loosed in heaven, and whatever is bound on earth will be bound in heaven.

The church responded often with enthusiasm throughout the pastor's sermon.

"Y'all, if I'm sick. I want somebody who's going to agree with me that I'll be healed. And the Bible gives us scripture to hold on to," McBride said. "That's what the Lord was talking about here!"

Garner, who disagreed with McBride, remained quiet. He was hardly impressed by McBride's presence behind the pulpit nor was he impressed by the content of his sermon. He tried hiding his displeasure by holding Kadrece's hand.

Just before McBride gave the benediction, Garner asked Kadrece for the keys to her car. "I'll bring the car around to the front of the church for you." He left the sanctuary without speaking to anyone.

As Kadrece made her way to the rear of the sanctuary, Levi intercepted her. "Sister, it was nice meeting your fiancé. But the honor was still in being blessed by your presence here this morning." He extended his hand out to her; however, she felt uncomfortable with the way he held on to her hand.

"Thank you, brother," she replied, turning her attention for the front door. "It looks like my ride is waiting for me."

Kadrece let out a loud sigh once she settled into the passenger seat. She asked Garner for his impression of Mission Grove; he did not immediately respond.

"Did you not hear me?" she asked.

"Yes I did," he finally answered.

"Pastor McBride's a trip, isn't he?"

Garner offered a smirk. "All I will say is that he misled the congregation with his sermon."

"What do you mean?" she retorted; she now shifted in her seat and stared at him intently.

"We had a study of that same verse with Pastor Lanier. And I found out it had nothing to do with prayer or the potency of a person's words. It had everything to do with, in proper context, how to deal with an offended person," he explained to her. "To be offended, in the Greek is the verb *scandalon*, which means to scandalize; someone who has been tripped up, duped into sin."

"So where have you all of a sudden become some scholar?" she derided him. "I don't remember you ever reading a Bible around me."

He smiled. "As I was saying, I understood that to mean the extent by which an individual makes restitution on earth—which is what to bind means—will be acknowledged in heaven. And the extent by which an individual is forgiven on earth—to be loosed—will be acknowledged in heaven."

"So what did two people in agreement mean?"

"It's simple. God is a God of peace. Wherever there is peace established by His people, He will always be in the midst of it."

The depth of Garner's response astonished her. "Well, excuse me," she finally said. "By the way, what do you think about my car?"

Garner never changed his countenance. "I like this car," he said, looking around in the cabin. "I think you made a very good choice. This is definitely more like you. Classy. Sporty. Elegant."

Chapter 22

Most of the major details for Kadrece's wedding had some organization to it, but there was one that she still lacking—she still had not arranged for a meeting among her, Garner, and McBride.

Desperate to cross that off on her checklist, Kadrece insisted that Garner make it a bigger priority. She then added, "Pastor McBride said the last weekend in March will be a good day for him, or possibly the weekend after Easter, to marry us."

"Can I get back with you on all of that?" he replied.

"Okay, but we need to move on this. I've got a lot of things that I need to do since I'm not paying anybody to plan this wedding. My sister, Kamryn, is going to help me with most of it."

None of what Kadrece mentioned resonated with him. He complained, "We're taking it week to week at the station covering some of these teams, so it's going to be busy. We've got Byrd College, which advanced to the second round of the national tournament. Now the station's talking about us traveling to some unknown place outside of Indianapolis."

Kadrece was not to be denied. "Well, you've got a fiancée who's trying to take care of everything since you don't live here in Spartanburg. Can you at least spare a few hours out of your day to meet with the pastor and go back to Columbia?"

It took all of Garner not to disparage McBride as being unfit fit to be a pastor, uncouth, uninformed, and, in his opinion, an untrustworthy shepherd of his congregation's souls.

"What's your problem, Garner?" Kadrece reacted. "I'm here in Spartanburg and I'm damn near paying for everything pertaining to this wedding:

"Five hundred dollars for the pastor, who has agreed to do our wedding either the last weekend in March, or the week after Easter; another three grand for the photographer, rehearsal dinner, and invitations; and a deposit on the reception hall, my wedding dress, and a dress for my sister, Kamryn. And you're . . ."

"All right, I'll find some time and meet with you in Spartanburg!" He took a deep breath, willing himself to say, "I'm sorry that I've not done more by helping you with our wedding. I wish that I've not been so busy."

That brought a smile to her face and some diffusion to her anger. "Baby, when I look at this ring on my hand, you've already done a lot."

There was an ivory white Mercedes E350 alone in the parking lot where Kadrece entered from Blackstock Road. She breathed a sigh of relief once she noticed that Garner had not been far behind. He just made a wide left-hand turn into a parking space directly across from the church's entrance. She rushed to join Garner as he emerged from his car. They gave each other a light kiss before they walked inside, hand-in-hand.

They guessed that McBride's office would be off to the right among a second row of doors. They were correct. His door was open, but he was in a phone counseling session with another member.

"Sister, I've got an appointment that should be here at any moment," he said. "May I call you back perhaps tomorrow? My schedule will be pretty wide open."

McBride allowed the member to talk for several seconds. He remained quiet the entire time amid nodding his head and scribbling some notes. When Garner approached the door, he motioned for them to take seats at the table adjacent to his desk.

"Sister, I'm going to pray the prayer of faith right now that you will see God move on your behalf, all right?" he finally said. "Now it's up to you to believe God, too, for your victory."

McBride immediately stood up and greeted Garner and Kadrece with his trademark gapped-tooth smile. He wore a long-sleeved beige collarless shirt and matching slacks; there was a study book and a Bible in front of them.

"Sister, I think this is the first time that we've really talked. Brother, didn't I see you in service here lately?"

"I was here the previous Sunday as a guest of my fiancée," Garner answered; he thought to himself that the only reason why McBride might have recognized him was because he was the closest to a white person in his service. He immediately replayed in his mind snippets from McBride's sermon that he emphatically disagreed with.

"Pastor," Kadrece spoke up for both her and Garner. "I really do appreciate you taking time out of your day to talk with us." She then reached over and held Garner's hand.

"Well, that's what I'm here for."

McBride asked questions about where they're from, whether they attended college, what professions were they in; and most importantly, were they believers?

"I feel that I'm held accountable by the Lord if I'm marrying two people who are unequally yoked," he said. "And I cannot have that happen. If you want to see two people show up in your office no sooner than they marry, have a believer and unbeliever get married."

Garner nodded while Kadrece spoke. "I agree, Pastor. Is there anything you'll need from us on the day of our wedding? I'll be getting the license from Spartanburg County this week."

"That's excellent, sister. I do have one thing: Now I just want to know if both of you will be attending this church once you're married?"

Unenthusiastic about the direction of the conversation, Garner allowed his mind to drift off to the one that he had with Pastor Lanier regarding Kadrece's insistence that he attended church with her.

Brother, don't worry about me. You just serve God. I don't have any right to be guarding the doors to this church," he explained to Garner.

"You are free to come in and out and find pasture anywhere you feel you're led to go."

Garner recalled telling Lanier that he did not feel led to attend church in Spartanburg, but that he knew it was necessary to keep peace with Kadrece.

"Brother, I can't tell you what to do. But if you love the woman that you've asked to marry you, God will honor the intent of your heart. Just remember that."

The conversation that occurred in McBride's office lasted for about a half-hour—Garner's mind remained far from there.

"Garner, you seem to be the quiet one of you two," McBride said, jostling him out of his semi-daze. "Is that right, sister?"

"Actually, I'm the quiet one, Pastor. And Garner's really the talkative one," Kadrece said, smiling. "You should see him conduct interviews. He's really good at them."

Garner smiled, reached over and held Kadrece's hand. "Well, you know, Pastor. I've gotta save my voice some days just like I'm sure you have to do when you're behind the pulpit. Today's one of those days."

"Oh, I see," McBride said, laughing while he stood up. "Well, if that's it, I would be honored to marry you two. And I'm already praying blessings upon you."

Chapter 23

With no more local teams left in postseason play, Garner arranged to take the rest of the week off following Tuesday's eleven o'clock broadcast. Kadrece had already sent him an enticing e-mail earlier in the day.

> Baby, when you come here tonight, I'm going to have your towel ready for you to take a shower. I'm going to have some massaging oil next to the bed, and I'm going to be lying here waiting for you with my legs wide open ready for you to be inside of me.

Kadrece's place was dimmed and she had scented citrus candles burning in her living room and bedroom in anticipation of Garner's arrival. She wore a black, crotchless fishnet body stocking. She had a bottle of white wine chilling in an ice bucket on the night stand to the left of her queen-size bed. And she had the entire place filled with the lively, yet seductive sounds of the late Teddy Pendergrass.

Just as Garner entered her place, he was met by "Turn off the Lights." Kadrece handed him his bath towel and she gave him a light peck on his cheek. He attempted to place his hands on her waist, drawing her near him, but she touched his forearm in a polite protest.

She said, "I'm not going anywhere; you just do what you have to do."

"Well, at least let me touch your wet pussy. I know it's already drenched."

"Okay, just a touch. But you need to do what I've already asked of you."

So, she glided over to the sofa where she bent over and offered him her round, succulent ass that he'd been so mesmerized by all these years. He rubbed his crotch against her cheeks then he reached around her waist, plunging his fingers between her most cooperative lips. She cooed and let out a moan knowing, too, that if she allowed him to do as he willed that her best plans would go for naught.

She then straightened up and pointed at the bathroom. "That's enough. Go take your shower."

There was nothing that Garner did that kept his mind off Kadrece—his dick remained erect while he showered. He knew that it would serve him no good to come out with a towel draped around his waist.

Thus, he decided to have some fun with it by doing a mini-male stripper routine: He tipped out the bathroom running the towel across his broad chest, over his stomach, and then allowing it to hang on his dick.

"Ooooh, baby!" she exclaimed. "I've got ten dollars if you can give me a lap dance!"

Then he took two long strides over next to her. He turned around and wiggled his body making sure that his gluteus muscles flexed before her. Kadrece was tempted to grope for him, demanding that she got a free sampling of his dick.

"See what you've done to me?" he joked with her. "You've got me doing things that I've never thought of doing for a woman."

"Hey, I'm going to be your wife in a few days. You're supposed to think outside of the box with me."

She then ordered Garner to mount her despite his inclination of wanting to tease her clit and taste her pussy. She whispered as he entered her "the next time I feel your sweet red dick, baby, I'll be Mrs. Kadrece Renee Davis."

He kissed her on the forehead, adding, "That has a nice sound to it."

Kadrece was so caught up in the moment of prenuptial seduction that her body convulsed as she reached orgasm within a matter of minutes after his entry. Not to be outdone, she appealed to Garner's lust by keeping her long, thick legs spread wide for many of the strokes that he gave her. Then she turned over on to her stomach and held her ass cheeks apart as he entered her doggy style.

"I've gotta give you something to keep your mind on me until Saturday," she said between his thrusts. "Can you handle it?"

Garner clutched onto her hips and pushed harder inside her; he felt her body tensed again. "Can you handle it?"

"Shit, baby. You're going to make me forget that I'm a saved woman!"

"That's all right. God knows your heart," he answered; he then gave her ass a playful smack.

"Mmmm, do that again!"

Smack!

"Don't you wanna cum inside this sweet dark chocolate pussy?" She then pressed her face into the mattress and gave him a higher, deeper target to fuck. "Or are you trying to hold out on me?"

"Nah, baby. It just feels so good. I wanna stay in here as long as I can."

"It's all right. I'm going to be your wife. It's okay that you give it to me right now. I want you to—"

Kadrece took the initiative by rolling onto her back, beckoning him to mount her in the missionary. She clasped her legs around his waist and drew that desired moment of climax out of him. Her body was most sensitive to Garner's torrent of cum that splashed against her inner walls.

For the next several minutes, Kadrece cradled Garner's head into her bosom. Then as he rested his head upon the pillow next to her, she whispered, "I just wanted one more time with you before we're married. Now wasn't that worth driving across the state in the middle of the night?"

Kadrece was about to drift off to nocturnal bliss nuzzled up to Garner's embrace when the thought became too great to avoid. She sat up in the bed, startling him. He was closer to drifting off than she was.

"Baby, can I ask you this question?"

Rubbing his eyes, he was slow to reply. "What is it you want, another round?"

"No. Besides, I think I'd wear you out."

"Are you sure about that?"

Kadrece reminded Garner that she was the youngest of five, and she had nine nieces and nephews. Her father, Hilton, was the second-oldest among six in his family and her mother, Johnette, was the oldest among three in her family.

"I don't want to sound insensitive, so what's your point?" he asked with hunched shoulders. "You're establishing that you come from a large family?"

She responded with a kiss on his forehead. "My point is that I just want to know what your thoughts are about starting a family?"

Garner rubbed his eyes once more and he ran his hand through his hair. "You know that I came from a dysfunctional family, but I want to do things better than what I saw while growing up."

"That doesn't answer my question about having a family." She knew that her patience was on the brink of being tested. "You know that I love children, and I'm always talking about my nieces and nephews."

"I know that I didn't say anything about kids," he said. "But I'll tell you this much: I want you to be the happiest wife that you've ever known of. That's my goal."

Sighing, Kadrece kissed him on his cheek and rolled over on her side. Then she bade him good night.

Chapter 24

Garner's nervousness was not easily hidden while he paced the luggage terminal inside Greenville-Spartanburg Airport in anticipation of Delta flight No. 1184's arrival via Atlanta.

He breathed a sigh of relief when it was announced over the intercom that flight had landed. Now it was a matter of minutes before passengers would be making their way down to pick up their baggage. He folded his arms, leaned against a newspaper rack, and he watched others greet those whom they had been waiting for their arrival.

Nobody could have predicted to Garner that he would be inviting his mother, Miriam, to be in attendance of any wedding that involved him. So invariably, he wanted everything to go right on his end—even her arrival in South Carolina.

He nodded and smiled once he saw Miriam look to her left, then right, appearing a bit lost. He decided to make it easier for her by waving for her attention.

Miriam saw her tall, handsome son from a distance. She picked up her gait. They soon met each other in a warm embrace. She also kissed him on his cheek. Tears filled her eyes.

"Why are you about to boo-hoo?"

"I don't know. I guess I'm just glad to see you."

"Well, we need to get your luggage. Did you bring a lot?"

They began walking towards the luggage carousel.

"Look here, I'm only going to be here until Sunday, so it's not like I prepared to stay here for a week."

"Now that's my mother."

As they stood there watching the luggage appear through the chute, an older guy who had been checking out Miriam from a distance moved to a spot next to her. "So you're here visiting your brother?" he asked, looking over his shoulder in Garner's direction.

Miriam smiled. "Thank you for the compliment. But I'm here for my son's wedding."

"Did you say son's wedding?"

"That's right."

Garner had now joined Miriam. He gave the man a suspicious glare. The man's eyes soon scaled upward along Garner's six-foot-two frame.

"Well, congratulations to you, sir," he said, attempting to save face; he glanced off to his left. "And here's my luggage. I hope you enjoy your trip, ma'am."

As they walked out to the parking garage, Garner wasted little time telling Miriam about Kadrece. He reminded her that he'd known her since college, but it had only been within the past year that they became serious.

"If my memory serves me correct, little boy, wasn't it about this time last year that you were dealing with that crazy police woman?"

Garner bristled at being reminded about Vernise. "Why do you have to bring that up, mom?"

"I guess things have happened so fast, so soon. I always hoped that you would find yourself somebody."

"Things happen, don't they?"

Garner mentioned to Miriam that she would be staying at the former Renaissance Hotel that was located on the first Business Route 85 exit past the I-26 interchange. He also noted to her that it was not far from Mission Grove, where the wedding would be held, and the Westgate Mall that was just beyond the railroad tracks.

She commented the Greenville-Spartanburg area appeared to be not that large in geography. The entire corridor from up above reminded her of being back in Wilmington, minus the water.

"Do you think you'll be happy if you had to live here in South Carolina for a long time?" she asked.

"I don't know. Right now, I guess I'm just trying to make it day to day," he answered. "I'll think about career after we get back from our honeymoon in the Virgin Islands."

"Now that's a nice place. I went there a few summers back." Miriam paused to reminisce about the tempting supply of men that were eager to be at her disposal. She then asked, "Have you met Kadrece's parents?"

"Once, but that was several years ago."

"So you really don't know what they think about you?"

"Does it really matter?"

"You're not only marrying Kadrece. But in some ways, you're marrying into their family just like she's marrying into our family."

Garner looked over his right shoulder, changing lanes on I-85 northbound. "I'll have a chance to speak with them at tonight's rehearsal dinner. Actually, both of us will."

Miriam soon got quiet and she stared somewhat aimlessly out of the window. Her countenance had changed from jovial to melancholy. Several moments had passed before Garner recognized it.

"Did all the flying make you tired?"

She sighed before pondering the way she'd form her comment. "I'm feeling fine. I've been taking pretty good care of myself."

"I know. That nosey man offered his two cents' worth."

"That's right. And don't you forget that as long as you live, until further notice, I'll always be forty-five."

They both shared in a laugh. Then Miriam turned serious. "I just want to know, Garner, are you really happy?"

He took a quick glance at his mother. "Am I happy about what?"

"You know, marriage. Marrying Kadrece—"

He inhaled deeply through his nose, allowing the air to dissipate back out at a slow rate. He pushed his head into the headrest. "Yes mom. I am."

She reached over and grabbed his hand, nodding in approval. "That's the most important thing, that you're happy about your decision."

"You know mom, I've been thinking lately that if something ever were to happen to me here in South Carolina I'd be a John Doe," he said, looking straight ahead. "Nobody would know who I am and who to contact because I have no family here. That's unless they're able to contact you." He then glanced over at Miriam.

She was not sure where Garner was headed with his rationale, so she allowed him to continue.

"The way I see it, at least if I'm married, there is somebody that's here for me." He paused to chuckle at his next thought. "You know, it's tough sometimes being by yourself."

"I understand what you're talking about," she interrupted him. "But do you not know there are times that being by yourself isn't a bad thing? I hope that's not your reason for getting married—"

Garner shook his head. "It isn't."

"Are you sure?"

"I'm sure."

She persisted with her question; her voice was in a serious tone. "Are you really happy about marrying Kadrece?"

"I am."

This was not the kind of conversation that Garner envisioned that he would have with Miriam less than an hour after she landed in South Carolina. But he figured it was probably for the best. He then queried, "Do you have any idea how my father, Garrett, might have felt about me getting married?"

It was a poignant moment. Miriam's eyes welled at the thought. Inwardly, Garner had often wondered if God had allowed him to live out something vicariously for his mother.

Leaning back into the seat, Miriam did not bother to answer. She reached out and grasped Garner's hand. Then she glanced out of the window, allowing a tear to escape down her cheek.

Chapter 25

Everyone who was invited to the rehearsal dinner was expected to meet at Europa's restaurant near the Westgate Mall in about forty-five minutes. It took everything within Kadrece to restrain herself from cursing out her parents.

After being apprised of her engagement to Garner for several weeks, Kadrece's parents still had not changed in their opinion about him. Her father still expressed his reservations about his youngest child marrying a light-skinned man whose features could be mistaken for being white. It also did not help that her mother shared a similar sentiment.

"You know what?" Kadrece vented. "You don't have to worry about me after this wedding. I've got nothing else to say to you two!"

Incensed, Hilton Sr. stood up and shook his stubby finger at his daughter. "Kadrece, we care about you. You're our daughter, and we want you to be happy. We don't have anything against him, per se, but there's just something about those light and bright skinned guys; they can't be trusted.

"Isn't this the same fella that you used to sneak off and date on the side when you were dating other men?

Kadrece stormed off towards the kitchen. "So what that has to do with us marrying?" She poured herself a glass of wine, hoping that would settle her nerves.

From her vantage point on the sofa, Johnette decided she needed to intervene. "It says a lot. Your sister Kamryn told us that he was willing to sneak behind his girlfriend's back to see you. Didn't you tell him that you were involved with somebody else?"

"Uh-huh. But I also wanted to see him," Kadrece answered, placing her glass on the kitchen counter. "I'll tell anybody that I believe it was the Lord's doing that brought us together. That's what is most important to me—"

Hilton Sr. smirked at Kadrece's response. "If you say so . . . Your mother and I don't think so, and Kamryn doesn't, either."

She stopped just shy of where her father had taken a seat in the comforter to plead her case to him. "Yes, I say so." But her anger had taken over. She shook her finger in his face. "I just want you two to know that you're just here only because I've asked you to be here!"

Now Johnette's anger was stoked. "Listen here, girl. We're your parents. You don't talk to us like this, you understand?"

"Yeah, I know y'all my parents," Kadrece responded, sighing. "But you also better realize that y'all are in my house. And I don't have to put up with either of you. Y'all can stay with Kamryn since she's so busy telling you my business—"

Sensing their conversation had gotten out of hand, Johnette reverted to offering a voice of reasoning for all of them.

"Hilton, this is still Kadrece's life, and it was her choice to marry Garner. Let's not ruin this for her." He waved her off, grumbling.

Kadrece was determined to have the last word in this conversation. She went back into the kitchen and poured herself another glass of wine. "I knew this would happen," she said in between sips. "That's why I've paid for everything that has to do with this wedding because I refuse to let you two wash my face with that jive nigger-slave talk."

Hilton Sr. stormed into the kitchen behind her. Nostrils flaring, he had the look that conveyed if she said another disparaging comment that he would slap her.

"Listen here, girl. I'm your father. Don't you be calling me some nigger slave. Not any of my children, including you, have ever gotten too old to be reminded who's the parent and who's the child. Do you understand?"

Kadrece walked off towards her bedroom in a huff. "And don't you go around disrespecting my husband.

"Do you understand?"

She slammed the bathroom door behind her and buried her face into a bath towel, sobbing.

Chapter 26

Kadrece nervously waited for Garner, peering through the door. She sat on one of the benches with her arms folded and patting her foot. In a quick moment of inspection, she used the reflection from the glass to brush her hair to the side. She also glanced back often at her family, monitoring them.

Seconds later, a stately woman walked in and just behind her was Garner. Kadrece jumped to her feet once she recognized the strong resemblance between the two.

"Mrs. Davis, I'm Kadrece," she said, beaming.

Miriam reacted with a pleasant smile. Both moved to embrace each other. "I've finally gotten to meet you, Kadrece." She looked back at her son. "Garner has told me so much about you. She's really a beautiful young lady." She then turned her attention to Kadrece. "Why did Garner keep you a secret for so long?"

"I'll have to talk to your son about that," Kadrece answered, chuckling. Appearing relieved, she then asked, "How was your flight?"

"You know how it is these days . . . you're in a long line and the flight seems even longer."

"Well, my family's waiting for all of us. Let me introduce you to them."

Garner slipped between both Miriam and Kadrece and escorted them to the large table setting off to his left. There was a reflection of pride on his face being able to walk with what he knew were the two most important women in his life.

They got to within five paces of the table when Kadrece's father was the first to stand up. He appeared slightly uncomfortable, adjusting his jacket. But then he brightened up once he set his eyes on Miriam.

Before Kadrece could form the words on her lips, Kamryn blurted over everyone, "This must be Garner!"

Kadrece felt like melting into the carpet. She cut Kamryn a glare that had the intensity of a laser. But Kamryn countered, waving her off, "Oh, girl. You know we've all been waiting to meet Garner. So you might as well get it over with."

Exhaling out of annoyance, Kadrece went ahead with introducing Garner and his mother counterclockwise to her family, starting with Kamryn and her husband, then Kanitra and her husband, her brothers Wesley and Hilton Jr., and then stopping just to Garner's left with her parents.

Miriam was the first to be seated, which was next to Kadrece's mother. Her father managed to cut a sly glance over at Miriam, admiring her beauty and hoping, too, that the rest of his family did not pick up on it.

"Kadrece had said Garner was a very handsome man," Johnette mentioned to Miriam. "Now I see where it comes from—"

Hilton Sr. then spoke up: "I hear you are a sports guy. I know a few important folk in Atlanta. Have you ever met, uh, Hank Aaron?"

Garner nodded. "I certainly have— once—during spring training."

"Is that right?"

"Yes, Mr. Kendricks. He's not much for talking to the media, but I'm told that's just Hank being Hank."

"You don't say?"

After the dinner, Garner and Hilton Sr. had a moment to themselves while Miriam and Johnette conversed. Hilton Sr. brought up another quick story on Hank Aaron, noting that they used to play golf together. That elicited a nod out of Garner. Then he bore down on his most pressing thought.

Leaning towards Garner, he asked, "What provoked you to ask my daughter to marry you?"

Garner reared back in his seat. "I asked Kadrece to marry me because, first of all, I'm madly in love with her.

"Secondly, I feel that your daughter is the woman that I want to spend the rest of my life with. I have never considered asking any other woman ever before."

"I see," Hilton Sr. replied, nodding. "Do you have any kids?"

"No."

"None?"

"That's right, none."

Hilton Sr. looked Garner over again, studying his mannerisms. Meanwhile, Garner never flinched. He remained composed.

"And you say this is the first time you'll ever be married?"

"Yes, first time."

"Never came close before?"

Garner sat more erect, maintaining eye contact with his future in-law. "Never considered anyone else other than your daughter."

Hilton Sr. cleared his throat, apologizing that it's gotten dry on occasion. He explained, "I recently had a procedure."

"I'm aware of that," Garner replied. "I offered to come and visit while you were in the hospital, but Kadrece insisted that I not cancel one of my assignments."

"She didn't tell me that?" Hilton Sr. reacted, with raised eyebrows.

Garner elected not to elaborate. Rather, he extended his hand towards him. "Mr. Kendricks, I know you're proud of your daughter. I hope you'll be just as proud to give her away to me tomorrow."

Chapter 27

There was no bachelor's celebration for Garner on the eve of his wedding. It was a sleepless night in which he tossed and turned. He finally gave in to fatigue around 6:25 a.m., and he woke up around midday.

Although he was fully convinced that marrying Kadrece was what he wanted, he felt obligated to contact Pastor Lanier early that afternoon.

"Are you nervous, brother?" Lanier inquired; he mused that there was no doubt that he was on his wedding day with Turquoise eighteen years ago. He prefaced his next comment with a light chuckle. "But it's going to be *alllll* right later in the day!"

"I'm sure it will," Garner commented. "I think that's the easy part."

Lanier paused in another moment of reflection. "I don't know about that, brother. Since I've been a pastor, you know that I've been told many stories." He also chortled at that observation.

Then he turned serious with Garner. "So, how have you been since you started attending your fiancée's church?"

Garner sighed. "I don't know. It's definitely not the same as attending Divine Grace." There was some resignation in his voice.

"Just know, brother, that no matter wherever you go in life that you'll always have a home here with us, okay?"

"Thanks, Pastor."

Lanier excused himself to handle Turquoise's popping into his home office, which she apprised him of some church matters. He returned to Garner without leaving him hanging for an extended duration.

He said, "Brother, you'll understand very fast once you're married that whenever the wife asks for your attention, give it all to her."

"I see."

"Did you attend any pre-marital counseling with her pastor?" he asked.

"Uh-huh."

"Well, I'm not going to ask what the pastor covered, but I do want to share with you that marriage is probably the second-most important confession that you'll ever make this side of heaven."

Lanier then related to Garner that he based his teaching on a passage that discussed an individual's confession of faith being made to salvation. The information brought about another heavy dose of sobriety upon Garner, but he was not deterred. In fact, he embraced wholeheartedly what Lanier had imparted to him.

"I never saw it like that," he said, nodding. "I know that I've done a lot of things that I'm not proud of, but I've never been ashamed of my decision of faith. And I'm not ashamed of asking Kadrece to marry me."

If there was any tension in their conversation, both Garner and Lanier expressed to each other that they were glad to speak before his wedding ceremony.

"Brother, don't forget us when you begin adding to your family," Lanier said. "We would love to have the privilege to offer a prayer and blessing for your child."

To the contrary, Kadrece spent the remainder of her last night as a single woman with Kamryn and Kanitra. The Kendricks sisters went out for a late movie in Greenville—a rare occasion among them.

They left the theater around 12:45 a.m., and Kadrece chauffeured her sisters around town for a bite to eat at the twenty-four hour Jack N the Box off Woodruff Road. She eventually dropped off her sisters at their respective hotels around 2:30 a.m.

Kadrece was aware that Hilton Sr. and Johnette decided to get themselves a hotel room of their own in retaliation to their falling out from the day before. That enabled her to reclaim her condominium back to herself. It did dawn upon her while she was stretched out on her bed that within twenty-four hours she was likely to consummate her marriage with Garner in that same position. That brought about a bit of excitement over her.

"God, I don't like doing this," she lamented, "but I need something to take the edge off me or I'll be doing something that I might regret in the morning—"

Kadrece sprang up from her bed and turned on her computer. Once it booted up, she logged on to TheBlackNFreaky.com, where she clicked on to The Booty Call video room. There, she perused the various video clippings uploaded by couples. A male-female-male threesome was the one that captured her attention: a light-skinned woman accommodated a male of caramel complexion in the doggy position while she sucked off a dark-skinned male.

The nineteen-minute segment apparently was more than enough to heighten Kadrece's arousal as she began rubbing her breasts, which was followed by running her hand across her stomach, before settling at her pussy.

"Mmmm," she moaned. "I didn't realize how horny I was."

She paused and reversed the video back to the point when the two men switched spots. She then leaned back in her chair, resting her left leg on the desk. She rubbed her pussy at a rate that matched the strokes the dark-skinned man had been fucking the woman.

"Damn, I love a big, thick dark nigga with a big, thick chocolate dick," she hissed; she also slid down in her seat, making it easier for her to insert a finger inside her pussy. Aroused by the sound of her pussy's juices, she stopped to taste some of it. She smacked her lips in approval.

Her thoughts had actually wandered off to Winston Culpepper, whom she had maintained a brief affair from about four years earlier. Culpepper was a successful businessman in the Orlando, Florida area. He was also eight years her senior—and married. But the man had charisma. He loved displaying her among his friends, and she often accommodated his freak side by wearing short skirts that revealed her thick, shapely legs. He even once fulfilled a fantasy of his by tonguing her asshole in a department store dressing room and then she responded by giving him a blow job to completion.

Moments later, Kadrece had taken her self-pleasure to another level as she digressed to the night that she and Culpepper fucked in a park that was less than a half-mile away from his family home. She often savored the memory of when she brought him to the point of ejaculation, she dropped to her knees and allowed him to deposit inside her mouth.

"Oh, shit, Pepper! Work that big, thick dick of yours," she said, increasing the rate that she stroked her clit. "Damn it you bastard, fuck me the way you want to fuck me!"

She inhaled deeply through her nose and gritted her teeth at her moment of release. Then as she rubbed her closely-cropped pussy in the afterglow, she reasoned to herself that God would understand, and from the next day forward much of her sexual experiences would be seen as honorable before all because it would be covered under her marriage covenant.

She actually thought about calling Garner to see if he was still awake; she decided against it thinking that she would break marriage tradition.

Kadrece had planned for a non-formal wedding despite her attire: an ivory beaded lace split front A-line gown with beaded embroidery at empire waist; she also had a sweep train. Garner wore a traditional formal black tuxedo with matching trousers. He wore a white tuxedo shirt, a black bow tie, and cufflinks. He opted for a vest instead of the cummerbund.

There was no music, just a quaint gathering at Mission Grove's sanctuary. But Kadrece did allow for Kamryn to stand as her matron of honor. She also asked that Hilton Sr. give her away.

The wedding ceremony performed by Pastor McBride lasted for all of about twenty minutes, although it did have its dubious moment. Some of the invited guests—about two dozen in all— gasped when Hilton Sr. balked not once but twice when he was asked by whom was Kadrece given away.

McBride eyed down Hilton Sr. until he finally announced in a less-than-dignified tone, "I, Hilton Kendricks, Sr., and Mrs. Johnette D. Kendricks—"

Giggling, McBride corrected Hilton Sr. "The mother and I would be sufficient." Hilton Sr. then tugged at his jacket and repeated what McBride suggested much to the amusement of the audience.

As McBride commenced to explaining the significance of the wedding vows, Kadrece began choking back tears. Garner, who remained stoic, reached over and grabbed Kadrece's hand in support. He also offered his handkerchief, which she accepted.

Meanwhile, Johnette rolled her eyes in derision at her daughter's timing. She also gave her husband a slight elbow jab—he acted as if he were about to doze off to sleep.

"I feel much honored to be standing here before all of you in this event of holy matrimony that I might lead the two of you in the exchanging of your vows," McBride continued. "And now, Garner Michael, do you take Kadrece Renee to be your wife . . . in sickness and in health 'till death do you part?"

Garner cleared his throat, answered "I do." He then looked over to his right at Kadrece, beaming with pride.

"And do you, Kadrece Renee, take Garner to be your husband . . . in sickness and in health 'till death do you part?"

"I do." She closed her eyes, dipped her head briefly, before she raised it to cast a loving smile at Garner.

Later in the ceremony, Kadrece's heart pounded furiously once McBride asked if there was anyone in the audience that had any objections to her and Garner being married. The ten seconds that McBride allowed felt like ten hours.

When McBride went to the next part of the ceremony—the benediction—Kadrece took a deep breath in relief, allowing it to dissipate slowly. She wiped another tear that had streamed down the left side of her face.

Then McBride declared that Garner and Kadrece were now married, but she did not wait until he gave them permission to kiss. She moved boldly and pressed her lips fully on Garner's. She was also quick to push her tongue inside his mouth, forcing him to suck her tongue for several moments before she withdrew. It was not what Garner had in mind, but it was what it was—an obvious prelude to later that evening.

"Well, praise God," McBride said, seemingly bashful for them. "I now present to you Mr. and Mrs. Garner Davis."

And so it was done.

After the post-wedding pictures, Johnette and Miriam had a brief exchange before they left out of the church. Both appeared visibly relieved that their child had now embarked on a new course in life.

Johnette welcomed Miriam as her newest in-law. She then inquired, "Is this your first child to marry?" She mentioned to Miriam that she noticed her shedding a few tears as Garner repeated his vows—something that she admitted to doing when Wesley was the first to marry off nearly twenty-three years ago.

"It is," Miriam acknowledged, nodding. "I guess I could not hold it any longer."

They embraced each other. Miriam then thanked Johnette for her being so welcoming to her.

"No problem."

They found a seat along the back-row seat pews. Johnette paused to scan the church before she went on to say, "I've prayed for Kadrece since I knew that I was pregnant with her. I even prayed about the kind of husband that she might have—"

She followed that with a sigh that hinted at some resignation on her part. That provoked Miriam to listen to Johnette even more intently. She forced a smile and nodded while Johnette went on to talk about how she also had done the same thing for her other four children and their future spouses.

The interaction that she had with Johnette prompted memories from her own marriage to Aaron: On that summer day back in 1971, she was not particularly cared for by his family members; they seemed pained to accept that a marriage had taken place.

Sighing once more, with Johnette intoning in her subtle South Georgia dialect, she took the liberty to mention, "You really do have to pray for your children these days because you just never know—"

Miriam finally interjected, "You don't say?"

"Uh-huh. I mean, there's just so much out there. You know we, the parents, well . . . You know . . ."

"No, I don't know," Miriam spoke matter-of-factly to Johnette. "But it is interesting that God has a way giving people just what they need?"

Miriam then glanced over her shoulder and spotted Garner standing near Kadrece. She excused herself from Johnette's company. First, she offered another round of congratulations to Kadrece. She added, whispering into her ear, "Please take care of my son. Would you do that for me?"

Kadrece returned a half-stunned reaction. She was careful to say, "Thank you, Mrs. Davis."

"Miriam."

"Sorry . . . Miriam. I'll do just that. You've done well preparing Garner for me." Kadrece mentioned that she wanted to catch up with her mother before she left. "I'm sure we'll talk again soon."

With her arms held out for him, Miriam beckoned, "Little boy, come here." Just as they embraced, she gave way to her emotions. There was so much that she wanted to tell Garner.

He joked, "You're not the one who got married this evening."

"I know," she answered, wiping away tears from both cheeks. "I just want you to know that I'll always be there for you. I want you to always remember that, you hear me?"

Chapter 28

Three weeks later

Kadrece openly flaunted her newly married sex life among her sisters and Johnette. She made it known to them that their post-nuptial romance had been mind blowing and earth shattering even more so than before they were married.

That was met by relative silence by Johnette. She reminded her daughter, "Hilton and I weren't exactly like you and Garner, but we do have five children to show for it. That accounts for something."

"Oh, mom, can't you just be glad for me?" Kadrece protested. "I'm in love with my husband and I can't wait to show him how much I do love him every time that I see him."

"That's nice. You just need to know that your marriage can't survive on sex alone."

"I know that, mom. But what are two newlyweds are supposed to do?"

Kadrece huffed out of frustration when she realized her conversation with Johnette was not headed in the direction that she desired. She became fidgety. Her mind drifted to other topics like a case that

that had been waiting on her desk since she returned from a week in the Virgin Islands.

"Look, Hilton and I have been married for forty-four years," Johnette attempted to reason with her daughter. "I still don't know him, and he doesn't know me. You'll never entirely know your spouse even after all these years. You're still learning who they are. That's how you build a relationship, and it doesn't happen over night after a couple of times in the bed."

Kadrece began shifting her feet. She was on the brink of erupting. "Are you trying to say that Garner and I never had a relationship?" She stood up and paced the living room.

"I'm not saying that, Kadrece."

"I've known Garner since we were in college—over thirteen years—and that's longer than any man I've ever been involved with," she said, cutting her mother off. "And you know there have been a lot of men in my past."

That was about all Johnette could stand. She knew this conversation with her daughter was at the brink of a fast ending.

"Kadrece, I'm not doubting you at all. So don't go off on me like you did before your wedding," Johnette reminded her. "Just let me ask you this: How can the two of you get to know each other as man and wife, and y'all live and work in separate cities?"

"I'm going to say this much before I get off the phone with you. You're getting a little too nosey. And to answer your question, I will be seeing *my husband* and I plan to make love to him tonight. Then I plan to spend the rest of the weekend with him plus a couple of more days.

"So I'll have a chance to get to *know* my sexy, fine husband quite well for a few days. Love you, mom."

She then hung up.

Kadrece and Garner still had not come to any agreement on how they would manage their long-distance marriage. But they did have a loose agreement that they would alternate spending off days at each other's place until further notice. This weekend happened to have been hers to make the ninety-minute drive to Garner's place in Blythewood.

During her early-evening drive, Kadrece brooded long and hard about what Johnette tried advising her. But she immediately dismissed it all, noting to herself that she was a grown-ass woman who was soon to be thirty-seven years old.

"Everyone's situation is different," she spoke loudly, sighing.

She then searched for her cell phone. While driving at seventy-five miles per hour, she scanned through her picture gallery and settled on a recent picture that she'd taken while feeling horny.

Smiling mischievously, she punched in the phone number to her intended recipient. It was just a matter of moments before she received a response.

"Is this how you'll be letting me know that you've missed me?" Garner greeted her.

Kadrece snickered. "Why not? It's yours."

He flipped open his cell phone again to sneak another peak at Kadrece's shot of her shaved pussy. He felt an erection growing in his slacks—it was a good thing that he was sitting at his desk at the station.

Nodding he replied, "You're right. It is mine, and I'd like some of that tonight."

"Your wish, baby, is my command. I'm just passing the Clinton exit on I-26. While I'm at it, is there anything you want from the store?"

"Actually, no. Just what you sent me."

Garner then felt his phone vibrate. Kadrece had sent him another provocative picture. This time, she had two fingers inserted in her pussy. He felt his dick become rock hard in response. He also realized that it had been five days since he last seen his wife.

"Uh, Kadrece, what are you doing to me?"

A familiar thought pierced Kadrece's thinking. It was a reminder of the picture that she e-mailed Garner nearly a year earlier that started it all. "Oh, I don't know. Guess I'm just feeling a bit frisky as the old people might say." Her face yielded a smile that was more representative of her reflecting upon the past.

"Definitely frisky. But I love it, and I love you!" He volunteered to her that he would probably grab something at Gallardo's, before he stopped off at his place between shows. "Would you like for me to pick up something for you?"

"Are you sure you don't have a taste for anything else?" Kadrece interrupted him. "I'm sure that I can accommodate—"

Shaking his head, Garner answered, "Well, I must admit that you do have my mouth watering."

"Now that's what I'm talking about. See you soon."

Kadrece felt a sense of justification the moment that she set foot inside of Garner's place. It did not matter what her mother had to say, she thought, because this was still her life. She reasoned to herself that times were different from back in the 1960s when it was almost unheard of that couples maintained long-distance marriages. Not to mention, she mused about how it was still taboo for women to talk openly about sucking their man's dicks and having sex in public.

She also felt like she was an equal partner in Garner's life. While on their honeymoon, he volunteered to her information about his computer passwords, personal e-mail accounts, and even his phone messaging passwords. She remembered him telling her that he had nothing to hide from her. She volunteered to give Garner similar information, but he declined.

Nonetheless, she exercised her spousal and female curiosity by checking Garner's phone messages. There were three messages. The first two were from media relations contacts regarding possible interview dates. The third one was unexpected.

"Hi Garner, this is Tamira. I just want to congratulate you on your getting married. I wish you all the luck. You deserve it," she said, pausing to sigh. *"To be honest, I know things didn't work out like we tried to make it work. But I do miss you a lot. If it's all right, give me a call. I just need to get some things off my chest so that I can move on . . ."*

"Who is this bitch?" Kadrece exclaimed in reaction. "Uh-uh. I ain't having this shit. I know we fucked around on each other, but it ain't going to be like that now!'"

She played the message again. She recognized that it came from a private number so she could not trace it. She felt compelled to contact Garner about Tamira's message, but she decided to wait for his arrival. She slung her bag on the sofa and she plopped next to it, seething. She folded her arms, rocking, and she mumbled a few more expletives.

Humph. He has nothing to hide. We'll see about that!

Not willing to wait idly, she flipped open her cell phone and called Nedra. She knew that it was slightly later than usual, but she needed the outlet.

"Kadrece, I'm so glad that you called," Nedra answered. "I'm so sorry that I couldn't make it up to South Carolina for your wedding. I know you were counting on me, but I hope you understand that my mom [Charlotte] was hospitalized and they discovered a couple of blood clots near her lung."

"Nedra, you don't have to explain anything to me," Kadrece answered, feeling herself calm down for the moment. "I completely understand. I would have done the same thing had it been my mother."

"Thanks for understanding. So what's new, married lady?"

Kadrece inhaled through her nose before commenting. "Nothing's new other than my last name. I decided not to do the hyphenated thing. I'm just Kadrece R. Davis." She nodded her head. "Yeah, that's about it."

Nedra also explained the noise in the background was one of her sons at baseball practice. She mentioned they've started early this year. Usually, baseball starts right when school ends in May.

"You'll see once you have kids just how expensive things can be," she said. "Nothing's free."

"Haven't you forgotten that I come from a family of five, girl?"

"Kadrece, I think I know you about as well as your sisters. And how's Kanitra and Kamryn?"

She sidestepped the answer by talking about her honeymoon in the Virgin Islands. Then she mentioned that she was in Garner's condominium and they were going to spend a nice, quiet weekend together. "He said that there were no assignments this weekend, so why not I come to Columbia?" She pursed her lips. "So here I am—"

"Well, that's nice. You know that I pray often for you. Even for Garner. And how has he been?"

That produced an uneasiness with Kadrece, considering that she had been venting her sudden displeasure. "I'll be right back. I just got here. And Garner should be coming home in a few minutes—he's in between shows and he comes here to hang out."

Nedra saw that as her opportunity to get out of the phone call. "Hey, I better get going, any way. I see Cosby and his teammates running to the pitcher's mound. That usually means they're about through with practice." She offered her best regards to Garner. "Call me maybe on Sunday, okay?"

Kadrece flipped her phone shut, and she began fidgeting with her wedding ring. She shook her head wondering why Garner might already be up to no good. He seemed to be such a changed man during their courtship, she thought. It was as though he had transformed into a thoughtful, caring, and kind man.

This quickly became a moment that she sought a spiritual answer to a perplexing and heart-wrenching scenario. Just as she adjusted herself on the sofa, she heard somebody fitting a key into the lock.

"Garner, is that you?"

The door opened with him poking his head in first. "Yes it is, my love."

That was all that Kadrece could withstand. She snapped to her feet and confronted him just as he entered.

"Who is this bitch Tamira?"

Garner reacted as though he was frozen in time. It took him several seconds before he composed himself to respond. "Can you at least let me inside my own place?" He then walked past her.

"The fuck you mean *your place*?" she yelled. "Uh-huh, you're goddamned right it's *your place*, but this is *our marriage* and I want to know who in the hell is this trick bitch Tamira?"

She followed him to the kitchen. Garner caught a quick glance over his shoulder. The fact somebody hovered behind him brought back memories of his childhood in Richmond.

"Kadrece, it's not what you think," he responded.

"Then what in the fuck is it?"

He went ahead with pouring himself a glass of water, taking a couple of gulps from it. He placed the glass on the kitchen counter—amid Kadrece shadowing him and her nostrils flaring—before he walked past her again, stopping off in the living room.

"Did you not hear me, Garner?" She began speaking slowly and forcefully. "I want to know who in the hell is this bitch Tamira?"

For a moment, it amused him that Kadrece would demand so much from him considering how he had gotten in trouble with Sabryan and a couple of other women while he was single. He never confided in her how he took the brunt of their wrath by allowing them to go off on him in order to protect her.

He ran his hand through his hair. It had been already a rather long and intense day. He had actually looked forward to Kadrece's arrival so that maybe he might get in a quick fuck and relieve some stress. Then he planned to make it up after the eleven o'clock show by really doing the romantic stuff with her.

Kadrece stood up in front of him, pushing her finger in his face. He gently pushed it to the side.

"So you're not going to answer me?" she huffed, placing her hands at her waist. "Well you know there is such a thing as an annulment because I'm not going to put up with any of this shit with you. I know how big of a goddamn whore that you can be."

"And I know just how big of a whore you can be, too," he countered. "I was the one you went off to fuck on the side, in case you've been quick to forget."

Kadrece's eyes were bugged and she flailed her arms. "Oh no you didn't, you light-bright nigga. I want you to call her ass right now—in front of me—and tell her not to call here again. Do you understand?"

Tilting his head, Garner went into cool mode by folding his arms.

He felt this should pass if he could just remain calm. Inwardly, he seethed because he knew that this was all Spencer Watts' doing.

And this is the thanks that I get for inviting his old, crazy ass to my wedding? he internalized. *That old motherfucker . . .*

He finally stood up, moving to embrace Kadrece.

"Don't you touch me!" she reacted, jerking away from him.

"Why can't I touch you?"

"Ain't shit happening until you answer why in the fuck did this bitch named *Tamira* had called here. Why don't you just listen to the message?"

She stormed over to the phone near the bar nook. She punched in the code to retrieve messages; she also placed the phone on loudspeaker.

"Kadrece, I hadn't responded to anything that you've accused me of because there isn't anything between Tamira and me," he explained. "I was involved with her briefly off and on for a few months, but I had not spoken to her in months, maybe nearly a year."

"Do you think that I was born yesterday?" she reacted. "Uh-uh, I want you to call her ass right now!"

Garner walked off to the bathroom, stopping to take a piss. He locked the door behind him, making sure that she did not attempt to barge in on him. He returned to the living room where she stood there still fuming and with her arms folded. She also patted her foot.

As he sat on the sofa, she handed him the phone.

"I don't remember her number," he answered.

"Do you expect for me to believe that?"

"I do."

"You really must think that I'm stupid?"

Amid her histrionics, they entered into a staring showdown. Garner decided to end it, shaking his head.

"So what did she say?"

She quickly dialed in his code and replayed the message. Afterward, she took a couple of steps towards him while she pointed back to the phone. "I want you to tell this bitch not to call here any more." She then sat down next to him. "Now, do I have to find out where she stays and what her phone number is, being that I'm an attorney?"

"Baby, you've got to believe me," he said, standing up. "I'm guessing the only reason why Tamira called me was because ol' man Spencer Watts told her about us getting married. I promise you that I've not had any contact with her since last year, and I'm talking before you and I got back together.

"You have to believe me."

Kadrece stared at Garner for several moments and pondered his response. She then took a deep breath. "Why did you let me get all riled up acting like a fool?"

He chortled. "That is your prerogative. But seriously, what reason have I given you not to believe and trust me?

"Damn you, Garner!" she answered, pounding him on his chest. "I knew something wasn't right with that old man at our wedding. Now I know."

Garner grabbed her hand after she hit him a third time. He led her over to the sofa, sitting her back down. He then went on to explain that Spencer had played the role of a match maker nearly two years ago when he gave him Tamira's phone number. He also explained again that they did go out on a few occasions, and they were involved sexually off-and-on for a brief period.

He added, "Don't ask me how the sex was because the only person that I'm concerned about when it comes to sex is with you, okay?"

She brought her right hand up to her temple as she began to pace the living room carpet. She asked, "Baby, why didn't you tell me anything about her?"

"There was nothing to say. When we got back together, that was it. I've been committed to you in every way that you can imagine."

She then returned to him, and they entered into a tender embrace.

"Please, Garner, don't do that again," she begged him. "Please don't let something get out of hand like that. We don't need any stress and confusion."

She paused, exhaling. Then her emotions got the best of her. A tear streamed down from her right eye. "You just don't know how many haters that I have out there. I never realized just how many have wished that we don't make it, baby." He cradled her head into his chest, apologizing to her.

"I bet there are a few people out there," he consoled her. "I bet there are."

Kadrece broke their embrace and dropped to her knees. She unbuckled and unzipped Garner's slacks. His dick sprung forth through the slit; she eagerly enveloped it between her lips as she squeezed his ass cheek with her left hand and tugged at his dick with her right hand.

While staring up at the ceiling, Garner began meeting her suction with some intermittent thrusts inside her mouth. Kadrece was so into sucking her husband's dick that she was oblivious to him helping her out of her clothes. She was completely naked before him by the time he moaned that he was nearing ejaculation.

She stopped long enough to help him slide his slacks down to his ankles. With his lower body exposed, she playfully slapped his ass.

"Damn baby! This feels *sooooo* good!" he reacted while he resumed fucking her mouth. "Oh, shit, I'm gonna cum! Whoooo, baby I'm gonna cum!"

Kadrece arched her head back and relaxed her gag muscles, enabling her to accept his offering of personal protein. His knees buckled from the intensity of his ejaculation. She looked up at him; her eyes sought his approval. She smacked her lips, chalking that up as an experience that she would consider bragging to those same haters.

Chapter 29

The view from behind was more than inviting to Garner. Kadrece, wearing just a black slip, stood in front of the dresser braless while she worked on her hair. Her breasts bobbled and jiggled much to his visual delight. He drew nigh to his wife and nuzzled his semi-erect dick against her full ass cheeks. She wiggled against him for a different reason.

"Garner, you know that I hate showing up at church after everything had started," she said, shooing him off as he caressed her breasts. "Why haven't you dressed for church?"

He gave her a playful slap on the ass. He liked it so much that he gave Kadrece another one. Hell, if he had it his way, he'd bend her over against the dresser for a quickie. But Kadrece had already balled her fist and shook it at him.

"I told you about us being late. Maybe I need to hold out on you the next time you want some of this—you just might get the message."

"You wouldn't do that to me?" Garner made a move for their walk-in closet where Kadrece's clothes took up roughly ninety percent of all the available closet space in her Spartanburg residence. She allowed him only a small section for his clothes—enough for him to hang up maybe a suit, a couple of slacks and a shirt.

"That seems to be the only way that I can get your attention on Sunday mornings," she answered. "Don't you know that husbands and wives need to not only have a good sex life but also a good spiritual life? And they can't do it not being at church when they're supposed to be there."

Garner rolled his eyes while he grudgingly went ahead with stepping out of his thin pewter colored athletic pants and into his gray slacks. He was also quick to slip on a starched white dress shirt. But if it were left up to him, he would prefer to show up at Mission Grove around 12:55 p.m. as the benediction was being given and call it a day.

He turned back around and noticed that Kadrece had not only gotten her hair looking quite stylish, she had covered her dick enticing breasts in a black lace bra and she had just stepped into a black thong.

"Baby, can you toss me those stockings just to your left?"

"And what do I get in return?"

"You get my most sincere thanks. Now hand them to me."

He tugged at his slacks. "Just remember when you're in the mood next time. I might have some stipulations attached to this." He checked the time on the Weather Channel. It was 9:24 a.m.; the early service started in six minutes.

"Garner, didn't I tell you to get ready?"

"I am getting ready." He had now taken his light blue silk tie off the clothes hanger and he had already created a knot for it. "You're the one who needs to hurry up!"

Exhaling loudly, Kadrece figured this was just as good as any opportunity to voice her latest concern. Although she had not suspected any questionable activity, it was her rationale that things could be even better. She walked with some urgency over to the closet, pulling a black leopard print dress over her still hourglass-shaped body despite having gained back twelve pounds.

"Baby, don't you think we could have fewer excuses about doing things together like going to church, and me not having to sleep here all alone?"

"What you're getting at?"

"Well, I was just thinking," she answered, searching for the right pair of dress shoes that might complement what she was about to wear.

"Thinking about what?"

"You looking for work here in the Greenville-Spartanburg area—"

"Are you crazy?" he reacted. "I thought we had a pretty good understanding about this: I don't tell you where to work, and you don't tell me where I need to work."

She walked back over to the dresser, applying a coat of lipstick. "Garner, look, you don't have to make a big deal out of nothing. But I was just thinking. I'm sure you could find something else do to, if push came to shove and it was a decision about your marriage versus everything else." She looked back at him, noticing that he was now fully dressed. "You do value me and your marriage over anything else?"

Garner had headed towards the living room door, delaying his response. "You know something? I've tried keeping my mouth shut about many things. But this is not one that I'm keeping my mouth shut." He raised his voice, making sure that she heard him from where she was in the bedroom. "You don't tell me how I pursue and further my career. If anything, it's obvious that you have some flexibility. All of a sudden you have a job here in South Carolina—I thought you had a pretty good gig in Florida?"

She had now joined him in the living room. "I did. But this was a better opportunity. Just how many opportunities have really come your way since you got fired in Houston? Just there in Columbia."

"For your explanation Ms. Know-It-All, I've not tried looking for anything just yet. I actually turned down an offer just before I asked you to marry me." He waited for Kadrece to walk past him before he closed the door behind them.

"So you would consider moving to this side of the state if it meant making sure that our marriage went even better?"

"As if things were bad before?" he asked. "Kadrece, let's not make something out of nothing. You're creating issues that, as best as I know, do not exist."

She exhaled in disgust mumbling rather loudly that Garner was selfish and only out for himself. He stopped in mid-stride, but she kept walking in the direction of his G-35.

"Hey, I heard that! If I were so selfish and out for myself, I'd still be going to *my* church than having to force myself into going to a place where the pastor doesn't know jack shit what he's talking about. Humph. You know what? I'm shocked that you would settle for a place like Mission Grove."

Garner clicked the doors for Kadrece. "I hadn't settled for just anything!" She plopped into the passenger seat, her slamming the door muffled the remainder of her response. "It's a good church. I think it's even better than the one I attended back in Tallahassee."

This was the first time that she had heard anything to the contrary from Garner about her church. It had been her belief the best way to portray a nice, wholesome picture of them as husband and wife was by transmitting a message of unity to her detractors.

"So what you're telling me is that you had been looking for an opportunity to wash my face about coming to a church that I liked better than your place out in the middle of nowhere among a bunch of rednecks?"

Garner, who had already driven to the driveway exit, was visibly annoyed.

"That church you say that is out there among a bunch of red-necks teaches its members with more substance than your so-called church." He huffed louder for more emphasis. "I can't believe that I'm still going through this for you today.

"Humph. The problem is if I don't go your church [then] I won't hear the end of it from you. You'll just do like every other wife around this world does: *nag, nag, nag, nag . . . nag!*"

She threw her head back into the headrest, folding her arms. "It means that maybe you husbands need to listen to your wives. And if you husbands were smart enough, you'd understand that if the wife ain't happy, nobody's happy!" She pursed her lips and stared out the

the window. Neither of them spoke for the remainder of the drive to church.

Like many church couples that had their differences, both Garner and Kadrece managed to put on their best face and appearance of unity by the time they turned into the parking lot.

After finding a parking space much farther away than usual, Garner paused to collect his thoughts before he turned off the engine while Kadrece gathered her purse. He had previously agreed to join Mission Grove this week.

"I hope you understand that I'm going along with this because I love you, and I want you to be the happiest of wives," he said, assuming a more serious facial expression. "I know that some things are important to you, and this is one of them."

He held out his hand for her. Then he leaned over and kissed her gently on her cheek, smiling. "If erections were the only sign, I think that I'd be off the charts right now."

In a single effort, Garner had put Kadrece at ease by saying words that were effective for the moment.

"We better get inside, baby," she said. "We might only be fifteen minutes late. Next week, can we get here on time?"

Garner sat during service replaying the interaction he had with Kadrece from earlier in the morning. It enabled him to dissociate himself from another message by Pastor McBride.

He knew that joining Mission Grove also meant he had given up another piece of autonomy for his wife's sake. He wondered how many other husbands would do something similar for a wife. Only God knew that answer.

From time to time, Garner glanced over to his right at Kadrece. At least from the exterior she appeared content. She even maneuvered her hand under his folded arms, allowing her fingers to tease him by how close they could reach his dick. Things could not be as bad as she described them to be, he thought, yet they were in church.

As anticipated, McBride did offer attendees an opportunity to make a decision of faith shortly after his sermon. Only two people stood up in response. He then invited attendees the opportunity to join Mission Grove.

"We're not about pulling and twisting people's arms to join here," McBride said. "We're excited about the possibility that y'all would consider being among us. Are there any here wishing to join?"

Kadrece squeezed her husband's hand before she stood up. He knew this was his cue to follow her to the front of the sanctuary—or else. They were met by a polite smattering of applause.

"Do we have others who desire to become a part of our experience here at Mission Grove?" Two other men and a woman also joined the Davises. "God bless you. This is what I'm talking 'bout. God is faithful; He is good, and His mercy endures forever."

McBride started by announcing the names of the two other men. "And we also have here a couple that I've come to know lately because, well, I married them. "We have here Sister Kadrece who joined our church a few months back—"

Garner was inclined to react with complete surprise, looking his wife over as if she had done something much to his consternation. But he opted for a much cooler tact. He kept his attention square on McBride.

"We also have here husband, uh, Arlen—"

"Garner."

"Oh, I'm so sorry, brother," McBride reacted, looking back at the congregation. "We have here Sister Kadrece's husband, Garner, and I guess that she wanted to make it official by coming up here to be with her husband.

"I invite all of you to come back next week between the first and second service and we'll have a session for you with me and Sister McBride, my wife. At that time, we'll go over some things about our church. Right now, I would like a couple of sisters and a few of you brothers to come up and greet all of our new members."

Five women of varied degrees of beauty and shapes almost sprinted to the front of the church. LaFreda Arrington, in her late thirties and nearly as tall as Kadrece, standing about five-eight without heels, could not contain her glee for having made it ahead of the other women.

"Welcome to Mission Grove, brother," LaFreda moved to hug Garner. What she did not expect was Kadrece's intercepting her telegraphed move my jutting out her hand to shake hers.

"Oh, I didn't see you, sister—"

LaFreda was reduced to nervously shaking Kadrece's hand before Garner's. The other four women also followed suit. There would be no hugs or other subtle moves made towards Kadrece Renee Davis' husband, if she had anything to do with it.

Meanwhile, Garner still showed no emotion. If anything, it dawned upon him how he rarely bothered to acquaint himself with anyone during the past several months that he attended Kadrece's church.

Humph.

"Brother, welcome to Mission Grove," a familiar face had stuck his hand out to Garner, who was slow to accept.

Garner was amused by Levi Harriston's attire—a black suit jacket similar to felt cloth material, a red shirt and black tie, and a black handkerchief stuffed in the jacket—that reminded him of somebody who just stepped out of a time warp from the Blaxploitation film era.

Levi broke out in a wide grin the instant he released his handshake with Garner and moved in front of Kadrece. As they made hand contact, Levi milked the moment for all it was worth by holding Kadrece's hand a fraction longer than he should have.

"Sister, we're glad to have you and your husband here at Mission Grove," he said before he returned to his post at the back of the church.

McBride had all the new members to remain in front of the congregation while he proceeded with the benediction. No sooner than "Amen" was uttered, Garner grasped for Kadrece's hand so they might make a bold move for the door. This was about all of the compromising that he could stand for a week.

Before they reached the rear of the sanctuary, a familiar voice attempted to hail down Kadrece.

"Now I can really call you brother, huh?" Levi mentioned to Gar-

before he deviated his attention at Kadrece. "The pastor didn't mention it this week, but we have cell groups that meet once, sometimes twice a month, at some of the member's homes. Some are held on Saturdays and some are on Sundays. You're invited to attend the one that I'll be having at my place not this Saturday, but next week—"

"Uh, thanks for the invitation," Garner interrupted; he also gave Kadrece's hand a light squeeze. "We'll get back with you on that."

Kadrece smiled. "Thank you, brother."

On their way back to Kadrece's place, Garner made light of it being obvious to him that Kadrece had a secret admirer at Mission Grove. "I didn't know you were off into partially bald yahoos that dress like Buckwheat?"

"What are you talking about, Garner?"

"Who's that clown that seems to be off in your face almost every opportunity when you go to that church?"

Kadrece waved off Garner. "Oh, he's Levi Harriston. He's one of the church ushers. He seems to know everything that goes on there." She then flipped the conversation on him. "Well, for someone who never says anything to anyone at church, you sure have a few fans of your own." He returned her a confused look while she added, "Well, Ms. LaFreda certainly knows who you are. But I just had to remind her who I was."

The comment well taken, Garner made a snap comeback of his own. "Yeah, just like I had to remind your friend Mr. Levi who I was. He thought he could invite you to something at his place next week without approaching me—I think not."

Chapter 30

When Kadrece last visited a doctor for her annual checkup, she was in the midst of reacquainting herself with Garner. Her weight was down in the one hundred fifties, but now that she had been married for nearly six months the nuptial bliss had translated into her gaining back about seventeen of the nearly thirty pounds that she lost.

Apparently, it still had been all good with Garner because he had yet to complain or make any odd observations. He still groped and fondled her at every opportunity. But the weight gain did not go unnoticed by her new physician, Dr. Anne Ridgeman of the Piedmont Medical Group in Spartanburg.

"I was browsing your records . . . Has your eating habits changed any, Kadrece?" she inquired, tapping through files on her touch screen computer.

Kadrece hunched her shoulders. "I don't know. I guess being married since my last check up and commuting between Greenville and Columbia has cut into my time for exercise."

"Well, that is a possibility. But there's no need to panic," Ridgeman said. "You are still well within your desired weight range."

"Whew! Maybe it was a good thing that I did lose all that weight the last year and a half?"

Some of Ridgeman's questions also went beyond the usual medical ones. She remarked, "You know, I got married right after I completed my residency. How long is your commute to see your husband?"

"He's in Columbia, and I'm here in the Spartanburg area and I work in Greenville."

"Well, it can't be as bad as when your spouse's working in northern Virginia, and you've just completed your training in Atlanta. There was no Internet or unlimited cell phone calling plans back then."

The mention of Atlanta piqued Kadrece's curiosity. "I'm originally from there, and my parents and the rest of my brothers and sisters live there. How have you managed to make your marriage work?"

Ridgeman reacted matter-of-factly, noting that her marriage lasted for less than four years. "It was very tough on us. Issues of trust began to creep in. Sometimes, we tried to meet each other halfway in North Carolina. In the end, we realized that we had made a great decision but at the wrong time in our lives."

This was the first time that Kadrece related anything about her marriage to anyone other than her mother, Kamryn, or Nedra. "I guess you had your share of haters telling you that you should have never gotten married in the first place—"

Ridgeman tapped through other folders on the screen before she responded. Sighing she said, "The hardest thing to do is not listen to everyone who has an opinion." She then took a seat adjacent to the examining table that Kadrece sat on.

"I've been pretty good about that. I had to get my parents straight before I married my husband, and I've had to limit my contact with my friend from college," Kadrece answered. "Other than that, things have been fine between me and Garner."

"Hmmm, Garner. That's a different name—"

"He's a different guy all together. But he's my husband. That's all that matters."

"Well good for you," Ridgeman replied; she also mentioned in passing that Kadrece's cholesterol, blood pressure, and mammogram all were normal. Finally, she queried, "It just dawned on me, Kadrece, that you're thirty-seven years old. Have you ever been pregnant?"

"No ma'am."

"Have you and your husband ever discussed starting a family?"

Somehow, that question hit home with Kadrece. Tears welled up and she bowed her head. Ridgeman reminded Kadrece that based on her pap smear and other information that she had the body of a woman in her late twenties. "If you are thinking about having children now would be the time—"

Kadrece raised her head, wiping away the tear that streamed down her cheek. Inwardly, she wanted to curse out Garner who had been non-committal as long as she could remember about starting a family.

"I'm sorry, did I upset you?" Ridgeman asked.

She shook her head. "No you didn't." She squirmed uncomfortably on the examining table's hard pad. "I know you doctors tell us that we don't need to rush things, but aren't there risks with having children later in our child bearing years."

"Women are having children late these days. But it is my opinion that now is the time," Ridgeman informed Kadrece. "May I ask you one last question, actually two?"

"Sure."

"Has your husband showed any signs of change in his sexual appetite?"

"Oh no, Dr. Ridgeman!"

"Call me Anne."

"Okay, Anne. Garner's not changed since the first time we met back in college." She paused then chuckled. "That's one of the things that I've had to get on the haters about my husband."

"So you're saying that your sex life is fine?"

Kadrece felt that if she were a different skin shade that she would have blushed at the question. "We may not agree on everything, but when it comes to sex my husband and I are always on the same page." She nodded emphatically to Ridgeman.

"Well, that's great." Ridgeman answered. "I guess for you two things might happen when they might happen. Who knows? Maybe the next time that I see you congratulations may be in order . . . You're free to go."

Kadrece's conversation with Dr. Ridgeman weighed heavily on her mind for the remainder of the day. She decided to surprise Garner that evening by commuting to Columbia unannounced. She awaited his arrival dressed in one of his older baseball warm-up jerseys. She lit a couple of scented candles in the living room area. That was about as far as she anticipated on him entering.

Apparently, Garner did not notice her BMW out in the parking area when he arrived. It had been a typical long day during the football season. When he entered the living room, he was taken aback by the candles on the coffee table and on the lamp stand next to the sofa.

Kadrece's familiar alto voice declared, "All I want you to do is come over here and fuck me. Is there any problem with that?"

He froze in mid-step, pointing in the direction of the hallway. "Can I at least go to the bathroom first?"

"Sure. Just remember where I am after you come out." She slipped a finger inside her pussy. She licked one side of her finger and she offered him the other side to him. "That's just to remind you why I'm here on a Tuesday night to see you—"

Kadrece moved to position all three of Garner's sofa cushions on the living room floor. She awaited his return lying outstretched on her stomach. As his footsteps became louder, she hiked his jersey over her hips.

Lured by her obvious attributes, Garner knelt behind Kadrece and proceeded to press his face into her dripping pussy, making slow and measured tongue flicks around her clit. And as she began working her hips to his oral mastery, he made his enjoyment more audible.

"Baby, you love licking my asshole, don't you?"

He moaned in acknowledgement.

Sucking air through her teeth she responded, "I love it when you lick my ass—"

In the spirit of her request, Garner had now figured it out that all the loving and sensual shit was for another time. He reared up and positioned himself behind Kadrece, pushing his dick between her slippery folds.

Kadrece offered no resistance, only a loud moan. "God I love you, baby!"

"Tell me why you want this dick?"

"Because I got horny talking about it today," she answered as she began meeting his long, deliberate strokes inside her. "I told you that I didn't want to discuss much of anything; I just want you to fuck me—"

He gave her a playful smack on her ass before he placed his hands on her hips, increasing his thrusts.

"That's what I'm saying, damn it!" she shrieked. "Oooh, you're hitting my spot!"

Kadrece's pussy felt unusually wet, but Garner knew there were ways of avoiding a quick release inside her. So he suggested for her to lie on her back while he rested her legs on his shoulders, giving him a deeper angle to fuck.

She reached around and clutched his ass. "Mmmm, baby. There you go. It's all yours to fuck!" He held her legs father apart while he stroked deep inside her; she reacted in a sultry tone. "Whooo baby, you're going to make me say some shit that I . . . "

He placed her legs back on his shoulders. He knew that he bottomed out by the way Kadrece screamed out his name and other obscenities. After they spent several moments fucking in that position, he suggested that she mounted him. Kadrece worked her pussy up and down his shaft, but she did not last long.

She leaned forward, panting in his ear. "Baby, you're beating up my kitty. That's why I talked about you so much."

"Is that right?"

Suddenly, her face contorted, and she squealed in reaction to the quaking that she felt between her thighs. Garner was not far behind as he released his nut inside her.

After their moment on the living room carpet, Kadrece confided in Garner, "I know it had been only two days, but I just really missed you."

"If you miss me that much, have you considered moving to Columbia maybe in six months?" he countered.

Kadrece sat up straight. "You don't understand that Duggans and Chattell have a lot of money tied up in me, and you can be damned sure they're going to try and get all they can out of me."

She then tried a different tact with Garner. "Have you considered at any point finding work in Greenville?"

He smirked at her suggestion. "Uh, haven't you recognized that we're in a down economy, and in my profession the only movement has been people being bounced to the curb because they were laid off?"

"I understand. But I can't afford right now to be viewed as a Gypsy in my profession," she countered. "I'm sure we'll work something out—hopefully sooner than later."

Kadrece nuzzled her partially sweaty body against Garner's. He reached around and cupped her breasts, savoring the moment with his wife. "This is better than I could have ever imagined."

She thanked Garner for the compliment. Then she shifted the conversation to her doctor's visit from earlier in the day. "Dr. Ridgeman says that I have the body of a woman in her twenties."

"I agree, that's for damned sure!" he answered, rubbing his dick.

She chortled at his response. Then she mentioned, "The doctor also asked about our sex life. I told her now we might not agree on everything, but we've always been on the same page when it comes to sex."

Knowing she was about to broach a more serious topic, Kadrece slid off Garner and sat upright next to him on the cushions. She leaned against the other portion of the sofa, yawning. "Dr. Ridgeman also asked me if we were considering a family." She felt Garner withdraw his attentiveness.

"What am I supposed to say?" he reacted.

That sent Kadrece into a conniption. "That's the fucking problem with you, Garner. You don't say any goddamned thing when it comes to important stuff like starting a family. Now I see why I started crying when she asked me that question."

Garner returned her a stunned look.

"Yeah, I said it," she hissed. "And I'll say this too . . . You're a selfish motherfucker. Really selfish!"

"What are you talking about?"

She stood up and placed her hands at her waist. She paced the living room. "Isn't that one of the reasons why people get married? You know, to have kids—"

"Why are you saying that I'm selfish?" he protested.

"Why don't you just listen to me," she said, pointing emphatically. "So are you telling me that family isn't important to you?"

Garner had now stood up and confronted Kadrece face-to-face. "Will you stop putting words in my mouth?" His chest rose and fell noticeably with each breath.

She rolled her neck, commenting, "Then why don't you speak up. Be a damn man and not just with your dick!"

His eyes widened. Rage had now consumed him. To better deal with it, he stormed off to the kitchen where he attempted to calm down alone. Moments later, he returned to the living room where Kadrece had now sat in one of the two living room comforters. He knelt beside her, reaching out for her hand. Then he leaned forward to kiss her on the cheek.

"Hey, baby," he said, smiling. "I'm glad that you came here tonight."

That incensed Kadrece even more. She stormed away from him, stopping off in the kitchen. "Will you stop avoiding questions, Garner? I'm not one of those people that you can make them sound dumb!"

He followed her stride-for-stride, and he was right upon her when she turned around. "Why don't you stop trying to think for me, damn it?" He demanded that she sit down, shut up and listen to him. "If this is your idea of having some romantic night with me, the shit just backfired." He walked off to the dining room before he returned to the kitchen. "While I'm at it, thanks for the pussy. I really needed it.

Hope you got all of the dick that you wanted."

She flipped him her middle finger. "Fuck you, Garner! Fuck you!" She stormed off to the bedroom. Along the way, she openly mumbled that maybe all of the commuting had already run its course.

Sucking her teeth she said, "Humph, I still have time to get that annulment. It isn't too late here in South Carolina."

"Too late for what?"

"An annulment!"

Garner rushed back to the bedroom. Ignoring him, she made haste to get dressed and repack her bag. He attempted to pull her close to him; she wanted no part of it, jerking away from him. "I don't know who you've been talking to, but you better check yourself and fast." He pointed forcefully in her direction, yelling, "And I'm getting tired of your bullshit, blowing up at me for some of the most immature things. Tonight, it's because I didn't give you a fast enough answer, and on a subject that we really hadn't talked about."

She walked past him, bumping shoulders in the process. "No, you need to listen. If I wanted just a sex partner, I would have stayed single."

In the living room, she searched for purse and her keys.

"I accepted your marriage proposal because I thought that you wanted me to become your partner in life—"

"I did," he interrupted her. "But I also expected for you to consider my side of things too. This ain't all about you!"

"Well, maybe it should be. You just might realize what's also important for your wife, and not just for yourself!"

Kadrece stared at Garner for several seconds, expecting for him to come to his senses. But he merely walked off to the bedroom. Thoroughly pissed, she slammed the front door and returned to Spartanburg.

Chapter 31

For most of the next day, Kadrece nervously waited for Garner to call her. She fully expected him to apologize and eventually beg her for some pussy. There were no calls that came from Columbia bearing his voice.

Her her conscience got the best of her. Grudgingly, she punched in Garner's number at the station. But she hung up just before it rang. Then she did the same thing with his cell phone.

"Fuck it," she hissed, hanging up again before it rang. "He's the one who's wrong, not me!"

Stressed, Kadrece felt compelled to talk about her situation with someone, but that might come with some unwanted grief. She reasoned that contacting Nedra would be an admission that she married the wrong person.

If she contacted Kamryn, she thought it would have been a sign of little sister not being mature to handle marriage. She cringed at the thought of contacting Johnette after their heated exchanges. And Kanitra was out of the question because she never discussed relational things with her eldest sister.

Tears welled up in her eyes—a couple landed on some of her case paperwork. Now struggling with her emotions, Kadrece made it a quick work of gathering her briefcase and purse, calling it a day. She managed drive away from the law office before she allowed her tears to freely stream down her cheeks.

Still sulking, Kadrece felt that she had a righteous cause to take up her complaint to God concerning Garner's reluctance to starting a family.

"You know my heart," she prayed. *"All I've wanted was to be loved and happy. This is not the way I thought it would be—"*

She wiped away her tears, although she still choked many back. The thought that next entered her mind involved her attending Mission Grove's mid-week service. She actually smiled at the idea.

Being among the congregation of the righteous was supposed to have been soothing to Kadrece's mind and soul. It turned out that Kadrece felt just as guilty as she had been throughout the day.

She spent little time paying attention to Pastor McBride's sermon, which he highlighted the importance of patience and the preservation of a person's soul. He gave reference to two passages: the first spoke of how patience leads to the perfection to an individual's character, and that person may be seen as mature; the other was presented to the sparse congregation as a direct commandment that impatience could lead to a person losing his or her soul.

"We all are going to be faced with trials and tribulations," McBride said. "But how we deal with it is going to tell whether we come out like pure gold and silver, or we might be consumed by the mighty burning fire—"

He paused, scanning the congregation. "Amen?" There were few that followed him.

For Kadrece, it did not help, too, that she found herself annoyed feeling even more vulnerable and wishing for her husband's security. She was eager for the service to end. And after the benediction, she was unable to leave unnoticed.

"Sista," the familiar male's voice beckoned Kadrece from behind; she was reluctant at turning around. He went on to say, "I saw that you weren't really into the service tonight. Is there anything wrong?"

Damn, she thought. *Amazing what some people pay so much attention to?* She was curt with her reply. "Nothing; I do thank you for asking." She began leaving.

Levi managed a weak smile, almost letting out a chortle. "Well, uh, if you need anything, don't hesitate to call me—you do have my number?"

"I'm sure if I there was something wrong, I'm sure that Pastor McBride would be the first that I'd contact."

She hurried out to her car.

By the time she settled in her BMW, she could no longer deal with her uneasiness. She checked her watch. It was about 8:45 p.m., and she guessed that Garner was either at his place or at Gallardo's between shows.

As she made a left-hand turn on to Blackstock Road, she punched in Garner's cell phone number. She held her breath while it rang.

"This is Garner—"

She was slow to respond.

"Hello, this is Garner—"

She recognized that there was a loud television off in the background. "Hi, baby. I'm sorry about last night." Her face actually brightened up in anticipation of Garner's response.

"Oh you are?"

"Yes. I am. I could have handled our conversation better especially after us making love."

Garner nodded, retorting, "I'm glad you recognized that." He excused himself for a few moments, explaining that he was walking outside. "All right, I'm back . . . Now when did you think you could just talk to me just any way?"

Kadrece let out a long breath. She slowed her car down so that she could handle both their conversation and the relatively thick traffic between the Westgate Mall and Dorman Commons areas. "Baby, I don't want to talk about that any more. I miss you. I hadn't heard from you all day, and I've been worried about you."

"Well that's nice to know," Garner retorted. "For a while, I wasn't sure."

She exhaled again. "Baby, didn't you hear me? I hadn't heard from you all day, and I've been worried about you. Why didn't you bother to call me?" She leaned back into the driver's seat; the light had just turned red at Reidville Road.

"So why didn't you call?" she persisted.

There was a lengthy pause.

"Garner, baby, please. We need to talk this thing out."

"If you happen to remember, you were the one who left Columbia all bent out of shape," he responded. "Yeah, you pissed me off and I felt the best thing that I could do was keep a cool head by not talking to you."

"Are you still pissed at me?"

"I don't know."

"Well don't be, please—"

Garner got around to explaining that he was not comfortable arguing with her. He said, "I didn't marry you to be fighting over silly shit. I know life isn't perfect, but I don't like that kind of drama." He went on to say that he grew up around his parents who fought and argued often, but he promised himself to be different. "I said I would never create that kind of drama when I get married."

"Point understood, baby," Kadrece answered. "But I still think you should have apologized."

He retorted, "And you should have checked your attitude at the door."

Sighing, Kadrece conceded aloud that they were getting nowhere. She went as far as to complain that Garner still did not understand why she was upset.

"Understand what?"

"That I'd like to start a family."

That provoked Garner to anger—his eyes narrowed and his eyebrows furrowed. He delayed his response, hoping that he would not resume cursing at her. "Well, why didn't you say that?"

"Because you weren't listening to me."

Garner shook his head. He felt that nothing like this had ever come up. In his opinion, the only pressing matter had been her birthday, which he bought her a session at a spa that was known for pampering women for an entire day.

He offered to drive to her place after the 11 o'clock show. He explained that it would be his way of showing unconditional love.

"Just call me when you're close to here."

Kadrece remained awake for Garner when he arrived at her place after 1 a.m. She met him at the door wearing a black and red camisole. Her nipples were eager for his attention, and her pussy throbbed for his tongue and dick. She stood on her toes as she gave him a warm, sensual kiss.

When they separated, she showed him a seductive look and a smirk. "I still think you were selfish, but I'll forgive you." She curled her index finger, beckoning him to follow her into the bedroom.

But Garner balked at her invitation.

"Selfish? If I were selfish, I wouldn't have driven here in the middle of the night to see you." He folded his arms, patting his foot. "Maybe you're the one who's selfish."

Confronting him face-to-face, Kadrece first pushed her index finger into his chest. "Garner, I'm not going to stand here and put up with that." Then she snapped her finger in defiance, rolling her neck. "Humph, you can sleep in the living room tonight. And don't bother about asking me for any pussy tonight!"

Kadrece left only a trail of her fragrance in her wake as she sashayed away from him.

"That's fine with me," he hissed. "I'll be out in the morning. Early!"

Chapter 32

Kadrece was headed to her car after working out at Sweat Room, a popular gym located next to The Door Christian Supply store on Reidville Road in Spartanburg. She wore a pair of long athletic pants with a matching silver sweat jacket over one of Garner's old baseball warm-up jerseys.

Even as she was not at her usual sexy best on this early fall afternoon, it was still enough to catch the attention of at least one male in the parking lot.

"I can use a workout partner," the man shouted in her direction; it was accompanied by a hearty laugh.

Levi Harriston's voice resonated with her. And of all things, after not speaking to Garner since their blow-up, a mischievous feeling came over her. She stopped just shy of her trunk and smiled back at him. "You know what, Brother Levi? I don't think that you could keep up with my workout program." She tossed her athletic bag in her car.

Meanwhile, Levi had already looked her up and down from his vantage point inside his beige 2001 Chrysler 300M, sucking his teeth.

"You must don't understand the power of prayer."

She quipped, "Whatever it takes—"

Levi placed his car in PARK. "Uh, sister, if you're not doing any-thing, would you like to fellowship at McDonald's over some cof-fee?" He nodded in the direction of the fast food place located at the far end of the property.

"It's on me."

Taking a deep breath, Kadrece found it easy to rationalize that what Garner didn't know wouldn't hurt him. It was only an innocu-ous conversation with someone from church over coffee—in her case, an iced tea.

"I've got a few minutes," she said, exhaling. "I forgot to get some-thing to drink before I left the gym, anyway."

Levi was beside himself. His forehead radiated from his giddiness. "I guess I'll meet you over there in a few, huh?" His car jerked no-ticeably whenever he put his car in DRIVE, but he was mindful not to take off in a rush.

After Kadrece settled in the driver's seat, she glanced down at her wedding ring, mulling her options. Then she stared straight ahead. She searched her memory for a verse that might justify her decision to meet with Levi. Nothing came to her. She also contemplated con-tacting Garner, but her pride decried fuck him.

She eventually crept across the lot despite protests by her inner voice. Even as she parked next to Levi's car she was well aware that she had time to change her mind. After she collected her purse and keys, each movement that she made seemed to go against gravity.

"I guess it would be the Lord that we'd cross paths today," he said, adding a weak chortle to his comment. "You know it says our paths are ordained by Him—"

She walked past him towards the restaurant's entrance. But just as she attempted to open the door, Levi lunged ahead of her, pushing the door. Their bodies grazed. An unusual sensation triggered an unwanted reaction within her. It was the kind that marked much of her single life leading to mischief.

She glanced back over her shoulder, thanking him.

"You're quite welcome," he replied, smiling again. He found a table near not far from the rear entrance. Feeling very much within his element, he was mindful not to portray himself as some sanctified predator.

Nonetheless, the lustful thoughts that he entertained were the foundation to what he fantasized while he masturbated on a couple of occasions. So many times he wanted to tell Kadrece in passing *chocolate come in all forms and colors. There's nothing like the real milk chocolate candy bar with lots of nuts in them.*

Now she sat across from him. Surely God answered prayer.

"You know, I could tell from a mile away that you're not from around here," he said. "But I still can't place where you're from."

Kadrece took a small sip from her cup, shaking her head. "Ugh! They say this is sweet tea?" Before she could go into a rant Levi had excused himself and retrieved for her several packets of sugar.

While he was away from the table Kadrece turned around and made a quick inspection of his goods from behind. It helped that he wore a pair of brown slacks and a light blue business shirt. She found it intriguing that he had a wide girth.

As he sat down, Levi resumed his query. "You never mentioned where you're from?"

She found Levi's attentiveness appealing. He seemed genuinely interested. That was something that rivaled Garner.

"I came here from Florida, but I'm originally from Atlanta."

He made a gesture with his index finger. "See, I knew it! I could tell in the way that you talked that you weren't from around here."

Taking on a more demure tact, Kadrece leaned back in her seat. She found his exuberance in sharp contrast to Garner.

She inquired, "So, are you from around here?"

"Born and raised."

He took a moment out for himself by pouring in three containers of crème, stirring it into his coffee. He mentioned along the way that he grew up on Spartanburg's east side of town—opposite of where they were—and he explained that much of the city's old money from the textile industry was based over there. He was also proud to mention that he attended the city's namesake high school, and he played on the football team, lettering all three years. He also volunteered to her that he had been attending Mission Grove since 1998. The church moved the same year from a smaller place from near the downtown area.

She noticed that he sucked his teeth on a frequent basis, but she dismissed it as just one of his quirks. "Now I see why you know so much about what goes on at Mission Grove."

"Well, you might say that to be true. I've been with the ushers since 2000. I've preached from time to time since 2005," he answered, pausing. He then hunched his shoulders. "Hey, I was taught that if you want to be blessed you need to be close to the man of God."

"Well that is impressive, Brother Levi—"

"Just call me Levi; that's what everyone else calls me."

"All right, uh, Levi—"

He tried to portray himself as being bashful, but in fact she had played into exactly how he expected to run his game. He figured here was his chance to sprinkle some sugar on top on his conversation.

"May I call you Kadrece?"

She nodded.

"I know your husband has to be a very proud man to have you as his wife. I know I would be if you were mine—"

The inner voice of reasoning within Kadrece suggested that she should end her conversation with Levi, yet her anger towards Garner prodded her to continue. She managed a slight smile.

"I'm sure you've used that line on a few women that have come through church. It's not like I was born yesterday, brother."

Levi threw up both hands. "So if I have, are you going to hold it against me? I bet a few other guys have told you the same thing. They're right. You are a very attractive young lady." He paused for a quick sip before he continued. "And how old are you anyway— twenty-five?"

"You're so silly, Levi. I'm not twenty-five. I think I was that old when I, uh, never mind."

"Never mind what?"

She shook her head. "It's nothing to talk about." She resisted telling him that was about the age she and Garner were booty-call partners.

Sensing the timing was right, Levi volunteered to her that he had been twice married and divorced. He had a teenage daughter who was a high school senior attending a school in nearby Duncan. When she didn't react, he also sensed he could proceed with his other personal factoid.

"I'm engaged, but then again I'm not engaged because we've not yet set an actual wedding date," he said. "You probably know who my fiancée is."

She returned him a puzzled look; her words were very measured. "I'm not sure if I'm familiar with her—"

He leaned back in his seat. "Oh you know her because she knows who you are. She was probably the first person that you met when you first came to Mission Grove."

She shook her head, still unsure.

"You know Carnette Flemming?" he said.

Kadrece still showed no reaction. What she did muse to herself about Carnette was that she was definitely not someone to be mistaken for a model, or as curvy as she.

"Well, congratulations. I'm sure you'll be sharing that with everyone when you two will set that date."

"Probably, it's all in His timing."

On their way out of McDonald's, Kadrece stalled just shy of the door. That produced another awkward moment because Levi unknowingly bumped up against her from behind.

"Oh, I'm sorry," she said, stepping out of his way. "I had thought about turning around to get me something for later this afternoon."

Levi rushed ahead of her, offering, "I'll get that for you." She thanked him for holding the door open for her. But the moment had triggered another lustful digression within her. In better times, had that been Garner, she might have gone out of her way to wiggle her ass up against him, and there would be no telling what might ensue.

Meanwhile, Levi tried every trick he knew to keep his mind off Kadrece's ass. He prayed that she would not notice the bulge forming in his slacks. He was careful not to walk so close to her as he followed her to her car.

Out in the parking lot, he thanked her for joining him. Despite battling her conscience, she accepted Levi's handshake, smiling.

"Maybe we could do lunch sometime?" he offered.

"Please say hello to Carnette for me," she countered. "I think she's a very nice lady. She's always made me feel welcomed at church."

"I'll be sure to tell her that," he said, walking towards his car. Before he opened his door, he figured that he'd take a final shot. "I never asked where you worked. I hope that I'm not being too nosy?"

"Hold on." Kadrece made sure she was inside of her car, ensuring that she was less conspicuous. Then she lowered her window. "I work for a law firm in Greenville . . . Duggans and Chattell."

Levi's eyes widened. "You work there? I see their commercials on TV all of the time. They're a big-time place around here. Do you work as a secretary or something like that?"

That moved Kadrece to laughter. "I'm one of their attorneys. They offered me a better situation than the one that I left in Florida." She looked over her shoulder, preparing to back out. "Nice talking with you today. I'll see you in church!"

Chapter 33

All throughout this silence, Garner had maintained to himself that he had no problem about starting a family. Even for his limited exposure at sustained relationships, he had overheard several conversations in which both the husband and wife expressed frustration that they were not able to start a family on their own terms. Usually, it was when they just decided to let things happen as they may that they became bearers of the good news—that's what he hoped for him and Kadrece.

When he approached Kadrece's condominium, he paused and let out a long breath. He noticed as he opened the door the lights and television were off.

So Garner went ahead with placing his bag on the kitchen table, and then he searched the refrigerator for something to drink. The only thing that he found appealing was one of her Smirnoff coolers.

By the time he returned to the living room, Kadrece stood in the hallway with her hands on her waist.

"What brings you here?" she inquired. "But since you are here, can't you at least say hello when you arrive?"

He placed the cooler on the coffee table, and he plopped on the sofa. He beckoned her to join him, sitting on his lap. Her fragrance was most welcomed just as her soft dark mocha flesh.

"I didn't want to disturb you," he answered, pausing. "I just wanted to be here with you. I can't believe that we've gone this long without speaking to each other."

She wrapped her arms around his neck. "Baby, let's not look back. Let's look ahead. I miss you." She gave him a kiss on his cheek. He returned with a warm, wet kiss on her lips.

When they came up for air, Garner volunteered, "I brought a couple of things for you."

Her eyes widened in anticipation. He excused himself and headed over to the kitchen, returning with two items in his hand.

"You did this for me?" she reacted.

He nodded.

"I really don't deserve this—I mean, I acted so much like a bitch to you."

Garner was determined to exercise restraint. He apologized to her for not fully understanding why starting a family was important to her. "I really don't know all the reasons, Kadrece, but I told you before we got married that I wanted to do everything that I can to make you the happiest wife."

"Thank you, baby," she responded; she then sat upright like a child waiting for her birthday cake to be served. "So what did you get me?"

He felt extremely proud to present to her a fourteen karat gold bracelet along with a "Missing You" card. Tears immediately welled up in her eyes. She stood up and nuzzled her body against his. She kissed him on his neck and then she pushed her tongue inside his mouth. He eagerly sucked it and offered his in return.

When they separated this time, Kadrece helped remove Garner's clothing and he returned the favor removing her oversized bed shirt. Then she led him by the hand back to the bedroom.

They needed no foreplay. Kadrece lay supine for Garner with her thighs parted for him. He mounted her and delivered slow, strong thrusts inside her.

She clasped her hands around the back of his neck, whispering,

"Oh baby, that's it. Give it to me right there . . . I miss your sweet red dick." Then she held up her legs, sending the message that she wanted him even stronger inside her. "Mmmm, I love you Garner Davis . . . damn it, I love you!"

He replied, "Don't say anything else, baby. Just fuck me back."

She worked to match him stroke-for-stroke. "Is that what you want?"

"Yeah, that's it."

By the time Garner had reached under to grasp a healthy handful of her ass, Kadrece had begun squirming and writhing below him. Tears also escaped her eyes as her body yielded a much-anticipated orgasm with her husband.

"Baby, don't pull out tonight," she requested of him. "I want to feel *all* of you tonight. All of you, baby—"

Garner increased the rate of his strokes; they never changed out of the missionary, which was atypical for them. But the occasion seemed entirely appropriate. Kadrece teased him by gripping and releasing his dick.

"Are you going to give it to me?" she asked him.

He was more than willing to oblige. Moments later, he moaned and let out a loud grunt.

"Mmmm, shit! This pussy is so fucking good!" he rambled to her. "Here it comes, yeah. Here it comes!"

She clasped her legs around his trunk just as his body went rigid atop of her. She lunged upward to kiss him fully on his lips just as she felt a strong spurt of his cum settle inside her walls. She closed her eyes in fulfillment, and she actually thanked God for receiving Garner's cum.

Early the next morning, Garner stared up at the white-textured sheetrock ceiling. The ceiling fan, which operated at a low speed all night, made it a cozy existence for him and his wife, who clung contentedly onto him.

Instead of waking up to feeling that all was well, guilt had already taken hold of him. He wondered whether he actually made the right decision by committing his life to Kadrece.

Had he been a single man, he might have slipped out of bed, gotten dressed, and driven back to Columbia never to speak to her again. But he was married. About seven months, to be exact. And of all the thoughts that he entertained, he never imagined that Kadrece's suggestion for an annulment was not a bad idea.

Chapter 34

Once again, Garner was hardly attentive while Pastor McBride preached. Nor did he really care that he was fast forming a reputation appearing as if he'd been dragged to church by his wife, and he was forced to be on his best behavior—or else.

Michael Smiley, owner a local glass installation and repair shop, approached Garner after service.

"Hey brother, you're doing all right?" Smiley inquired.

Garner returned him a suspicious glare.

Smiley still offered Garner his hand to shake; Garner was slow to accept.

"I was just wondering if you had any time next Sunday afternoon. We're having a men's fellowship at my place, and you're more than welcome to join us," Smiley said. "We'll probably look at the football games, have some snacks, share some word, and encourage one another."

"That sounds nice, but I commute from Columbia to Spartanburg and I'm not sure what my wife has planned."

"Who's your wife?"

Garner nodded in the direction of Kadrece, who was in a converversation with Carnette a few rows away.

"Oh, yeah. I remember you two. Y'all joined here not long ago?"

"Yeah, we did."

"Well, in that case, if it works out in your schedule feel free to stop by. I can give you directions today. Better yet, do you have a business card?"

Garner reached for his wallet, but then he placed it back in his pocket. "I'm sorry. I left my cards in Columbia."

"Well, here. Take one of mine. I'll put my home number on here just in case you get lost. I'm out near Cannon Campground Road. It's not really that far away."

As he passed by their conversation, Garner overheard Carnette keeping Kadrece at bay explaining to her how her brother Lucious had been in a car accident and he needed representation.

"Child, he's really hurting right now. He's been out of work now for a couple of weeks, and he's already out of sick leave," Carnette said. "The person who hit him is some Indian guy who runs a pharmacy out in Wellford. But he's trying to settle out-of-pocket and what he's offering isn't even going to cover the repairs for my brother's car. So he's really in a pickle."

This was not the first time that Kadrece had ever been approached with similar legal matters. But she knew her limitations. She acknowledged Garner's head gesture that he would be waiting for her in his car.

"I'm flattered that you would come ask me, but I deal with mostly business clients and their legal issues," she explained to Carnette. "I've not been here in South Carolina long enough to meet other attorneys that specialize in accidents and personal injury cases.

"But I'll tell you what I'll do. Since I'm a part of the Bar Association, I can talk to some people in Columbia who might be able to recommend some attorneys for you to contact. I should be able to have that list by Wednesday or Thursday of this week."

Carnette was elated. "Levi said you might be helpful. I really appreciate what you're doing [by] taking time out of your day to do something like this for me."

She then looked over her shoulder and surveyed the sanctuary. She lowered her voice so only Kadrece might hear what she had to say next.

"Girl, we have three or four other lawyers right here in this church. Not a single one of them have even bothered to tell me yea or nay that they could do anything for me." She shook her head in dismay. "I guess because I work in the lunch room at an elementary school that I don't make enough money for them."

Kadrece shifted her purse from under her right arm to the left and took the first step towards leaving. But Carnette constrained her for another minute. "Sister, just so you know, I feel like I can really trust you."

"Why that's very flattering. I don't know how much help that I can be, but I thought that I can do at least that much for you. I'll make sure to ask the Bar if these are lawyers that would accept you *pro bono*, or at least they would not charge any fees unless there's a settlement."

"Bless you, sister."

Garner was more than glad to be leaving Mission Grove's parking lot. He almost did not bother to stop for oncoming traffic as he made a quick left-hand turn on to Blackstock Road.

He suggested that they go to California Dreaming for dinner. "I found out that they had a restaurant in Greenville; I've gone to the one in Columbia on a couple of occasions and the food's pretty good."

That did not settle well with Kadrece. "You're telling me that you've gone to some place in Columbia a few times without telling me?" She squirmed in the passenger seat and looked out the window. "What else are you keeping from me?"

Not again, Garner lamented. He did not respond until they were on I-26 headed towards the I-85 business route, which took them to the main I-85 thoroughfare. He then glanced over at her, perturbed.

"How can you say that I'm keeping something away from you?" He hissed and focused his attention back on the traffic. "I've been in

South Carolina for two years. What makes me some expert of this entire state?"

"I thought a husband's role is to always look out for his wife. You're not looking out for me by mentioning in passing, 'Oh, by the way. I've gone to a restaurant a couple of times in Columbia. I found out they had one in Greenville.' That doesn't make any sense."

By now, Kadrece pouted and sulked, and she stared out of the window.

"Hey, don't you work near Greenville?" he queried.

She glanced back at him. "Yeah."

"How far are we from Pelham Road?"

"Maybe about ten minutes. Why do you ask?"

He pointed just off to his right. "The directions they gave me at the restaurant in Columbia were that I'm to take I-85 south until I reached the Pelham Road exit. I'll see the California Dreaming right from the freeway."

"Did you say Pelham Road?" Her eyebrows were raised. "I've passed by there. Why didn't you tell me?"

He snorted in disgust. Rather than reacting with incendiary words, he merely internalized them and kept driving.

Chapter 35

If Kadrece had it her way, she would rather not trouble herself with another labor law case such as Grady Minton's. Her desire had been to take on those involving contracts, torts, takeovers and mergers.

Minton, a Simpsonville-based milk dairyman, spoke so fervently about his pending legal matter with employee Fred Gist suing his business for negligence that his ears had turned a bright reddish pink color.

"The last thing that I need is my family being dragged in the mud by some scheming white trash from Belton," he huffed. "Hell, I've known his family since grade school."

This is what pays the bills, Kadrece reminded herself. Maybe Garner was right that she might want to consider moving to Columbia. But she would be damned to do it. Let him move to Spartanburg and show how much he loved her.

"Mr. Minton, now you're saying this employee, Fred Gist, wants a half-million in compensatory damages for what?"

"He fell off a damn ladder and he claimed that he suffered two herniated discs, and it might require at least six month's worth of rehabilitation. Not to mention, there's the distinct possibility that he might not be able to work again."

Kadrece pursed her lips, exhaling. She toyed with her ink pen and scribbled a couple of notes: check for maintenance records for all dairy equipment, examine Gist's work and attendance records, and examine all medical records. Then she needed to interview any people who may have witnessed the accident.

The case was not as bad as it sounded. The way she saw it, there was definitely no reason to be crying over any milk that might have been spilled by an employee especially if the employer's willing to pay the $350-an-hour billing fee. That did not include a running tab for phone calls, faxes, mailing, and other related costs.

"I'll say this much, Mr. Minton. It seems in this economy everyone is looking for some way to get out of their financial doldrums. I've heard more and more of cases of these kind are popping up everywhere."

Minton ranted that Gist still might be costly to his business in the long run even if he won the lawsuit. There was a worker's compensation claim that had not been reconciled. And since the company's health insurance policy was self-insured, it was liable for at least the first five thousand towards the loss limits.

"All I can worry about is making sure that this here guy doesn't make it bad for the rest of the one hundred and forty-six people and their families whom I'm responsible for," he said. "All it takes is one bad apple to ruin the entire barrel. And he's one of them. I wished that my daddy hadn't done a favor for Gist's daddy by hiring him."

After a while, Kadrece felt more like a psychological counselor rather than Minton's legal counselor. She spent more time trying to calm Minton down than apprising him of his legal options and her preliminary case strategy.

Minton left shortly before lunch. But then Tawny Carpenter, the front desk attendant, flagged Kadrece down for another incoming phone call.

"*Lord, I promise that I'll be more understanding,*" she begged. "*Just let me get through the day.*"

On the other line was Carnette. This was not a call that she had expected.

"Sister Davis, I just want to thank the Lord for you. I'm here to tell you that my brother has found an attorney—one from the list you had sent to me—and he's agreed to take the case. He won't charge us a single dime unless we win the case."

"That's great. How sure is he that you have a case? And may I ask who's representing your brother?"

Kelvin A. Horetmer was the attorney that told Carnette's brother that he had a winnable case, and he expected to file a lawsuit within a week. He was most notorious among South Carolina attorneys for his relentless work.

"Sometimes these cases never reach a judge's desk because they're withdrawn before then," Kadrece warned Carnette. "The reason is that a wrongful party might be out of a lot more should a case be heard, and the party is found guilty and liable. There are punitive damages that can really be overwhelming."

"I don't understand, sister—"

Kadrece erupted with loud laughter into the receiver. "I'm so sorry, it's hard to separate talking legalese and regular, every-day talk," she explained. "So let me translate it: Your brother's attorney seems confident that they might get more money in an out-of-court settlement rather than face a trial."

That was all that Carnette needed to hear. Now it was time for her to do what she did best—gossip.

"You know, I really thank the Lord again for you, sister. Levi said there was a sweet spirit about you."

"Thank you."

"Yeah, uh-huh. I hear that you've not been married long and Pastor McBride was the one who married you and your husband."

Kadrece shook her head with much consternation. She felt obligated not to give Carnette reason to spread vicious rumors that she copped an attitude and ran her off the phone.

"Well, knowing men like I do," Carnette went on to say, "I bet your husband's tapping you on the shoulder at 3 a.m. every chance that he can . . ."

There was no immediate response.

"You know, I'm believing the Lord has finally positioned me to find that man that He has ordained for me."

Kadrece finally spoke. "It's been everything that I thought it might be, and more. I'm glad that Pastor McBride was the one who married us. I really thought his pre-marital counseling session really helped our marriage so far. We both get it."

Humph.

Carnette's been known as one of Mission Grove's oldest brides-maids at age forty-eight, having never married or had children.

"Really?"

"My parents have been married for more than forty years," Kadrece said. "I think they've also given me a good example on what marriage should be."

"Well, that's great. You know, Levi's got his faults. But he's really a caring man." Carnette paused to add with a laugh, "He's really attentive and he can also be really romantic."

Kadrece glanced at her wall clock. It was ten minutes before noon. She realized that in a matter of twenty minutes, Carnette had divulged to her life story how she got saved at the age of eighteen, which she went on to say how the Lord had brought her from a mighty long way.

Additionally, she had held out being a virgin for the Lord until she was thirty years old. She claimed that her first-ever experience was with a minister who promised to marry her, only to say that he was no longer interested after they had sex a couple of times.

She said that led her to a depression syndrome that caused her to withdraw from men and be highly non-trusting of them. But then she turned forty. She realized that she had been missing out on so much in life. So for about two years, she made up for lost time with a series of sexual romps that only left her feeling separated from God.

"Now I'm vigilant and sober," Carnette said. "And I'm trusting in the Lord that He'll be faithful to send me someone who knows I'm not a perfect vessel, but a yielding one."

By now, Kadrece had prayed for some divine intervention. It came in the form of Tawny buzzing her with another phone call.

"Sister Carnette, I better take this one. We'll talk again soon."

"Yes, sister, we will!"

Catching her breath, Kadrece stomach growled just as she picked up on line four.

"Sister Kadrece?" the male's voice inquired. "This is Brother Levi."

She cringed and looked upward at the ceiling, shaking her head. She wondered how he knew when to contact her at work.

This, too, shall pass, she affirmed to herself.

"What can I do for you, sir?"

"I was just checking up on if Sister Carnette had called you. She seemed really happy about what you'd done for her."

Kadrece rolled her eyes. *If he only knew*, she said to herself.

"You have a very nice fiancée," she said. "You're so lucky that she thinks so highly of you."

"Is that right?"

"Yes. She absolutely worships the ground that you walk on."

Levi threw his head back chortling at the thought. That was more than a welcomed stroke to his ego. "I just called to say thank you, but I also wanted to show you how much I really meant it by inviting you to lunch. I insist on it."

Suddenly, she also recalled how things had been rather frosty of late between she and Garner.

"All right, I'll take you up on your offer since you insist—"

"Good. It's, what, going on 12:30 [p.m.]?" he noted. "There's a buffet place over on Laurens Road near the Haywood Drive intersection. Can you meet me there at one o'clock?"

"I'm over on Wade Hampton before you get to the college. How far is it from where I'm at?"

"If you leave right now, you'll get there right at one."

Chapter 36

Levi had been waiting in Prine's Café parking lot for fifteen minutes, scanning for any signs of Kadrece's arrival.

Goodness!

He'd now noticed in the immediate distance a tall, regal ebony figure emerging from her stylish BMW wearing an off-white pant suit and black blouse. He found himself wiping his palms on his lap. More so, he took a deep breath as his heart raced in anticipation of their meeting.

There's no need to rush, he said, composing himself.

For a little bit of suspense, Levi waited a couple of minutes before he decided to go inside. There, he spotted Kadrece immediately to his right. He smiled.

"I guess you thought that I'd be late, huh?" he said, approaching her. "I saw you as you drove into the parking lot, but I was on the phone with my manager."

Kadrece stood up, smiling back at him. She extended her hand out to him. "It's really nice of you to offer lunch," she said; it was her way of maintaining a businesslike approach.

"The pleasure is mine. I feel much honored to be in the presence of such a beautiful queen—again."

They sat back down and waited for a hostess to seat them.

"Uh, Sister Kadrece, did anyone tell you that you had a very sweet spirit? You know it speaks of how we are to be the fragrance to this world—"

"I've never heard of it that way before."

"Oh it is right in the good book. It is. But few people leave a fragrance that's like their personality. You're one of them."

Kadrece found herself thinking of the last man to gush with such platitudes for her was Winston Culpepper. He also was somebody whom she was not particularly attracted to, but there was just something about the way that he carried himself that she found to be most appealing. It turned out that she was right because they had enviable sexual chemistry. She wondered if the inner struggles that she was having were reminiscent to Winston. She allowed her instincts to take over.

"Come to think of it, Brother Levi, what do you know about fragrances? I bet the only thing that's ever made sense to you is Right Guard."

He chortled. "You'd be surprised what I know, sister." He looked her over once more with subtle eye movements—he almost gave himself away once he focused in on the hint of cleavage that she revealed.

"Yeah, I bet."

He squirmed on the bench, looking over his shoulder. "What's wrong, can't take a compliment? You know we are to speak truth, in love. And I'm doing exactly what the word teaches me to do."

She returned him a suspicious look. "Right now, what you're saying is subject to interpretation."

The hostess had now come to lead them to their table.

After they sat down, Levi asked if this was her first time coming to Prine's Café, to which she nodded it was so. He gave her a brief rundown about it being a chain restaurant that actually started in Spartanburg, but it had since opened restaurants all over South Carolina, eastern Tennessee, and Georgia.

"Are you just trying to impress me with your vast knowledge of eating establishments?" she queried him. "How do you know so much about this place?"

"I worked for them when they had just three stores. I was an assistant manager until I decided that I could no longer baby sit a crew of nineteen- and twenty-year-olds who couldn't think for themselves."

"Interesting."

Levi then volunteered to Kadrece that his departure from Prine's also occurred about the same time of his second divorce. He did not disclose that his marriage to Jarinda Bell Harriston lasted for less than six years. They divorced over him having inappropriate contact with Pilar Sherman, an evangelist in Burlington, North Carolina. The marriage was also troubled by Jarinda's constant complaints about him calling other women, those same women calling him at their place, as well as her contention that he was emotionally and verbally abusive to her.

He sat back and studied her reaction, but there was none.

"You know there are some church people that will look down on a brothers or sisters who have divorced," he volunteered. "I'm glad that Pastor McBride hasn't been like that. I'm also glad that Sister Carnette is one who sees me for what I am now, and not for what I once was."

"How long have you and Carnette known each other?"

"We became friends not long before I left Prine's," he answered. "But it took a while for me to get my act together. We didn't really begin dating until three years ago."

Kadrece stared at her wedding ring, hoping it might serve as a reminder that she married Garner for the long haul despite some of the scrutiny from those who knew her best. "I've known a few men that were divorced. None of them seem quite proud that ever happened in their lives." She took a sip from her water with lemon.

"I'm not especially when it's happened not once, but twice," he said, folding his arms. "I thought when I got married the second time around that I would do things better than I did the first time."

He glanced off to his right, shaking his head. "It didn't work out that way." His eyes dimmed and became downcast. Exhaling, he announced, "That was then. The Lord has dealt with me and I feel like I'm a new man. He said the latter house will be greater than the former house, and that's me. I'm a better person today than I was yesterday."

Kadrece's ears perked at Levi's references to spirituality. If there was any complaint that she had about Garner, this was not something that he readily indulged, although he had proven himself to be quite knowledgeable.

In her many conversations with Nedra, her friend had often made references to the importance of both the man and woman being of equal yoke. It was one thing that both had made professions of faith, but Nedra said it was another thing if the man and woman had nothing else in common before the Lord—and in their relationship. This was a topic that Kadrece sidestepped to avoid further pre- and post-marital scrutiny of Garner and her.

The waitress had now stopped by, interrupting the flow of their conversation. Kadrece made a quick scan of the menu, deciding on the house salad with Italian dressing and grilled chicken.

"I'm not looking to eat much."

"Go ahead, get what you want," Levi insisted. "The honor and pleasure's mine."

"Well, in that case, thanks. But I'll stick with what I just ordered. I'll have a Diet Coke to go with it."

Levi reared back in his seat, stuck out his chest, and ordered a sampler platter that consisted of shrimp, chicken tenders, and an eight-ounce steak. He also ordered mashed potatoes and a house salad with honey mustard dressing. He ordered a regular Coke to go with his meal, although his true inclination was to order a Budweiser.

He chuckled at his own thought. "As you can see, I'm not one for cheating myself out of a meal." He ran his hands over his midsection.

"Hey, there's nothing wrong with a healthy man and a healthy appetite. I've been known to put down some food as well."

"I don't believe you."

"Oh yes, I lost most of my weight almost two years ago. I've done well sticking with my diet."

Levi leaned forward and rested his chin on his hands. "Sister, I doubt if size was ever a problem." He mindlessly licked his lips before he hid them behind his hands. "I kinda like my women with some meat on their bones."

She raised her eyebrows, adjusting her posture. "Oh you do?"

"Yeah, that's right. I like mine with some butter on their biscuits." He gave her an intense stare-down, nodding. "And it's obvious that your husband and I have the same taste." He even went as far as sucking his teeth rather audibly.

Kadrece's having a meal with Levi felt like a black hole of sin had opened up, and she had dangerously approached its circumference. Peering down into the deep lure of perdition, she knew what to do to keep from falling into it, but everything about her went against all common sense.

She remembered Nedra once mentioned how she never went on lunch dates with men other than her husband unless there was a clear business objective. She sighed at Nedra's past preaching.

I'll never be like her. Nothing happened when we met for coffee at Mc Donald's, so what suggests something might happen today?

She also thought about Garner. This time, she was pissed off at him because he was too engrossed in his job. She complained that he had not been e-mailing her, text messaging her, or calling her like he did before they were married.

Garner explained that basketball season had just started. The Chanticleers men's team was nationally ranked in the pre-season polls, and they were deserving of a lot of attention. But as she persisted, he reacted with anger, cursing back at her that maybe she was the one who had not been treating him like she once did before they were married.

"*Don't you think you're being disrespectful to me?*" she remembered confronting him. "*This is not how you're supposed to treat me, your wife.*"

"*Then how in the fuck am I supposed to treat you?*" she recalled him snapping back at her. "*Obviously, gifts, my time, [and] the obvious sacrifice that I've made commuting aren't enough.*"

When they slept, she brooded over how they had become magnets of the same charges. They rarely touched each other unless they were just too damned horny. Even then, there was much emptiness from sex. She thought she would do better just masturbating.

Earlier in the week, Kadrece had also confided some of her marital problems in Kamryn, who advised her younger sibling that they were just bumps in the road.

"*Do you think that any marriage is perfect?*" Kamryn tried reasoning with her. "*I know that I did my dirt early on, but now I regret it. All I really needed to do was talk to Kevin. Now I've got my own struggles with trust. It could have been averted had I only opened up to him in the beginning.*"

Fuck all of them, Kadrece cursed to herself.

As confusing and troubling Levi's lunch invitation was, Kadrece thought it just might be what she needed. Variety's the spice that always goes nice with anything in life.

"Sister, is there anything wrong?" he inquired.

Kadrece snapped back. "Oh, I'm fine. I guess my late-morning appointment with my client has me really thinking."

"About what?"

"It's a classic worker's comp claim case with a suit brought on by the employee. In the countersuit, my client, the employer, is arguing that his employee was just plain reckless. And if anything, he should have been fired for not adhering to strict company policy."

Levi was impressed by the way Kadrece spoke such fluent legalese to him. He had always aspired to attend college, but he never had the financial backing. He also found women like Kadrece to have much sex appeal. That meant he searched to talk on more universal terms—and at his level of intelligence.

He folded his arms again. "I know if I were a lawyer going up against you, my whole game would be thrown off."

"That sounds sexist."

"I'm just paying you a compliment. I bet it's not the first time that you've heard it."

"No, it's not. But each time I've had to remind the other person that his observation was very sexist. How would you like for some white person constantly making references to you being some big black guy?"

"I am a big black guy. So what's up with that?"

Kadrece shook her head. Knowing this conversation might not get too far, she conceded that his mischief was noted and well taken.

"I don't know about the sexist talk, but speaking of sex . . . do you think that church people talk enough about sex?"

Now that caught her attention. It was a conversation piece that Nedra would not openly have. She reacted, "Why don't you explain to me why there's not enough talk about sex so that I might have a better understanding?"

He was more than eager to elaborate.

"Pastor McBride will only talk about it so much. And I understand his position. He's a pastor. It doesn't look good if that comes from the pulpit," he said. "But you do know that people talk about it. The problem is that so many of us make it sound so nasty if it's mentioned."

"I can't disagree with you on that. I've got a very close friend who stayed a virgin until she was married." Kadrece did her best to remain matter-of-fact with her conversation. "There are times that I wished I had remained a virgin, but things are what they are."

Levi made additional subtle eye movement looking her up and down. He also stole another quick glance at the hint of her cleavage. "Sister Kadrece, I bet you could do a great job explaining to couples how to communicate about sex. I can see it in you, through and through."

"I'm not the ministry type, believe me," Kadrece said, smiling. "It's enough being a wife while maintaining my profession."

He persisted. "Look, that's the thing. People are looking for others who are real in their message. I bet you know some real freaky stuff when it comes to sex. But you know what? People, if it's given the right way, would receive what you had to say . . . I know I would."

There were times before she recommitted herself to church that she considered opening a side adult novelty business. She figured with her legal expertise that she'd be able to keep everything she did legal, but while she pushed the envelope as far as it might go.

"Brother Levi, you know if I've been listening closely, you've wanted to talk sex around me all along. You just didn't know how you'd get there. What's wrong? You and Sister Carnette have kept too holy of a conversation?"

He ran his hand over his mouth, squirming in his seat. "I guess that I did want a lady's opinion—"

"That's all you had to tell me. What was so hard about that?"

"I guess it's not. It says that we have to open our mouths wide, and He would fill it."

The idea of discussing sex triggered something lustful within Kadrece. In her more promiscuous days, sex was one of the first three topics brought up in her conversation with men. She was so discerning of a man's sexuality and preferences that it took her mere minutes and seconds to figure him out.

That's what made her so bold and provocative around men like Garner, whom she felt his easiness for sex was a complement to her voracity for it.

"I think that your concern is whether Carnette will be accepting of the things that you would like to do sexually."

His facial expression reflected that she had guessed his situation dead-on. He leaned forward showing his full attentiveness. He commented, "She's a real sweet lady. But I hate to say it. She does have some real backwards thoughts about sex."

"Well, that's one thing I've not had to worry about with my husband. We both see eye-to-eye when it comes to sex."

"I bet y'all be doing some real freaky stuff."

The waitress had returned with their food. "Now I bet you ordered the sampler platter," she said, looking in Levi's direction.

"You got it!"

"And here's your salad."

Both were not as interested in their food. The sex conversation had them going. Kadrece paused and took a sip from her soda before she returned to his question. "Uh, Brother Levi, what gives you any reason to think that I'm off into freaky stuff? Besides, that's none of your business. That's between me and my husband."

"So what?" he countered. "What you and I are talking about is between me and you."

"You say you've been married twice, right?" she queried him. "And what have you learned after all your years of marriage?"

"I learned that I needed to pray for a woman to be sent into my life that can meet all my needs. I think the Lord knows that sex is important."

She pondered his response, nodding. A bit of the attorney in her emerged in her pace of questioning. "So if you say that you've prayed for a woman to be sent in your life, and you think the Lord knows how important sex is to you . . . Don't you think that maybe, just maybe, Carnette might be the person that you've needed after all these years?

"Certainly, if you're trying to live right as you allege you say you have, He doesn't withhold anything to those who walk upright before Him—"

That was one that flew past Levi's head. But he was not deterred. "Sister, you know what? I've been attracted to you ever since I first laid eyes on you." He didn't say another word, but rather studied her reaction.

This was the kind of temptation that Kadrece had prayed that she might be delivered from. But it seemed that God must have put her on hold. Her conscience was like a four-alarm blaze of lust.

Her provocative side convinced her that she could tease Levi without going too far. She took a deep breath before commenting.

"May I ask you this? What has been Carnette's response to you about oral sex?"

He shook his fork. "See, that's the problem. She doesn't think that oral sex is something that God ordained. She thinks like this TV preacher out west who said that was an unnatural use of our bodies. And that's just for starters."

He took a long sip from his soda, continuing, "She's got this thing that God only intended for men to ejaculate inside a woman. She mentioned about the story where God killed a guy for pulling out. I tried to explain to her there was more to why he pulled out. But she wouldn't listen."

Amazing what sex had done to the tone and tenor to their conversation. Both their perfunctory Christian walls were lowered and now they conversed like they had never gone to church.

"I don't think that I could have ever married a man who wasn't into oral sex, or he felt that the only place that he could shoot his stuff was inside me."

"Really?"

"Really."

There was a God. This had to have been ordained of Him, he thought. Passing up on finishing lunch might have been the last thing that he'd ever considered. But there was a first time for everything. He hailed the waitress for a to-go container.

"I've made a lot of mistakes in my time," he said. "But if you were my wife, I know that I would make love to all of you and not just your body."

"Brother Levi, you better shut up with your bad self."

"I might be bad, but it's the kind that they can get hooked on to." He straightened up against the booth's cushion, but then changed his mind and leaned forward upon his forearms. "If you got the time, I can prove it to you."

The gravity of a conversation on sex had pulled Kadrece into that endless orbit of temptation. She mindlessly added to the conversation. "I've got all afternoon to find out, counselor." She shuffled her feet on the carpet. Then she brought the Diet Coke up to her mouth, but in a seductive way. She allowed for her tongue to taste the soda first before she placed her lips on the glass.

Placing the glass back on the table, she added, "I've been thinking about you for a while, too. I bet you thought I wasn't paying attention when you bumped up against me last time?"

"Oh, I was just trying to get the door for you, sister."

"I see. So, in the process, were you trying to let me know you had a roll of quarters in your pocket, or something else?"she retorted.

A few beads of sweat formed on Levi's brow. In a matter of minutes, Kadrece had flipped the script on him and turned up the heat. Before their conversation had reached a frenzied pitch, he suggested there were a couple of motels just east of Prine's Café just off Laurens Road.

He was emphatic to insist the pleasure was his.

Chapter 37

Kadrece followed Levi over to the Montreat Inn, whose property was along I-85's southbound side. It all seemed surreal that she was headed there because she had not acted this impulsively with a man in more than three years.

It was as though another person had driven there. Even more inexplicable there was no serious courtship or continuous flirtations that triggered this response from her. But so many times in her past Kadrece had been a willing participant in these kinds of sexual mischief.

Levi had only hoped that Kadrece would not back out of it as he made a right-hand turn into the motel's parking lot. For once, he thought that he might indulge in a tryst with someone whom he truly coveted instead of accepting whatever pussy might come his way.

He parked near the motel's front desk, and he motioned for Kadrece to park anywhere she wanted. Then he got out of his car and he rambled in her direction, beaming.

Previously, he mentioned, "Carnette and me have kinda toyed around with sex, but we ain't do much more than some kissing, some fondling, and she let me suck on her breasts." He looked over his shoulder observing for any oncoming traffic. "She wants to hold out until God has married her with her mate."

In her own warped thinking, Kadrece empathized with Levi's frustration that some people might hold sex as hostage when there was every indication to believe that they wanted it just as much.

Humph.

Kadrece always knew that she controlled the fate of many of the sexual encounters that she had, and not once did she ever ascribed to any repressed attitude. Enticingly, she smirked at the possibility of the next time that she spoke or saw Carnette she might know more about her fiancé than she did.

Minutes later, Levi returned with instructions to follow her inside the hotel and meet him in room No. 235 on the second floor. Upon entry, he then turned on the heater and open the shades; it just so happened that his room faced an embankment and there was no driveway below.

"Are you all right with this?" Levi asked Kadrece.

She swallowed hard. "Just give me a few moments." She tossed her purse aside and took a seat in the mini sofa that was adjacent to the bed. After taking a deep breath and then exhaling, she responded, "I'm fine. You know, I'm just tired of the drama between me and my husband."

Levi managed a weak chortle. "I saw that the first time you two came to church. He doesn't strike me as knowing what kind of woman that you are—"

"Well it's nice to know that somebody knows what kind of woman I am."

"I may not have a lot of money. I may not own a home, which I hope someday that I will. And I'm working to repair my credit after my second divorce. But I've always known how to treat a woman."

She pursed her lips while she ran her hand along her neck, and then brushed her hair to the back. "Right now, my pussy is saying it needs proper treatment. I hope you're not some impostor of a man."

Spurred on by her comment, Levi removed his white long-sleeved shirt and black slacks, revealing his hairy, barrel chest; thick, but not muscularly defined legs like Garner's; a modest overhanging of his gut, and a dark gray pair of boxers.

Kadrece found herself turned on by his eagerness to prove what he could do with her—and for her psyche and attention-seeking pussy. She stood up and was careful to remove her business attire. She kept on her black upper lace see-through bra and matching panties.

Reclining back onto the mini-sofa, she paid particular attention to his thick erection of medium length that protruded through the slit of his boxers.

In a lower, but not quite sultry voice, Kadrece said, "As you can see, I'm not some little girl and not all men who claim to be men can really handle all of this sweet mocha chocolate." She then stood up and nestled herself into his chest. He wrapped his not-so-rock-solid arms around her. They stared at each other for several seconds. Had they listened any harder they might have heard each other's hearts beating.

"I never thought that I'd be doing this so soon, if at all," Kadrece confessed.

"I wanted you, too. But I can't say that I thought we'd be here."

She reached down and tugged at his dick; her eyes widened. "Hmmm, looks like somebody is glad to be with me."

Levi dipped his head slightly and gave her a light kiss on her cheek. She sucked air through her nose and closed her eyes. Then she opened her eyes and planted a light kiss on his chest. She followed that with a more substantive kiss on his lips.

He reached down and grasped her ass cheeks. "You're going to make me forget that I've been redeemed. You know he should have taken better care of all this—"

Her pussy moistening, Kadrece felt embolden by Levi's adoring, yet contemptuous words. For a wicked moment, she thought maybe what she needed all along was not someone at the perceived top of the pecking order, but maybe somewhere in the middle or just below. Perhaps those were the ones who would kill a motherfucker over her, and they'd worship the ground that she walked.

She placed her hand behind his neck, drawing him closer. She offered her tongue to him, which sent him into a mild case of delirium. When they separated, she excused herself to freshen up, leaving Levi alone to his increasingly lustful thoughts.

Minutes later, she returned and removed her remaining garments before him. Though he did not articulate it, he did think to himself, *Well, I'll be damn, good god to mighty!*

He then excused himself and went to the bathroom. When he returned, he noticed that Kadrece was already lounging on the mini-sofa. She then slipped her right middle finger into her pussy, then withdrew it and sucked her moisture.

She then announced, "Court is now in session."

Levi needed no further clue. He knelt before her parted thighs and pushed his tongue inside her pussy. She threw her head back and raised her legs higher. She also rubbed his bald pate, which she found to be even more of a turn-on in the heat of things.

"How sweet is this chocolate pussy?"

The room was filled with an enthusiastic moan. He looked up, face already glistening. "Happy is the man that delighteth in this!" He returned to licking and sucking her slit, making circular flicks with his tongue.

"I thought you'd like it," she replied, pushing her mound in his face. "Mmmm, that's the way I want you to make this kitty purr."

Levi took deep breaths, inhaling all of her scent. There was no doubt that he wanted to savor this for posterity, if possible. He noticed her pussy became even more accommodating to his tongue by the thicker flow of her nectar. But that was not enough for him. So he kissed her entire pussy region, causing Kadrece to squirm and shudder. Then he embarked on a light kissing trail along her inner thighs, then back up past her pussy, onto her impeccably cropped pubic hair, but stopping short of her navel.

"Mmmm, what you're trying to do to me?" she moaned repeatedly.

He looked up. "I want to show you what a man does to a woman when he truly appreciates her beauty and sexiness. He stays down there until she's fully satisfied."

She held her legs up and guided his head back down between her thighs. "That's what I'm talking about—"

He returned to offering her wide tongue brushes upon her clit, which provoked her to push her pussy harder in his face. Sensing that he had her going, he never left her clit until she shrieked and stiffened in his grasp.

"Now is that what you were talking about?" he inquired.

"Yes, that's what I've been talking about."

Catching her breath, she smiled and cast a desirous stare in his direction. "That's been overdue around here!"

"There's more where that came from. I can stay down there like there's no tomorrow."

"Well, you just might have a new customer, if you can keep on like that," she remarked. "But let me show you something."

She motioned for Levi to stand up, and she helped him step out of his boxers. She cradled his balls with her right hand and with her left she guided his dick past her lips. She did not stop until she felt it against the back of her mouth. Levi damned near ejaculated at the sensation of her tongue stroking the underside of his shaft and the softness of the back of her massaging his dick's head.

Lost for words, he merely placed his hands on her shoulders and reveled in her skillful manipulation. She knew that she had him right where she wanted while she paused and maintained a continuous sucking, tugging sensation on his engorged member for several moments.

"Oh god," he whispered twice. "Please, baby. Keep going."

She reached past his hips and squeezed his ass cheeks, inducing him to fuck her mouth, and it wasn't long before the tenor to his conversation had changed.

"See, now you really got me going," he said. "Suck this dick. Come on, suck this fuckin' dick!"

Kadrece savored Levi's abrupt transformation. But she had another one for him. She instructed for Levi to bend over against the mini-sofa. He glanced back over his shoulder unsure of what she wanted, but he went along with it.

Kneeling behind him, Kadrece first tea bagged his dangling, hairy sac and slipped her hand under him, stroking his dick. All Levi could do was close his eyes and shake his head in amazement. Neither of his wives ever did this to him, let alone any woman that he ever fucked.

"Mmmm, I like a nice, thick dick and a tasty set of balls," she said, before she resumed tantalizing him; she also pushed her face deeper into the crack of his ass. It was apparent to her by the way Levi bent his knees that he desired for more. So she went for it all, pushing her tongue up his asshole.

His body stiffened.

Whoooo!

"Damn, I thought I had a little freak in me, but you really are a freaky woman." It was not long before he began pushing his ass back to her forceful tongue fucking of his puckered entry. "I like this shit; I like this shit a hell of a lot!"

Kadrece noticed that Levi began oozing a noticeable trickle of pre-cum into her hand. She knew that she had the option of sucking his dick to completion and blow his fucking mind, or she could treat him to her married pussy and still blow his mind.

She paused again and made eye contact with him. "I bet you'd love to fuck this pussy, don't you?" His facial expression had said it all to her.

"A woman like me has many needs," she said, "and right now she needs to have her pussy well fucked."

She climbed onto the bed and reclined back, beckoning Levi to mount her. Her pussy was so aroused that his dick easily slid past her swollen lips.

Because of his girth, she could not easily reach around him and clutch his ass cheeks. But she made sure to send as many subtle messages as she could while he fucked by the way she placed her hands on his shoulders or on his lower back. Meanwhile, Levi had preoccupied himself by delivering a series of slow, circular strokes.

"If I wanted to be made love to, I would have asked you," she said. "But you know what you wanted to do today. Now do it!"

Taking her cue, Levi rose up on his knees and delivered long, hard strokes to her pussy, causing her to lift her legs and clasp them around him. Pussy had never felt as good as this. He was smitten and incredulous of it.

"What you got for me, baby?" she bantered with him intermittently. "What you got?"

A woman had never overpowered Levi, but it was not long before he unashamedly ejaculated inside of her. After he felt the last twitch from his dick, he buried his head into the pillow. Kadrece showed her appreciation by clasping her hands around his neck. She gave him a soft kiss on his cheek.

Although he had not yet withdrawn from her, he raised up to mention, "I guess we both have to get back to work?" Then he eased back out of her; both giggled at the amount of thick cum that had trickled back out of her pussy.

Initially, Levi thought about rushing to the bathroom and then returning with a towel. He changed his mind and simply positioned his face between her thighs and proceeded to lick and suck away their commingled fluids.

Kadrece was ecstatic. She held her legs up for him while he pushed his tongue farther up her pussy.

"Mmmm, shit, that's right, nigga," she remarked. "Lick that pussy clean. I like that in a man!"

When he finished, Levi slid atop of Kadrece, smiling. "I bet your husband had never done that to you?"

She leaned forward and kissed him fully on his lips. Their scent was strong yet it was a turn-on to her. She considered nudging him to return to lapping out of her pussy. Rather, she was content with knowing that she had a bonafied pussy boy.

While they took turns in the shower, Levi joked with Kadrece that he was capable of fucking for longer periods.

"Just wait until next time because you're going to think that I'm related to that bunny on the TV commercials," he quipped, while soaping down his body.

"Is that right?" Kadrece responded. "But you weren't bad today."

He managed a chortle while he rinsed down his body. "I told you that you needed someone that's going to make love to all of you."

"And that you did."

He turned off the shower water, emerging from it. She noticed from the bathroom mirror that his dick was fast regaining its erection.

"Next time, I won't be as gentle," she said, moving to kiss him on his lips.

After dressing, Kadrece took down Levi's home phone number, job number, and even his Interzero.com e-mail address. She explained to him that she could only give him her direct line at the law office and her upstatesc.com e-mail address that Garner was unaware of.

"That's fine with me. As long as I know that I've got some contact with you," he said.

Kadrece returned him a suggestive stare, rolling her tongue over her top lip. "We can work on that." She savored the thought of his eagerness to lap up the creampie that he left inside her.

She suggested, "I guess I better leave first."

"I guess so. This was definitely a high time today."

Neither of them questioned each other how they felt in the afterglow of fucking. But Levi was already longing for more. He waited several seconds before he followed her out into the parking lot. And while he did not walk Kadrece to her car, he watched in an admiring way as she entered hers and drove off.

Kadrece, meanwhile, felt no shame. If anything, she felt that she had been liberated from the person that she had tried portraying around Garner.

Chapter 38

Later in the week

While preparing for her afternoon appointment with Grady Minton, Tawny buzzed Kadrece about a caller from Tallahassee.

"She said you know her quite well. Uh, a Ms. Nedra Winslow is on line three."

"Thanks, I'll take that."

"Nedra?"

"Kadrece?"

"Don't even say it, girl."

"I know."

They both giggled into the phone.

Kadrece sat straight up in her office chair, reclined back, and crossed her legs. She was more than aware that they had never been separated from each other for any more than a couple of months since college. Now they had not seen each other in more than a year, nor had they spoken in several months.

Their conversation still flowed as if they had spoken to each other a few days ago. Nedra shared that she, Crennell, and the boys had planned to spend the Christmas holiday in Miami visiting her sister, Darletta. The next leg of the trip was over to Florida's west coast, stopping off in Tampa to visit her in-laws. The last stop they planned was for the boys: two days in Orlando.

"We had promised the boys that trip to Atlanta, but then mother was sick," Nedra explained. "So this is a make-up trip for them."

Kadrece said she was not sure what her holiday plans might entail. Since it would be their first Christmas as husband and wife, she hoped that they might spend a nice, quiet day together and then drive down to Atlanta to visit her family.

"Unfortunately, that's all up in the air because of Garner's job," she said, sighing. "We don't know where he might have to go covering a silly bowl game. It might be Memphis. It might be Atlanta. Or it might even be Orlando. Ironically, I remember him calling me from Tampa last year—"

While Nedra brought her up to date with the latest happenings from Cosgrove Baptist, Kadrece wandered off in a bit of mischievous thought. Maybe there might be a possibility of her spending Christmas with Levi; that was immediately dismissed because it was just too new of a happening.

Soon the conversation circled back to marriage. "I remember when Crennell and I spent our first Christmas holiday together. It was sooooo romantic. He bought me a book that had many of Smith Wigglesworth's messages, and we spent time reading several of them aloud. Then he read me a personally handwritten card and he gave me the diamond cluster ring that you've seen on my pinkie."

There was only so much preaching and testifying that Kadrece could stand. She found herself rolling her eyes upward into her skull. Nedra then caught her off guard.

"I feel that I can ask you this question," she said, pausing. "How are things with you and Garner? Are you two getting along all right?"

Kadrece went silent. She explained to Nedra that Tawny just popped in the office with some paperwork for her to sign. She then requested that Nedra called her on her cell phone. "I'd rather not for someone from around here to eavesdrop on me." That bought her a few moments to collect her thoughts.

Seconds later, her cell phone blinked and buzzed. "Thanks for calling me back. Funny that I've been here for over a year and I still don't trust any of these people that I work with. But you'll never be that way with me. Garner knows other than my sister, Kamryn, there's no one as close to me as you are."

"That's nice to hear. I say that with all sincerity of heart, K-girl. Just strange how time flies."

"I know. I guess life does happen . . . whether we're ready for it or not. Hey, I need to grab me a bite to eat. Say hello to my nephews and Crennell for me."

After Kadrece hung up with Nedra, the guilt that she suppressed from her tryst with Levi crashed upon her with full force. She could barely control the tears that began streaming down her cheeks. She darted over to lock her office door. Then she rushed inside her private bathroom. Her shoulders heaved and fell as she sobbed.

I've been married barely eight months . . . I'll never understand why I do things like I do. I can't tell anyone that I've already gone to bed with another man . . . I can't tell anyone that I came here for all the wrong reasons . . .

How do I make the best of any of this? God, help me! What do I do?

Chapter 39

The springtime marked a notable milestone for Garner and Kadrece. They managed to make it to their first wedding anniversary and without the drama and infighting that soiled the start to their marriage.

Garner felt so good about having made it through the first year that he even went as far as inviting Spencer Watts' old crazy self to lunch the day before Kadrece was to spend the day with him in Columbia. But Spencer insisted that Garner drive over to his place in Irmo.

When he showed up, Garner soon recalled that it had been his first time there since Vernise and he attended a Christmas party more than two years earlier.

Several moments elapsed before Spencer answered the door—with the help of a walking cane.

"I thought you had forgotten about me, young buck," Spencer bellowed as he opened the door to his red brick exterior dwelling. "I was telling Ms. Shirley how you had forgotten about us after you got married."

"Now how can I forget about you?" Garner responded. "What's up with you? You're finally realizing that you're old?"

He explained that he began suffering circulation problems in his right leg, which dragged badly when he walked. Doctors initially thought it was a blood clot; however, that was only part of his problem. He also was diagnosed with diabetes and an enlarged prostate.

"Shit, I can't even fuck now. Ain't that a bitch?" Spencer said, shaking his head. "Now none of my honeys even wanna be bothered with my ass. They've all gone off searching for new dick."

He sighed. "Even Ms. Raynee [Bickford] done damned left me. And we'd been fuckin' off and on for over twenty years."

This could be not the same Spencer Watts that Garner had at times admired him from a distance. He was careful with his words. "As long as I've known you, aren't you the same old motherfucker that bragged how he didn't need any colored pills?"

"Shit, I wish I can say that now. This hit me all of a sudden. I thought I'd been taking care of myself. Hell, I thought they said some pussy each day would help keep the damned doctor away. Motherfuckers lied to me, damnit!"

"Were you aware of any health issues?" Garner asked.

"Hell no," he snapped. "I'm telling you, it all started showing up out of nowhere. One day, I felt woozy. Another day, felt like my leg was giving out on me. I finally went to the doctor after Ms. Shirley got on my ass for hobbling around.

"I mean, I'll be seventy-five years old in a couple of months, but damn!"

Spencer went into detail how he was under doctor's orders to cease drinking all forms of alcohol, and he had to alter his diet drastically. That meant no more starches and excess sugar and high fat-content foods that he'd been used to. Lots of the basics like fruit, vegetables, and juices.

The worst thing, Spencer complained, was that he's had to take insulin injections. He lamented, "I thought that I had beaten the odds given my family's history with the shit. Seventy-four years and then I come down with this—"

Now Garner understood why Spencer insisted that he came over to his place. The man was lonely. All the friends that he thought that he had over the years proved not to be there for him in his time of need.

Looking him over, he noticed that Spencer was losing weight and his face was gaunt. His eyes seemed more tired, although it was hard to notice from behind his glasses. Creases were forming in his face. Aging was really setting in.

"How has Ms. Shirley been?" he inquired.

He was careful not to recount as soon as Shirley learned of his medical maladies she went as far as goading, *"I told you that God didn't like ugly. You thought you could go all these years messing over me. Now look at you. As soon as you can't do a damned thing for yourself, guess what? I'm putting your sick ass in one of those facilities."* His son and daughter have also maintained only minimal contact with him, as well.

But Spencer still tried to put a positive spin on his spouse. "Oh, she's doing fine. Since I'm not bedridden, she's still doing her daily things. But it is sure as hell different not being able to chase her around the place knowing that my shit can't get up."

Garner's last memory of Spencer was gawking and lurching to catch another glimpse of Kadrece's cleavage on his wedding day. And the time before that—about a month before his wedding—he had cursed out one of his friends over a game of dominoes at Sho' Fly Barber Shop on North Main.

The person he saw now sitting in one of the large recliners hardly paled in comparison.

"You know, I wanted to invite you to lunch because I wanted to celebrate with somebody the news of my first wedding anniversary," Garner said. "I remember you said some very nice things to me after I told you that I was getting married."

"That's all right, young buck," he replied. "I've learned the hard way that you've got to nurture a relationship always with a woman because there will come a time when she's through, she's through."

Spencer brought up Tamira. In his own thinking, he always saw her as the ideal match for Garner.

"She told me that she was glad for you getting married. But I could tell that she was kinda sad." He paused and clutched his cane. "This damned bad leg doesn't allow me to get out like I used to; I hadn't seen her since last summer."

Moved by compassion, Garner spent nearly three hours at Spencer's place. They shot the shit just as he had hoped to do at Ruby Tuesday's, although much of Spencer's contributions to the conversation were more about his past.

They also played a few games of dominoes. Although Spencer's body was breaking down fast on him, his mind remained sharp. He rallied from behind, defeating Garner by forcing him to pass with two dominoes left in his hand and fetch bones from the dog pound. He scored fifteen on his last play and got another twenty-five from Garner's hand.

"That's right, damn it! I've played this game a long, long time," he said, exalting in victory. "And the game of dominoes is much like life: You gotta play the bones you've pulled. It don't matter if you got seven doubles in your damn hand.

"Remember that, young buck!"

Chapter 40

The Davises spent a quaint and romantic anniversary night at Luria's, a bed and breakfast inn frequented by couples in Columbia's downtown district.

While reclining in bed, Garner pursed his lips and clasped his hands behind his head.

"I just feel like I was somewhere else in another time and place," he said.

Kadrece returned a curious stare in his direction. Sensing her reaction, he draped his left arm around her shoulder.

"A couple of days ago, I spent some time with ol' man Spencer Watts. He's not as well as he used to be." He sighed, drained of thought and sentiment. "You just have to know Spencer to understand where I'm coming from."

"Why don't you try?"

He shook his head. "It's probably not worth explaining."

Kadrece closed her eyes and breathed deeply. For the sake of the conversation, she chose not to mention anything about Spencer's wandering eyes and lustful gazes during their wedding.

"I'm sorry to hear he's not doing well. I didn't realize you two were that close."

"Sort of," Garner answered. "He's always kept a watchful eye on me since I've been in Columbia. He says he actually prayed for someone like me to be hired at the station."

"Humph, he didn't come across as a spiritual man when I met him. He was more like a heathen."

Garner chuckled. "Take this for what it's worth: Spencer has his ways. Sometimes, he even makes a lot of sense."

Kadrece leaned over and kissed Garner on his cheek. She mused to herself that in recent weeks he had not mentioned anything about her gaining weight or the added paunch in her stomach.

On her own, she noticed that her breasts had become more sensitive, but she dismissed it as Levi having titty-fucked her on a few occasions lately and that was preceded by him nibbling and gnawing on her nipples. What had amused her the most was that Garner had not been suspicious of anything unusual with her behavior.

Hell, she found it also fucking fiendish that, on her part, she continued having the audacity to interact and remain so cordial with Carnette, knowing whenever she was face-to-face with her that she'd been fucking her fiancé almost at will.

More so, she found it equally as scandalous that Garner had no damned clue that the man who often rushed to shake his hand and grinned in his face whenever he showed up at Mission Grove had been fucking her, lapping out of her pussy after he ejaculated inside her, and licking her asshole more often than him.

She finally asked, "Baby, are you sure everything is all right? You seem to have more on your mind—"

The mood lightened once Garner felt his erection returning. He thought of indulging in some anal sex, which they had not done in several months. So he nudged Kadrece to turnover on her stomach.

"Baby I'm sorry. Hold on." Kadrece jumped out of the bed and sprinted to the bathroom. Unbeknownst to him, she had felt nauseous for several minutes, but nothing came up. She inspected her face in the mirror, and then she checked the profile of her body.

Never lacking confidence, she always admired her curves and her full, round ass, as had so many other men in her past. She returned to the bedroom prancing and smiling.

"Now what was it you wanted to do?"

He pointed at the mattress. "Put your face down and your ass up."

She complied, looking back at him. "Like this?"

"Yeah, like that," he answered with a lustful smirk.

"Anything else you want?" she asked, wiggling her ass at him.

He clutched his dick and balls and knelt behind her, rubbing his engorged head against her puckered entryway.

"You like this sweet, sexy mocha chocolate ass, don't you?

He moaned aloud at the visual stimulation of his dick disappearing inside. He gave her a light tap on her ass cheeks.

"Mmmm, you've always been a freaky man, baby."

"That's what I'm talking about!"

Kadrece did manage to enjoy herself throughout the anal sex. She helped herself to her own orgasm by stroking her clit in concert with his thrusts. But it was not long into their afterglow that she felt another wave of nausea. She excused herself once again. This time, something did come up. She immediately thought about stopping by a store on her way back to Spartanburg in the morning.

When she returned to the bed, Garner expressed his concern. "That's the second time you've had to go. Are you all right?"

"I think so. It might have been that seafood. I think this was one time the crab salad may not have agreed with me."

On her way back to Spartanburg, Kadrece stopped off at a Rev-Con Pharmacy at the Highway 221 and Blackstock Road intersection, purchasing a couple of self-pregnancy tests. She rushed back to her place and sampled the first stick: it displayed two blue bars.

Stunned by the result, she waited until around midday at work before she took the test with the other test stick. That one also proved to be positive. Initially, she wanted to jump up and down in the bathroom, but then she was moved to tears.

Chapter 41

The drive over to Dr. Ridgeman's office seemed extra special, for it was a day that Kadrece had dreamed of in recent years. She inhaled deeply through her nose and exhaled just as hard once she turned off the ignition switch in the parking lot. She made a brisk walk to the medical building's lobby.

While she waited in the unusually empty reception area, she mulled what she might say each to Garner, Nedra, Johnnie, Kanitra, Kamryn, and her brothers. She figured whatever she mentioned would be generic, although it would be modified slightly for each individual.

Mentally, she practiced saying, "I hope you're ready for this . . . I'm pregnant." She envisioned what each person's reaction might be. Then she practiced her response: "Yes, I really am. I'm so happy . . ."

One of Dr. Ridgeman's receptionists clad in aqua colored scrubs opened the glass. "The doctor is ready to see you. Follow me to the back." She gathered her purse and followed her down the narrow beige corridor where she was led inside the third exam room on the left. The enormity of the moment finally hit her—she took another deep breath to compose herself.

"We'll need to take a urine sample from you."

"Okay."

"Dr. Ridgeman will be with you shortly after."

"Thank you."

Until she began showing symptoms of nausea, Kadrece recognized that she had been in denial about being pregnant. She had not experienced anything as close to a pregnancy scare since she was in her mid-twenties. That occurred while she was involved with Turner Middleton, a former college instructor of hers. Middleton was always insistent on not wearing any condoms. At the time they began fucking, she was late at resuming birth control pills. She prayed that if God would answer her prayer that she would break up with him. She kept her word and never saw Middleton again.

But this was different. In all the years that she'd known him, Kadrece and Garner never discussed birth control. Hell, the question was never broached once she and Levi began fucking.

She pretended that she was slightly startled when Ridgeman appeared in the exam room about twenty minutes after she'd given the urine sample. Ridgeman was as cordial with Kadrece as she was during her last visit. She also asked her a couple of perfunctory questions.

Then she smiled. "Congratulations, Kadrece."

A warm feeling came over her. She smiled back at Ridgeman. "Thank you. But do you know how far along am I?"

"We think you may be about seven to eight weeks. But an obstetrician would better be able to answer that question."

Ridgeman told Kadrece that the receptionist could provide her a list of obstetricians in the Spartanburg area. But that was the least of Kadrece's concerns.

"Are you sure you can't determine how far along I am pregnant?" she asked.

"Again, it's better for an obstetrician to give you a pin-point answer," Ridgeman said; she then placed the notes that she referred to back into Kadrece's folder.

"Is there anything else that I might answer for you?"

"I guess not."

Chapter 42

A few days later

W hile she changed into something more casual, Kadrece stopped to primp and pose nude in front of the bedroom dresser. She caressed her breasts in both hands. Already, they had become softer and more sensitive to the touch. Then she ran her hands along her side then across her stomach. Humph. If it weren't for the fact that she knew Garner would be arriving soon she might have reclined back on her bed and massaged her clit until she reached a tingling conclusion.

She decided on waiting for him by wearing one of her silk kimono-style robes. She thought it would be quite a sensual and loving moment to greet her husband in all of her early maternal glory and then get dressed in front of him just as she had done so many times before.

When she heard the key playing in the keyhole, she sprung to her feet from the sofa and positioned herself to where she would be the first thing that Garner saw once he opened the door. He was agape once he noticed Kadrece's exposed breasts.

"You missed me, huh?" she greeted him.

He searched for words to respond. Eventually he said, "Uh-huh . . . I guess it has been a minute or two since I kissed you goodbye from Columbia."

She nuzzled up to him, rubbing her body against his. He felt a searing, nearly combustible sensation. Mindlessly, he reached around to her backside and groped her ass cheeks.

"Obviously, you missed me, too," he said, regaining his composure. "Maybe we might need to take care of that before we go to dinner."

Kadrece kissed him on the cheek. Then she brushed his hand away. "Baby, I'm not going anywhere. It will all be here once we get back." She sashayed away, but Garner was in close pursuit. For added titillation, she allowed her robe to fall to the floor just as she reached midway in the bedroom.

"Are you sure you don't want to do something before dinner?" He readjusted his dick's position in his slacks.

"You said you were taking me to dinner and I'm going to hold you to that." She retrieved a low-cut blouse and dark slacks from the closet. "I'll be ready in just a few." She turned him around and dismissed him from the bedroom.

The happy expression from Kadrece's countenance nearly disappeared once they arrived at the London Broil Steak House located just off Business Route 85 and the I-585 exchange. She noticed Levi and Carnette were conversing next to a white Kia Sorrento SUV, and Garner had driven in their direction. Immediately, she bowed her head and began fumbling inside her purse.

"Is it usually as crowded over here on a Thursday night?" Garner complained.

When Kadrece glanced again, she noticed that Garner was forced to drive all the way to the back of London Broil's parking lot. Inwardly, she wanted to exhale in relief, but retorted, "Why are you asking me that question?"

"Because you live here in Spartanburg; I'm sure that you don't eat at home every night."

She shrugged Garner's comment. "That is true. But you need to visit this fish-and-fry place on Wade Hampton Boulevard in Greer on Friday nights. This is nothing compared to them." The temptation to dig at him further was too much to resist. "If you had considered finding work here in Spartanburg or Greenville, you wouldn't be asking that question—"

Garner returned a long glare, but he did not respond.

After they had finished the main course, Kadrece squirmed against the booth cushion, yawning.

"What's wrong?" Garner inquired.

"Nothing. It's just been a long day. Humph. A long week."

He nodded.

Aware of her pregnancy, Kadrece elected to have iced tea rather than her usual glass of wine. She placed the glass back on the table. Then she cleared her throat. "Can I ask you a question?"

He gestured with his head and eyes to go ahead.

"Just what would you do if I were pregnant?"

He returned a cold, expressionless glare.

"Did you not hear me?" she persisted. "Just what would you do if I were pregnant?"

Garner looked away.

Taking another sip from her tea, Kadrece nodded but internalized her rage. She felt even more justified for having not yet mentioned to Garner that she was pregnant—it had been three days and counting since it was confirmed to her and she shared the news with her family and Nedra.

"You did hear me, Garner?" she queried, shifting again in the booth.

He finally nodded. "I don't know. It's not something that I've been thinking about." He returned her a puzzled look. "Are you telling me something that I don't know about?"

She managed a wistful smile. "Baby, I wouldn't do that to you. But I was just curious what your reaction might be."

As they turned into her condominium complex, Kadrece could not hold back with her disappointment. She huffed and then glared over at Garner just as he placed his car in neutral and applied the hand brake. He happened to catch this out of the corner of his eye.

"What's wrong with you?"

She rolled her neck. "And what do you mean, what's wrong with me?"

"All of a sudden you look like someone's pissed you off to high hell . . . It can't be anything that I've done."

"Ah, but you are so wrong!"

He glared back at her.

"Yeah, I said that."

"Kadrece, just what are you talking about? I thought we had a nice dinner and we were going to have a nice rest of the night."

"Shit, keep dreaming!" She then sucked her teeth.

"Dreaming about what?"

"Did it ever occur to you that your lack of response to my question pissed me off?"

He shook his head. Then he opened the driver's side door.

"You see, that's why women feel like they're all alone in situations like mine. They have no support from the male." She emerged from the car and stormed off to her place. He walked casually behind her.

"Look, Kadrece. I don't know what you're talking about. But you better make yourself clear. Right now. I don't read minds!"

She waited until she reached the door before she faced him. "If you've not noticed or heard anything, I'm pregnant."

Immediately, Garner felt as though his heart, stomach, and sternum all collapsed to his feet. *She's got to be shitting me, right?*

"Yeah, that's right. I'm pregnant, Garner. I'm pregnant with our child."

Garner's lips parted, but that was all he could manage. Meanwhile, she opened the door and hurried inside. He finally collected himself and staggered behind her. When he recognized where she was, Kadrece had a glass of water and had plopped on the sofa.

"Did you say that you were pregnant?" He spoke slow and carefully.

"I didn't stutter."

"When did you know?"

"A few days ago."

"And you're now telling me?" he responded. "Kadrece, we talk on the phone every day, sometimes several times in a single day—"

"I've had a lot on my mind," she said, interrupting him. "I'm glad that we had gone out to dinner. I thought that would have been a perfect time to share the news with you. But you fucked that up with your dumb ass reaction."

Any stupor that Garner was in ended abruptly. "Just what in the fuck do you mean me being a dumb ass and fucking something up?" He placed his hands on his waist and stood directly in front of her, continuing, "You just asked me some arbitrary question, what would I do if you were pregnant?

"Hell, I wouldn't know how to answer to any shit like that. But now you're telling me that you're really pregnant. Why couldn't you have told me three days ago? What respect are you giving me as your husband?"

Jerking her hand and rolling her neck she yelled, "You get respect when you earn it, damn it!"

He shook his head. "I don't have to put up with this shit! It's one thing you're saying that you're pregnant. It's another thing that you're trying to play some fucking mind game with me, and I ain't the person to be fucking with!"

"Garner, you better leave *my place* . . . Right the fuck now, or I'll call the police on you!"

"For what?" he screamed.

"Verbal and emotional abuse towards me and your unborn child," she yelled back.

With fists clenched, Garner inhaled deeply and held it. He shook his head again, waved her off, and took two long strides toward the door. Looking back over his shoulder, he sneered, "Fuck you and your bullshit! I told you that I'm not the one to be playing silly games with. Pregnancy is nothing to be playing with."

And with that, he yanked the door open and slammed it behind him.

Chapter 43

This time, Kadrece had really gone too far, Garner fumed. The way he saw it, he'd put up with enough of her bullshit. Funny how people become another person once they're married. He'd heard the stories. Now he'd become a witness to it.

Of all the things, he pondered while he drove aimlessly around Spartanburg, why would she withhold something as important as being pregnant, and what other mind games would she attempt next?

Immediately, thoughts of Janine Dorsett, a sports anchor at Columbia's ABC affiliate WCSC, filled his mind. Janine, twenty-eight, showed no aversion to flirting with him while he hardly concealed his attraction and admiration for her height (six feet), model-like features, and hazel eyes whenever they ran into each other on assignments.

Your wife's a very lucky woman," she confided in him while she stood next to him at the last Chanticleers' annual spring football game. *"Do you know how many women in Columbia would love to jump on you for themselves?"*

"I've heard that before. Are you thinking of being the next one?" Guilt then seared his conscience. He realized that he'd relapsed into his former promiscuity. *"I'm sorry. I shouldn't be having conversations like that*

with you."

She smiled back at him. *"It's all right. Just know that you have a fan in me—even if I am the competition."* She slipped him her business card with both her cellular and home phone numbers on it. Then she walked off, allowing him to catch a view of her high-sitting ass as she strode like a female stallion.

Although there had been moments when Garner considered getting rid of Janine's card, he kept it stashed in his desk at work. He turned into the Walmart parking lot in Dorman Commons

Shit! Just my luck, he reacted to his cell phone ringing.

"Why did you leave here like that?"

For a moment, Kadrece's voice was akin to an out-of-body experience. "Didn't you hear me, Garner?" she yelled, catching his attention.

He reclined back in the driver's seat, sighing. "What did you expect for me to do? You threatened to call the police on me." He shook his head. "That ain't happening here."

There was a lengthy pause between them. Garner had no intention on elaborating. For that matter, he glanced at his dashboard clock and had already decided if Kadrece did not speak in the next minute that he would hang up.

The clock changed from 9:45 to 9:46 p.m.

"I expected more from you than some mummified reaction," Kadrece said. "You know better than anyone how important having a child is to me."

Inhaling deeply, he responded, "Yeah, and the last time we got into an argument over this we didn't speak for about a week. I guess your memory stands to be corrected."

"Do you not realize that I'm carrying your child—our child?"

"Was I supposed to jump up and down, roll on the floor, and break out with Mariachi music?"

"That would have been nice."

He maintained his composure with Kadrece. "Look, I don't appreciate every time you disagree with the way I respond to you that you want to curse me and kick me out to the curb."

"You're supposed to be the man in this relationship. There are certain things you just need to realize."

A fuse had now detonated within him. "Did it ever occur to you that your saying that you're pregnant may have triggered something in me?" He did not give her an opportunity at responding. "Did it ever occur to you that you might have triggered a bad memory? I've been through someone claiming to be pregnant. It wasn't a pleasant experience."

Kadrece, who had been lying in bed, began pacing the bedroom carpet. "I don't believe you just said that to me. And who's dick do you suppose been all up in my pussy and asshole?" She had now rested her left hand on her hip, breathing heavily.

"I'm not questioning you about that. Or should I?"

"Damn you!"

"Well damn you, too. This shit's all too familiar with me!"

Tears had now welled in Kadrece's eyes. Prior to calling Garner, she hastily contacted Kamryn in an attempt to explain her side of their argument. But Kamryn did not want any part in it. She openly questioned her younger sister's decision of having not informed Garner before anyone else; she dared not to think how Nedra would have responded to her.

"Baby, please, I'm sorry for reacting the way I did. I was wrong for yelling at you and telling you to leave. Please, come back home with me tonight," she begged, then pausing. Garner did not respond.

"Don't do this to us—your child. Stress like this is what causes women to lose their child. I've wanted a baby as bad as I wanted you to marry me. I know it took us a few years to get where we are. But I love you, Garner. I've always loved you. Don't let the haters have their day."

He shook his head. "What are you talking about?"

"You remember—"

"What does that have to do with us right now?" he retorted. "Right now, I've got flashbacks to something that was not a pleasant experience."

"Maybe I should be asking you what you are talking about?"

"I'm saying that before we got back together I had to deal with somebody trying to trap me. Fortunately for me, it backfired on her."

Kadrece interrupted him in mid-thought. "Now wait a god-damned minute," she huffed. "We've been married for over a year. So you better strike that shit from the record . . . Now!"

"As I was saying," he interjected, "I've got some bad memories from someone telling me that she was pregnant and there was a lot of unnecessary drama with it. All you had to do was give me the common courtesy of telling me first that you were pregnant. I thought that's what a wife would do for her husband. But now you want to blame me for this? That ain't going to fly."

"You're right. I was wrong. I should have told you first." She spoke in a calm tone. "So where are you? Are you already driving back to Columbia?" She now sat on the side of the bed.

"Why do you want to know? This is not the first time you've kicked me out."

"I want to know because I promise to be more mature about us. And I want you back here in bed with me where you should be."

The tension in Kadrece's condominium had eased by the time Garner settled into bed next to his wife. They were back in one accord espousing love and unity to each other. In the morning, she was awake before him and made breakfast sausage, pancakes, and hash browns for both of them.

While they conversed at the breakfast table, he conceded, "I never thought of myself even becoming a father. Who would have thought that I'd even get married?"

"It doesn't matter what others think," Kadrece answered. "We have what a lot of people wish they could have."

In her perfect world, that would have included Garner working on her side of the state. Thus she reminded him, "You know at some point my pregnancy will prevent me from driving to Columbia—"

He stood up and headed back to the bedroom. "I understand. I also told you that I'm going to do everything I can to make you the happiest wife on this planet." He stopped at the closet, retrieving a pair of brown slacks and a white Polo shirt with the station's logo on it. She stood in the doorway admiring his physique. "All I ask for you is to work with me. Just meet me a fraction of the way. Can you do that for me?"

They hugged and kissed.

"Baby, I'll do that and more," she answered, then pushed her tongue inside his mouth. "So how do you like sex with a pregnant woman?"

They shared a chuckle.

"Not bad. I can get used to it," Garner answered.

No sooner than Garner was on his way back to Columbia, Kadrece rushed to her phone in the bedroom. She was greeted by a voice with grogginess.

"This is not like you to call me so early," Levi answered. "What's up?"

She took a deep breath and slowly exhaled. "Nothing's really up. I just had to talk to you this morning. Is there anything wrong with that?"

"I don't know. You tell me?"

"Well, hubby and I got into it last night. But we're all right as of this morning. He just left."

"He's found out about us?" Levi inquired.

"It's nothing like that," she answered. "Or wouldn't I be telling you about a confrontation that we had?"

"Okay, then what is it?" His yawn was quite audible.

Leaning back against the headboard, Kadrece queried, "I was just curious. How would you handle things if I told you that I was pregnant?"

"Is that all you wanted to know?"

"Yes."

After a short pause, Levi responded, "First of all, I'd ask you if you knew who you might be pregnant for."

Kadrece felt her patience had already reached borrowed time. "Levi, why do you have to make this so difficult? Just answer the question." She hissed into the phone.

Scratching his scalp, Levi finally replied, "I don't know. I guess I'd have to say if it were mine, we'd definitely have to keep it between us. That's not something your husband should ever know. And if it's for him, well, I'd have to ask you if you still want to continue seeing me." He added a chuckle to his last comment.

"What's so funny?"

"Oh, nothing." Inwardly, he considered it would then be a luxury to ejaculate inside her without any further concerns. "Seriously, I'd want to know if you were pregnant would you still want me to continue seeing you?"

Kadrece sat up in her bed. "I hope you would want to continue seeing me because I am pregnant."

Chapter 44

Several months later

Another commute along I-26 westbound was being logged during Kadrece's pregnancy, which entered its thirty-eighth week. The loud vibration from Garner's tires riding over the emergency lane warning grooves had startled him. Jerking his car back onto the road, Garner blinked his eyes, shook his head, and rubbed his neck. He knew that he had just uncontrollably blanked out.

That wasn't smart, he chided himself.

Fatherhood was turning into a welcomed experience for Garner, who had now averaged at least three trips a week from Columbia to Spartanburg to be there for Kadrece. He promised himself long ago that he would always be tangible for the woman he'd marry and his child.

In keeping his word, he had attended virtually all of the scheduled doctor's visits with her, including the last one that was just a couple of days ago. Duncan Leibrandt, the obstetrician, informed Garner and Kadrece that he would induce labor if she didn't given birth by the end of the week. Officially, Kadrece was due anytime. Worst case, she was eight days away.

After passing the last Newberry exit, Garner still struggled badly with remaining awake. He resorted to a last-ditch effort. If that didn't work, he decided that he would pull over at the second Clinton exit just before the I-385 interchange.

"Are you calling to tell me that you love me and miss me?" Kadrece greeted him.

"I stand accused," he responded. "How about both?"

Lying on her side, Kadrece began rubbing her stomach and her breasts through her sheer chemise. "You're lucky that I like doing things like this." She then told him that she was fondling her pussy.

"Interesting how creative two people can become because of pregnancy."

"That's the beauty of it, wouldn't you agree?"

"Uh-huh . . ."

Kadrece mentioned to him that she still enjoyed him eating her pussy and tongue fucking her asshole late into her pregnancy. She also reminded him how she liked masturbating him or him fucking her swollen titties: she'd either lick his cum off her breasts or eagerly swallow his deposit.

"Shit, you've gotten me hard already," he exclaimed.

"I bet you were already that way." She sighed knowing that her clit had been extra sensitive; however, the intensity of her orgasms had become uncomfortable. "But you know I can't wait to take care of it once you're here—"

Garner called out for Kadrece as soon as he entered her place. He heard a faint response coming from the bedroom. "Baby, you know it's now January, the cold of winter, and you know once I snuggle up in bed, there are very few reasons why I'd get out. I'm sorry. Greeting you at the door isn't one of them." She then rubbed her belly and shifted to lying on her back.

A few minutes later, Garner joined her, nuzzling his nude body next to her scantily clad body. He mentioned to her that he was inclined to delegating coverage of the Chanticleers men's basketball game in Gainesville, Florida to his No. 2 guy, Dennis Rainey.

"I think the station will understand," he said.

"They just might," she answered. "But I want you to go ahead, do your job. You've already done so much for me. I'm so proud of your sacrifice." She reached for his hand to squeeze.

"What I've done is merely a labor of love. There is no sacrifice."

Kadrece explained that Carnette had offered long ago to be available if she ever needed any help should an emergency arise during her pregnancy. She then argued, "What would happen if you were in Columbia?" He hunched his shoulders. "It would be the same thing, different scenario.

"So I'm not going to insist that you stay here with me in Spartanburg when you have a job to do. It's only two days that you're going to be gone, not two weeks. I can handle that."

"Haven't you forgotten that you're due anytime?"

"Baby, I'm not some little girl. I was doing quite well taking care of myself before we were married." She winced and flinched. "I'm getting used to our child kicking around inside. It won't be long, that's for sure."

He shook his head, letting out a sigh. "All right, you've convinced me. I'll go. If it weren't for the fact Gainesville is so far away, I'd drive."

Deciding to change subjects, Garner mentioned that he spoke with Miriam earlier in the day. She told him that she missed them coming to Richmond for Christmas last month. "She said she'll be coming to visit us in a few weeks to help with the baby."

Kadrece felt she had managed to maintain a cordial, if not favorable relationship with Miriam. But she was always careful with what she said about her to Garner, and vice versa.

"I bet she's told everyone that she knows that she's about to become a grandmother."

"Uh-huh, knowing her, you would think that this was her first." Garner reminded Kadrece that Norris and Shalinda had their child, a daughter, last June. Miriam bought twelve fifty dollar gift cards— each from a different retail outlet—for baby clothing, supplies, and entertainment.

"Yeah, but you know your mom really talks about you the most.

Every conversation we've ever had your mother's mentioned something about you."

"I'm not surprised at all. That's Miriam Davis."

The campus athletic complex was not hard to find. But Garner also knew from previous experience covering football games in Gainesville that he still needed to be there at least an hour before tip-off. No sooner than he turned into the media parking section, his cell phone went off.

"Anything yet?"

The familiar voice reduced him to laughter. "No, mom, nothing yet. I called Kadrece before I left the hotel. She's fine."

"All right, you know me. Where are you?"

"Gainesville, Florida."

"Shouldn't you be in South Carolina?"

"Long story. But Kadrece is okay with me being here. She insisted on me coming."

"I see. Well, both of you are grown. You two have to make your marriage work, and I'm proud of you for that. Just call me if you hear anything."

"I will."

The Chanticleers trailed the third-ranked Swamp Gators 43-34 at intermission. The game was much closer until second-year coach Harley Dinkins was ejected from the game with two minutes remaining.

Rather than hanging out in the press room, Garner wandered outside just to collect his thoughts for filing his story at game's end. His cell phone went off again; he was not familiar with the female's voice on the other end.

"Brother Garner, this is Sister Carnette from church. Your wife just called me saying that her water's broken, and I'm on my way over to your place."

His eyes widened and felt his heart thump even harder. "How long will it take for you to get there?" He began walking back towards Simstone Coliseum.

"I don't know. I'm walking out of my place as I speak. But I'm sure that it won't take me long to get over there, and then take Sister Kadrece to the hospital."

"How did she sound?"

"Rather calm. I don't know if I'd been that way. Then again, I've never had a child and I doubt that will ever happen."

At that moment, Garner realized that maybe Kadrece had a valid point had she'd gone into labor while he was in Columbia. It still would have taken him about an hour to get there.

He tried contacting Kadrece as soon as he got off the phone with Carnette; her phone kept going to voice mail. For the rest of the night, he barely concentrated on the game. The best thing that happened was the Chanticleers, ranked nineteenth in the polls, were steam rolled 88-59, proving that they were not quite ready to be considered among the South Eastern Athletic Conference's elite. There were few good highlights to choose from. It made for a much easier story to file for the eleven o'clock broadcast.

It was about 11:45 p.m. when Garner finally reached Kadrece at her hospital room. He was greatly relieved to hear her voice, which seemed groggy and annoyed. "I tried calling you after I found out you had gone into labor—"

"I know. I was trying to call my family and let them know that I was headed to the hospital," she answered. "Well, you have a healthy eight pound, eight ounce baby boy. I'm really, really tired right now. Can we talk later?"

"Sure, I'll call you in the morning."

Chapter 45

Garner's first thought after he returned to his hotel room was to search his wallet for the black and white photo of Garrett Chaney, one of three that Miriam gave him after Aaron's funeral. He studied it—Chaney, a first lieutenant at the time of the photo, was in his military uniform—for several minutes. In this photo and the other two, Garrett wore his hair low and he sported a thin mustache where as Garner was the opposite wearing his hair moderately long and he was clean shaven. He relished in the thought of similar genes being passed down to another generation.

When he finally fell asleep, Garner experienced an unusually vivid dream of a newborn male child that startled him awake. He sat up in bed and tried to recall the child's features, but he quickly forgot. He wanted to call Kadrece and share what he dreamt. He reasoned that call could wait until the morning. Thus, it was a long, helpless night that did not end as he desired.

Despite the obvious fatigue, Garner willed himself to remain awake throughout his return plane flight back into Columbia, and then for the ninety-minute drive to Spartanburg. He took the long way over to the Regional Medical Center by exiting I-26 at Business Route 85, heading northbound to the I-585 exchange. There, he took the eastbound exit and drove past the Milliken complex until he reached the Route 9 exit.

Once inside RMC's main facility building, he asked a half-dozen people for directions to the maternity ward. Finally, on the fourth floor, he found room No. 425 where Kadrece was registered. The smile that Garner wore quickly disappeared, and he halted in mid-stride once he recognized the small contingent of people standing at his wife's bedside.

"Hey, brother. Congratulations!"

Garner did very little to hide his displeasure towards Levi and the three women whom he recognized as members from Mission Grove. He had expected—and gladly would have preferred—to have seen Kadrece's family.

"Uh, I think it's time for us to leave, Sister Kadrece," Levi volunteered. "So we're going to pray for you and the baby. Is that all right with you, brother?"

He glanced over at Kadrece, who raised the mattress to an upright position. "Sure, you can pray for her." He made a quick scan of the room. "Hey, I don't see my son in here?"

"You just missed him," Kadrece said. "They just took him back to the nursery."

"Okay, I'll go ask for him." He immediately left the room. While en route to the nurse's station, Garner fumed at the thought of anyone from Mission Grove being around his child. When he returned, he noticed there was just one of the Mission Grove women, Daphnie Braddock, standing near Kadrece's bed, and Levi standing not far from Daphnie.

"Sister, I'm just praising the Lord and rejoicing for both of you," Daphnie said. "It's such a blessing to become a parent. I pray great things for you and your child."

Garner cleared his throat, startling them.

"Look, baby. The nurse is back with our son," Kadrece alerted him.

He turned around and noticed the small cubicle with BABY DAVIS at the foot. The nurse picked up the child.

"You must be dad?" the nurse inquired, looking in Levi's direction.

He was quick to nod over at Garner before he made an even quicker exit from the room. She then placed the child in Garner's arms.

"Here's your son."

At first glance, the child's deep copper complexion and fuller lips were not what Garner envisioned in that dream. The moment was both surreal and humbling.

"He looks like he's going to be a big one," the nurse said. "His legs are so long."

I am really a parent, Garner acknowledged to himself. He then replied to the nurse, "I guess he has that honestly. As you can see, both his parents are tall. So how long is he?"

"Twenty-three and a quarter inches."

Garner forced a smile on his face. He took a step towards Kadrece's bed.

"Hey, baby, look at what we did here—"

"I know. Right now, I am the happiest wife in the world. I love you, Garner." He leaned over, still cradling the child, and kissed her on the cheek. "I'm still a little sore. But I actually feel pretty good."

They both admired the child who appeared so serene. Garner mused to himself that at some point he would no longer remain quiet but that he will demand for his parents' attention the only way that he knows best. He then queried Kadrece, "Have you thought of a name? I hope you weren't thinking of possibly naming him Garner Jr."

"Uh, I know you weren't thinking of cursing my child?"

He stared at her before he responded. "Then what did you have in mind?"

"I was thinking . . . LeKendrick Martez Davis." She sucked her teeth, savoring her thought. "The 'Le' part is spelled 'L-E' because in French male words have the 'Le' in front of it."

"He doesn't look like someone named *Le-Kendrick* to me."

Kadrece cast a loving gaze at her son. "I think he does."

Inhaling deeply, Garner then proposed, "I'll only go along with it if you change the middle name to Garrett."

"Why give him the name Garrett?"

He handed the child to her. Then he crouched down onto the seat next to her bed. "I've never told you this before." He stopped and pulled out the black and white photo from his wallet and held it in front of her.

"Okay, so what's so special about this picture?" she asked. "Is he related to your mother?"

He shook his head. "This man is my father. I didn't know he was my father until a couple of years ago."

Kadrece asked to hold the photo. She glanced down at LeKendrick, then over at Garner. Then she stared at Garrett's photo for several moments. Inwardly, she felt void of any energy and emotion. "Now I see where all the handsome features came from," she said, nodding. "Why you never showed me a picture of him?"

"I just never got around to it," he answered. "It wasn't intentional keeping it from you."

"I see," she answered, now rocking LeKendrick close to her bosom. "So that means your mother—"

"It does. But I'm okay with it." He looked over at LeKendrick, studying the child's features. "That's why I want Garrett to be included. I hope L.K., because that's what I'll call him, will be proud of me someday. That was one of the last things my father said to my mother before he died."

"I'm sorry to hear that."

"I actually visited his grave while I was in Richmond for Aaron's funeral." He then sighed. "As I was saying, I'm going to do everything I know good to make it possible for L.K. to be proud of me."

Kadrece smiled back at him. "I know that I married the right man." The child squirmed while in her possession; she joked about it being a familiar feeling over the past several months.

Chapter 46

The six-week check up was a more than welcomed milestone. At least Kadrece knew that she would stand to be given her doctor's stamp of approval to resume her old routine, which included sex.

She tried desperately to maintain a loving feeling towards Garner, who at times maintained his sexual sanity as he did late in her pregnancy by asking her to suck his dick, masturbate him, or by allowing him to fuck her lactating breasts. But she desired more to be in Levi's company—they agreed to limit their contact to just phone calls, e-mails, and text messages in the interim.

"You know it's killing me with you being where you are and I can't come by and see you or anything," Levi told her during a recent phone conversation.

"I know what you mean," she said. "My husband's a good man. He's better than I've probably given him credit for being. I'm just ready to get my groove on somewhere else."

For the first time, Levi confided in her a more personal feeling. "I can't explain it, but I, uh, actually felt like there was a bond between me, you, and your baby when I saw you in the hospital. I almost wished that he was my child."

Levi's comment stunned Kadrece; however, she knew something like this would be inevitable. She was slow at forming the words.

"Is there something wrong with what I said?" Levi inquired.

"No. We've been in each other's lives now for going on a couple of years, right?" She then let out a deep sigh. "I do have something that I want to tell you."

Over the past several weeks, Levi had limited his contact with Carnette to just a perfunctory phone call that had little to do with anything.

"I do miss you, Kadrece," he volunteered to say. "I've never been with a woman as sexy, smart, and [as] freaky as you."

She was moved to chortling. "I have thought about you, too. But what I wanted to tell you was that LeKendrick is really your son."

"What are you talking about?"

"The reason why you've felt that bond is because he's our child, not Garner's."

"You mean to tell me?" Levi felt a sinister, yet satisfying boost to his ego. It thrilled him knowing that he had been fucking Garner's wife, and now he had been apprised of the ultimate in being a son of a bitch.

"That's right," Kadrece answered. "It took me a while to figure it out even after the doctor told me long ago . . . Do you still remember the day you asked to eat my pussy while you held me upside down?

"Well, you came in side of me like you had burst a pipe. It was like I couldn't stop wiping away all that cum you left inside me the rest of the day."

"Heh-heh-heh, well you know. You've had a way of doing that to me—"

"And now you know," she said. "Can't you see in the way I named our child that you were the father?"

"I really hadn't paid attention."

"Le . . . Kendrick. The L-E is for you, Levi. The Kendrick part, well, that's in honor of my family's name," she said. "He definitely has your eyes, nose, and ears."

"So when am I going to see you and my child? You're not going to keep him away from me?"

"No, I wouldn't do anything like that. But you can't just act any way out in public. Do you understand?" Kadrece recognized the "Love's Holiday" ringtone that she set for Garner's incoming calls. "Look, we'll talk about this some more."

"I know we will. We better."

Miriam was ecstatic that Garner had insisted on inviting her to Columbia to visit him and his family. The timing of her trip also coincided with her celebrating her sixty-first birthday on Monday. Her male friend, Riley Couture, an attorney client whom she befriended within the past year, had offered to take her on a cruise to the Bahamas. But she politely declined. Nothing compared to visiting her son.

When she arrived at Garner's place, Miriam felt a wave compassion for Kadrece as she noticed her grandson in his mother's arms.

"It's good to see you, Miriam," Kadrece greeted her in the living room.

"Thank you, Kadrece." She then became wide-eyed. "Is this Le-Kendrick?" She glanced back at Garner, whose countenance was a portrait of pride; it was obvious that he savored the moment of being in the presence of now the three most important people in his life.

As she drew closer to Kadrece, Miriam mentioned, "I forgot to bring my tissues." She hugged both of them, stopping to plant a kiss each on Kadrece and LeKendrick's cheek. "Can hold him?"

"This is your grandson, LeKendrick Martez Davis," Kadrece said, placing him in Miriam's arms. She flinched and looked over at Garner. "I'm sorry, LeKendrick Martez Garrett Davis."

The compassion that Miriam felt from the onset gave way to an onslaught of emptiness. Never had she felt that way for her other five grandchildren. She also felt troubled by an indescribable disconnection with him. It took all of her to manage a smile.

"I don't think I raised a mama's boy in Garner."

Kadrece returned a puzzled look.

"What I mean is that I can see Le-Kendrick is really attached to you. How does he act around Garner?" Miriam went on to say.

Garner chimed in to say, "I'll show you."

"All right now," Miriam snapped at him. "Let's not fight over how much attention LeKendrick's getting."

"That's right, Miriam," Kadrece reacted. She suggested that everyone take a seat rather than stand around in the living room.

"How was your trip here to Columbia?"

"All the trips seem to be about the same these days. The difference is that I caught a good price for a first-class ticket—one hundred and forty-nine dollars round trip."

"You don't say?" Kadrece replied, sitting across from Miriam. "I don't know if I could drive to Richmond and back spending only one hundred and forty-nine dollars."

Miriam seemed adept at handling both a conversation and the child. But without warning, she stood up and brought LeKendrick to over where Garner sat near the dining area. "I think in a little while I'll have to start calling LeKendrick 'Little Man' because he's a big one."

When she returned to the sofa where Kadrece sat, Miriam divulged to her that Garner was no runt of a child, either. "He really took after me. My mother said that I was all legs and not much of an appetite. So was Garner."

"LeKendrick has a very, very good appetite." Kadrece spotted Garner sitting in one of the large living room chairs. "There's a bottle ready for him in the refrigerator."

Miriam's arrival gave Garner an opportunity to surprise Kadrece. About six o'clock he suggested that Kadrece wear something nice, but could be contrived as sexy in public.

"I don't have anything like that," she protested.

"Don't you do have clothes in the closet. Why don't you look? There might be something in there."

Reluctantly, she checked. There was a leopard print skirt and blouse that she could fit into; she had dropped only five of the nearly forty pounds that she gained during her pregnancy.

"Garner, I really don't have anything to wear."

"What's wrong with what you have in your hand? Try it on."

She returned him a sideways look. "What are you up to?"

"Nothing out of the ordinary—"

"Now tell, me. What are you really up to?" She turned around and placed her hand on his forehead. "Are you not feeling well?"

He leaned forward and kissed her on the cheek. "I'm fine. Horny, but fine." He placed both hands on her ass cheeks and gave them a firm squeeze. "You know it's really been a while."

"Oh, so that's what this is all about." Her eyes widened. "And we're going to leave LeKendrick with your mom?"

He nodded. "She came here for all of us this weekend."

"You told me that she was celebrating her birthday here in Columbia." She walked over to the bed and plopped down on it. "Do you really think that's the right thing to do? I don't feel right asking your mother to do something that's really our responsibility."

"What are you talking about?" Garner hurried to sit next to her. He was incredulous that she would even make a comment like that. "You've known since L.K. was born that my mother would be coming here to spend a few days with us."

She stood up in front of him, holding her hands out in protest. "Why are you making a big deal out of me voicing what I really feel?"

"How am I making a big deal out this?" he reacted. "Do you have a problem with us spending some time together? That's all the reason why we need to go out tonight. We've forgotten what it's like being a husband and wife and alone just for a few hours."

Sighing, Kadrece reluctantly agreed. She reached out for his hands, drawing him nigh to her. "You're right. I'll put on something." Then she took a step back. "But I get to pick where we go for dinner."

While they were out to Kazuki's, a newly constructed Japanese restaurant in the Village at Sandhill, Miriam initially occupied herself as a baby sitter by catching the second half of a Lifetime Channel movie. She was startled by the sound of a cell phone ringtone going off in the dining room area. Her immediate concern was whether it might wake up LeKendrick.

About an hour later, while she was curled up on the sofa and reading the middle chapters of *Temptation.com*, the ringtone went off again, startling her. The cell phone's going off had now piqued her curiosity.

Initially, Miriam thought that Garner had left his phone. So she used her cell phone and dialed Garner's number. *"This is Garner. You've caught me at a bad time. Leave me a message. I'll hit you up whenever I can . . ."*

Miriam smirked. "I've heard worse." The most telling thing was that phone in the dining room area did not go off—at least when she called. Now her curiosity was heightened. She stopped by and perused the white cell phone with silver trimming. A number from the 864 area code without any description was on the display screen; she also noticed that there had been five other calls from the same number.

Just for the hell of it, she used her phone and dialed the number to find out who would call so many times on a Saturday evening. The phone picked up on the third ring.

"Where have you been? I've been calling you all night," the male voice answered, not recognizing the call came from the 804 area code. "I'm calling when you said for me to call you."

Miriam was taken aback. But she was quick to react. "Oh, I'm sorry. I've dialed the wrong number."

The main course was taken away by the waitress at Kazuki's, and dessert was being served when Kadrece excused herself to go to the bathroom. She checked her purse and realized that something was missing.

"Oh shit!" she whispered under her breath. "I can't believe I did that!" She rushed to return to the table. "Hey baby, I called home and there was no answer. We need to get back."

"Do you think that maybe my mother might have dozed off?" Garner answered.

"That's when things usually happen," she said, sitting nervously. She exhaled loudly. "Look, I've had a nice time tonight and I don't want to ruin it. But I'd feel a lot better if we just went home so I can check on LeKendrick. This is the first time that I've been away from him, okay?"

Garner shook his head. "You really picked a fine time wanting to go home. We hadn't even gotten through half of our date." He ran his hand on his thigh. Then he balled his fist, pounding it on his thigh.

"I'm sorry. I'm still not used to being away from my baby," she said.

"Do I have to remind you that he's our child?"

"Look, just take me home."

When Garner and Kadrece returned around 9:45 p.m., Miriam had been up waiting for them.

"How did things go?" Garner inquired as soon as he entered.

"Oh, fine. LeKendrick went to sleep around seven. He's been asleep ever since," Miriam said. "It's like that now. Just give yourself a few more months. It won't be that way. They'll keep you up awake forever . . . so y'all are back early?"

"I know," answered Garner; he plopped down in one of the comforters and stroked his brow.

Meanwhile, Kadrece walked past Garner and Miriam and headed straight to the bedroom. But her preoccupation was not for LeKendrick, who was sound asleep. Afterward, she made a subtle, yet overt pass by the dining room area, retrieving her phone. Then she walked towards the kitchen. She showed no emotion once she recognized that Levi had called. She merely deleted his entry, made sure to reset her phone to meeting mode, and she locked her keypad.

Upon her return in the living room, Kadrece and Miriam's eyes met. It was as though Miriam had peered directly through Kadrece's soul, exposing her sin and her conscience that bore witness to it.

Chapter 47

Church remained an item of contention between Garner and Kadrece. She was insistent on attending Mission Grove, and she refused to go elsewhere.

"Kadrece, that pastor is nothing more than a pimp. He can't preach. He doesn't know what he's talking about more than half of the time, and all he cares about is how much you're giving," Garner argued. "Last time I spoke to him he's telling me that I need to make sure that I'm tithing.

"Shit, if I wanted that kind of preacher, I know at least a dozen of them who are just like him."

Kadrece had been in front of the mirror applying her make-up. She turned around and pointed at him. "You know what your problem is?" she fumed. "You don't have an ounce of commitment in you. I bet if you had the opportunity you'd be off with some trick."

"You know what?" he retorted. "Maybe I should ask you the same question. But I won't bother you with that silly shit."

"Ain't nothing silly about any of my concerns I have about you."

"Sounds like the pot's calling the kettle black."

She rolled her neck and looped her fingers in an "S" motion. "I know you're not talking about me being black. 'Cause if you are—"

"No I wasn't," he interrupted her. "All of a sudden you have amnesia about the things you used to do, hmmm?"

"I told you that God's dealt with me. That's another person you're trying to resurrect." She walked over to LeKendrick's room and checked on him. He seemed oblivious to his parents' tiff.

Annoyed with the direction of matters, Kadrece decided to drive her point with vigor. "It's bad enough after having a child and more than two years of marriage we still are separated."

Garner's eyes widened. "Separated?" He walked slowly towards her while she was in the closet changing into a skirt. "We're not separated. And I don't know who's been filling your fucking mind with that kind of foolishness. You need to stop while you're ahead!"

She buttoned her blouse and walked away from the close. "Pastor McBride says so."

Hissing and flapping his hands, Garner smirked, "Pastor McFucking Bride this . . . Pastor McFucking Bride that. Fuck him!"

"You shouldn't talk about a man of God like that."

"Hah!" he snapped back at her. "What you need to do is go over to Pastor Lanier's church. At least you know you're dealing with a godly man with a godly message." He paused for a few moments before he continued. "You've never told me why you never liked it over there?"

She stopped to sit on the bed and put on her navy blue stilettos. "Look, it doesn't matter what the reason is. Right now, it is what it is. We need to have more unity in this marriage." She stood up and stared at him. "You do understand that a house divided will fall, don't you?"

"I'm not some heathen."

"Could have fooled me by the way you were cursing just a few moments ago."

Garner bunched his lips. His chest rose and inflated like a balloon.

"Now, are you going to come to church this week for LeKendrick's dedication?" Kadrece queried him.

A powerless feeling came over Garner whenever Kadrece invoked God and LeKendrick in a conversation with him. She placed her hand on her hip.

"Well, are you going?"

He still had not answered.

"Now that's what I meant when I told Nedra about my fearing that I've been alone the entire time." She shook her head. "Garner, I don't understand you. You've never been supportive of me. All you've wanted is sex. And I'm tired of trying to give to you when you're not giving me anything in return."

"Fuck you!" he screamed.

LeKendrick began crying.

"I told you about us fighting around my child!" Kadrece reacted. "And you expect for things to go right for you? You expect for any of your prayers to be answered?"

She rushed into his room and took him out of his playpen. His crying was not the result of them arguing, but that he had dropped his toy outside of the playpen. As she comforted him while returning to the bedroom, she queried Garner, "Now are you going to be an asshole, or are you going to be a husband *and* a father today?"

> **Can't do it today. Garner and I were fighting. I'll explain when we talk again. He'll be with us today.**

Levi received Kadrece's text message shortly before he arrived at Mission Grove that she would not name him and Carnette as LeKendrick's godparents at least for now.

His heart raced when he noticed her with Garner and the child in the parking lot. He looked over his shoulder in the church's lobby to find Carnette, who was making conversation with another member. He cleared his throat and mentally reminded himself to portray a friendly and professional demeanor with the Davises.

He first greeted them with a grin. "God bless y'all."

"Good morning, Brother Levi," Kadrece responded; her diction was much like an attorney before a judge's bench.

Immediately, Levi extended his hand out to Garner. "God bless you, brother."

Garner was barely audible. "Hi." He turned to Kadrece and indicated that he'd meet up with her in the sanctuary. He excused himself. In the immediate distance he overheard a female's voice.

"Wow, look at you and your son!" the lady said. "He's really growing like a weed."

"It doesn't take long, Sister Carnette," Kadrece replied. "Soon he'll be running round here [and] getting in all kinds of trouble."

Kadrece, Levi, and Carnette all shared in a hearty chuckle.

Meanwhile, Garner spent several minutes in the bathroom. He stood in one spot, kept his eyes shut, and took several deep breaths. *This is not my idea of what family should be*, he mumbled to himself, hoping that nobody also visited the bathroom while he was there. Exhaling, he opened his eyes and stood in front of the mirror, peering into it. His displeasure for showing up at Mission Grove was quite visible. He tried thinking of better times with Kadrece. Nothing seemed to work. Finally, he convinced himself into thinking that he would not allow his difference of opinion with her come between them. He recalled from his personal observations that many couples merely used their differences as weapons of marital destruction.

Once he felt calmness, he exited the bathroom. But then he overheard two people talking just as he was about to turn the corner, heading back towards the lobby.

"You know you're right. He looks nothing like your husband. He favors someone else," the male's voice said.

The female responded, "I told you already who he favors—you." She then snickered at her comment.

Garner halted in mid-stride. He thought his hearing had deceived him.

"Sister, they're about to start service. We'll talk later, right?"

A child's squeal was rather audible. Garner immediately recognized it as LeKendrick's.

"You know we shouldn't be talking like this here." Garner had now recognized Kadrece's voice and she'd been chatting with Levi. "Come on baby, say bye-bye . . ."

Garner shook his head thinking, *I'll be goddamned!* He felt like he had entered into suspended animation. Nothing seemed to make any sense at that moment. He resumed walking—slowly.

"Hey baby, what took you so long?" Kadrece said, startling him.

"I thought you'd already be inside," he answered.

"No, I figured that I'd wait for my husband. How would it look if we didn't walk inside together?" She glanced down at LeKendrick before she continued. "Are you okay?"

"Yeah, I just had to leave my attitude at the door," he answered. "That's what we used to say and do when I played baseball."

"Well, I'm glad that you have. This is an important day for LeKendrick."

Humph!

The first thing that Garner did once he entered the sanctuary was seek out Levi just off to the right. He greeted him with the tightest handshake that he'd given someone in recent memory. He maintained eye contact with him during the entire exchange.

"Well, brother, the Lord's able, heh-heh-heh," Levi replied, making an awkward attempt at releasing Garner's grip.

Garner smirked. "Yes, He is." Then he walked off and joined Kadrece and LeKendrick in the section where they normally sat. He took LeKendrick out of Kadrece's hands and held him. For the first time, it became evident to him why he had felt disconnected with this child: LeKendrick bore no traits similar to him, and he had been oblivious to many of the other comments that were made over the past seven-plus months. But he wondered why in the fuck would such a revelation have occurred at Mission Grove, of all the fucking places?

After a brief survey of the sanctuary, he glanced down at LeKendrick and shook his head—it had nothing to do with the child squirming in his possession.

Chapter 48

The feeling was at best contemptuous being in Kadrece's company.

Shit, this was the same woman who once pontificated so much about the Lord's work in her life and only wanting to indulge with people of substance. And this was the same woman who periodically interrogated Garner on whether he was truly committed to their relationship during their courtship.

What a fucking joke. Shame on me, he cringed.

He knew whatever decision that he made had to be decisive. As it was during the Vernise ordeal, Garner needed to confide in somebody, although there were few people he knew.

"I just had to call you," he said. At that moment he felt a weight removed from his shoulders. "Before you say anything, now I see why you always told me to keep my eyes and heart open."

Miriam recognized that maybe a prayer had been answered. She elected to listen intently to what her son might disclose to her. "And all I'll say is that I'm your mother. If I can't tell you something that's right, who will?"

"I know . . ."

It pained Garner to tell Miriam that he suspected LeKendrick was not his child. He was careful not to say that he had been in denial,

"I hope that I'm wrong because what I'm thinking about doing won't be nice," he said. "But what made me realize Kadrece might be playing me all along was when I overheard her talking to some fat, baldheaded, stupid son of a bitch at the church she likes to attend."

Miriam sighed loudly into the phone.

"I know you don't like for any of us to be cursing this way," Garner said. "All I'm saying is that I ignored all of the signs. The entire time I've been attending that church with her, this ignorant motherfucker, Levi, would rush to greet me at church with one of those silly ass grins.

"Humph. He wasn't grinning. It was more like him laughing in my face. Like, 'Yeah, dumb ass, I've been doing your wife and you don't even know.'"

Miriam tried to calm Garner. "I should have told you that I've suspected Kadrece hasn't been right all along."

"How did you know?" he reacted. "And why didn't you tell me?"

"First of all, you needed to have found out for yourself. I didn't want to be blamed for accusing your wife of something that turned out not to be true. That's the easiest way of wrecking a marriage. I couldn't have that on my conscience. Secondly," she went on to say, "I picked up on a few things while I was in Columbia this last time. She knew I was onto something about her. She never looked me in the eye."

"Well, now I'm on to her."

"What are you going to do?"

"I've already planned on taking LeKendrick with me to Columbia one day this week. I told her that I want people at the station to see our child." He paused, sneering at the thought. "But while he's with me I'm going to take a DNA test. And if he isn't my son then I'm outta there."

"But what if he is yours?"

"I don't know. I might confront her, and I might not." He sighed again. "I don't think I have it within me to ever forgive her because I know Kadrece."

"Garner, just playing the devil's advocate, if LeKendrick is not your son, do you think that would be the right thing to do when a child's involved. Looking back, that might be the only thing I could ever give Aaron credit for in all his warped thinking."

That was the last thing Garner wanted to hear. Raising his voice, he countered, "She's never been with one man. Even when we first met, that's what made being around her so exciting. Both of us got off on whoring around on the people we were supposed to be involved with."

He went on to say that now he felt like eighty thousand people in a football stadium had been laughing derisively at him.

"Little boy, you can't be so hard on yourself. It's not like you're sixty-one years old like me. You're only thirty-five," Miriam said. "I'm only going to share this with you once, and only once: There are times in life you'll find that it's not a bad thing being alone. The right person will come along for you. I pray that it would."

There was silence between them for several seconds. Then Garner finally spoke up. "I guess that I've had my nose wide open once again, hmmm?"

Chapter 49

It had been several months since the weather was as cool in the Columbia area. An overcast and rainy early-October day in the low sixties served as a reminder that football season was in full swing, a stark contrast from temperatures in the mid-eighties just a little less than a week earlier. Garner mused to himself that he did not need any reminder with all the garnet, white and black flags waving from almost any place imaginable.

Upon his return from the weekly Chanticleers media session, Garner noticed the stack of envelopes just off to his right on his desk. Most were press releases from places he deemed as having no news worthiness to the WCAE audience; however, his heart began beating faster once he recognized a white envelope from Carolina Diagnostics and Testing. He dug into the envelope, but he was careful not to tear the two-page reply.

The second paragraph had the information that he had been waiting for since early September:

> The alleged father, Garner Michael Davis, is excluded as the biological father of the child named LeKendrick Martez Garrett Davis. The alleged father lacks the genetic markers that must be contributed to the child by the bio-

logical father.

Based on testing results obtained from analyses of 4 different DNA probes, the probability of paternity is 0.0% . . .

Immediately, Garner folded the letter and slipped it back into the partially torn envelope. He closed his eyes, folded his arms, and leaned forward. As much as he was relieved with the results, he was equally devoid of emotion much like the day he visited Kadrece and LeKendrick at the hospital for the first time. He then straightened up, rested his chin on his hand, and stared straight ahead.

In a matter of about five minutes, his life as he had known it now came to a moment of demarcation. A few seconds later he rested his left hand on his right forearm, and he glanced down at his wedding ring.

Amazing, he thought, *three years ago I proposed to her. Humph. I was so fucking in love with this bitch . . .*

"Hey, Garner, are you all right?" cameraman Pete DiCarlo queried him.

Looking up at Pete, Garner shrugged his shoulders, responding, "I'm doing fine. Guess I had to think a few things through."

Pete chortled. "You're one of the fastest thinkers I've ever known. Something's really gotten you to slow down. Hope it isn't too bad."

"Oh, no; not that at all—"

Patting Garner on the shoulder, Pete said, "All right, I expect for you to piss off a few fans tonight. I know how you are about those Chanticleers."

Garner smiled back at him. "Don't worry. They'll be plenty mad when I get finished with them." He leaned back in his chair, clasping his hands behind his head. "You know everyone's all giddy about them being four-and-one so far. Humph. Reality's going to hit them real soon. Or so I'd like to believe."

In a spur of the moment, Garner made a quick exit from the newsroom and station's building—without speaking to anyone—

and sought refuge inside his car. There, he reclined slightly in the driver's seat and stared straight ahead as his mind worked extra time trying to mull his options.

The more he thought about Kadrece and Levi the more his rage intensified. He decided before he did anything violent that he'd seek impartial but godly counsel in a time of need.

He was more than relieved that he was able to contact Pastor Lanier on his first attempt.

"I know it's been a while since we've talked," Garner said. "A lot of things have happened since then."

"Brother, I'm sure they have, but how are you?"

Lanier seemed genuinely glad to hear from Garner. "You know I watch your broadcasts whenever I can. I still think of you as one of my members. Sister Lanier often asks if I've heard from you. Now I can tell her that I have."

"That's good to know, pastor."

"Now, let me get this right. If memory serves me correct, you were about to get married. Your bride lived and worked and work in Greenville, right?"

The conversation went silent for a few moments. Garner used it as a chance to compose his thoughts. In the background, Lanier had reclined back in his office chair.

"That's right, Kadrece and I have now been married going on three years—"

"Has it been that long?" Lanier interrupted.

"Yeah, we're still commuting."

"Well, praise God. He has certainly given both of you much grace to make it work commuting as you two have done. But can I ask you this: Have the two of you considered living in just one place?"

Shaking his head, Garner knew his tolerance for the probing questions was fast reaching its limit. "Pastor, in my profession you go wherever your opportunities are. Why do you think I'm in South Carolina?"

"That doesn't answer my question," Lanier said.

"All right, to answer your question, I hope you understand in this economy I'm just glad to be working. But I also hope you understand that sports director openings don't occur just like that?" Garner snapped his finger for emphasis.

Shifting his feet, Lanier glanced back over his shoulder. He expected for his wife, Turquoise, to stop by at any time. "I see, so where are you attending church these days. Was it not Mission Grove in Spartanburg, your wife's church?"

Garner nodded. "I went there with her for about a year and a half, and I've since stopped going."

"You do know that a house divided cannot stand," Lanier said. "You know that both of you not worshipping at the same place—or at all—presents a problem."

"I don't know. I tried convincing her that we needed to go somewhere else. That caused one argument after another," he said, pausing to snort. "It was basically her way or no way at all."

"Brother, you know—"

"I'm just about fed up with attending church. There's been a lot on my mind since this child was born," Garner rushed to respond.

Lanier made a double-take reaction. "This child?"

"Yeah, I said it that way. This child."

"That's not a godly way of responding to one of God's blessings."

"Humph. It depends on who you're telling that to."

By now, Lanier began entertaining scenarios that he had been talking to somebody in a backslidden state. "Brother, let's slow this down again. How about that we start with you. What's really going on? Are you having second thoughts about being a husband and a parent?"

Garner's eyes began to widen. Also, his voice went up an octave or two. "Pastor, this is not about me shirking any responsibility. I'm looking at papers from a DNA test that I took that says I'm not the father of the child that was born in our marriage. There is ZERO probability that it's mine. It belongs to another man.

"That's the reason why I'm calling you is because I'm trying to keep my cool. If I were to do what I really feel right now, you would be viewing me on the eleven o'clock news and it wouldn't be good."

He let out a loud sigh. He then pressed his head back into the head-rest, staring upward at the roof.

"Brother, God is more than able to give you the grace to love both your wife and this child that may or not be yours," Lanier responded.

Garner countered, "I'm going to put it to you this way: What single man do you know of shows up in the hospital room of a married woman who just had a child, and he's not related to her?"

Lanier began shifting uncomfortably in his chair. "Tell me more."

"There's nothing more to say, really—"

"I can see how this appears to be suspect and distressing, but God is not the author of confusion."

"Pastor, before I say something to you that I'd regret, you have a nice day."

He immediately hung up.

Shit, that was not a good idea, Garner cursed to himself. He squirmed for several moments in the driver's seat before he settled on a new posture. Everything within him seemed numb. Things just did not seem to matter for the moment. He now contemplated taking the day off and driving to Spartanburg, but then for what?

He noticed the cell phone had gone off, startling him. Without paying attention to his caller ID, he responded, "Garner Davis—"

"Hey, where have you been?" Kadrece greeted him. "I've been calling you for the past twenty-five minutes."

"Why in the fuck do you need to know?" he snapped. "I'm a grown man."

In the background, LeKendrick could be heard cooing and making other noises. "Whoa, wait a minute. Let me start over again." Kadrece took a deep breath. Literally, she tried putting on her best facial expression. "Hey, baby. How are you? I've missed you and I was concerned about you.

"I called your desk, somebody answered, but he didn't know where you had gone. He offered to ask Mr. Redfearn; I told him that wasn't necessary. So how are you?"

He spoke deliberately to her. "I'm going to repeat myself only once: I'm a grown man. I know what needs to be done when it needs

needs to be done. And right now, I'm really not in the mood nor do I have the time to speak with you."

Sucking her teeth, Kadrece retorted, "Okay, now when you pull your dick from between your legs and out of your ass—"

The phone clicked before she completed her thought.

Kadrece was not to be out done or denied. She called him again between the evening broadcasts.

"Baby, I think us maintaining two households just isn't working out." She suggested that he drove to Spartanburg after work. "We need to have a serious talk."

"I don't feel like driving ninety goddamn miles tonight," he snapped. "Shit, I'm going to need a new car before long."

"Haven't you forgotten that you're a married man?" She walked from the dining room where LeKendrick was in his playpen over to the kitchen table.

"No, and your issue is?" A fire truck's siren blared in the background as it traveled eastbound on Garners Ferry Road.

"It's called doing what you have to do," she countered. "You have a son. You have a wife. It's called you have a family here in Spartanburg."

"Humph, whatever . . . "

"I know you didn't say that."

"You're damn right I did!"

There was no interaction for several seconds. Garner then broke the silence declaring, "I need some space. I've got to think some things though."

Kadrece could not believe it, reacting, "What are you talking about, Garner?" All of a sudden, many of the sentiments of skepticism she fought prior to and after them marrying began echoing in her mind. She then blurted, "You know what? You're just an ungrateful man. You've got a beautiful wife and son. You've got a happy family situation, and you just want to fuck it up, don't you?

"You know, maybe everyone was right. You aren't husband material. You sure had me fooled."

Garner erupted into laughter. "So now this is the way you've always thought of me?" He searched for the Carolina Diagnostics envelope he stuffed in his jacket pocket. Pulling the letter out, he focused in on the paragraph that detailed there was zero chance he was LeKendrick's father. He placed it back in the envelope and stared ahead, retorting, "Hey, that's fine with me. Say whatever in the fuck you want!"

There was no doubt that his behavior and comments were signs of the obvious, Kadrece thought.

"All right, so who's the bitch? Is it Tamira Lake? You thought I'd forgotten about her, didn't you?" She glanced over at LeKendrick, hoping that she had not scared him; the last thing she wanted was an argument with Garner and a child crying in the background.

He rolled his eyes and smirked. "It's whoever you think it is." For a moment, he wished it was Tamira or anybody, for that matter.

She placed a hand on her hip. "Listen, baby, I'm willing to forgive and forget all of this if you just come here tonight and be with me. I know sometimes we'll say things that we don't mean when we're mad." She took a deep breath, hoping that Garner would consider what she just bargained with him; he did not respond.

"Garner, I didn't move from Florida to South Carolina to be with some whore," she said. "I thought you had finally grown out of that."

"Whatever," he replied, chortling. "Think whatever way you want about me."

Kadrece attempted to reason once more with Garner. She offered that she understood about his upbringing was not the best of situations, and it may have affected his perspective on resolving relational issues.

"I'm okay with that. But I'm not going to let you jerk me around emotionally like some roller coaster ride." She began wagging and shaking her finger. "I won't put up with that shit! Now I'm asking you nicely. Please come to Spartanburg tonight and let's get this straightened out. This is obviously something that cannot be accomplished over the phone."

He remained defiant. "I'm not going anywhere. Not tonight."

Searching for some common ground, Kadrece suggested, "Do we need to see Pastor McBride for some counseling?"

"Apparently you're having difficulty understanding me." He slowed his speech again. "I'm not going anywhere near that city or anyone associated with that church."

Kadrece's eyes widened, but tears quickly filled them. "Garner, please baby. You don't know what you're doing to me." Meanwhile, he shook his head staring off with an incredulous look while she continued, "Do you not realize that I've had your back when others have told me that I was crazy for the decisions that I made to be with you?"

Jerking his head back, he responded, "Thank you for the support. But I still need some time and space."

"Garner—"

The phone clicked.

Immediately, Kadrece slammed the phone, snarling, "Fuck you, Garner. Your ass will come crawling back begging for all of this. Your whorish ass is too fucking weak to do anything else!"

Chapter 50

Later in the week

Garner exhaled loudly as he exited his car in the parking lot of Mercer & Dunlap's law offices on Assembly Street, which was located about six blocks from the Columbia Police station. He arranged for an appointment with Candace Mercer a couple of days after learning of his blood test results.

He did not appear nervous or uncomfortable as he entered the red brick exterior building. Rather, he kept telling himself that it was necessary. There was no other logical solution.

"Please fill out this questionnaire and hand it back. Attorney Mercer will be with you shortly," the receptionist instructed him.

Garner returned it within five minutes and plopped back on the couch in the reception area. He folded his arms, closed his eyes, and arched his head back.

"Mr. Davis?" the receptionist said, startling him. "Attorney Mercer will see you now." She led him to an office near the back, its view being the half dozen or so tall office buildings that comprised Columbia's downtown skyline.

A white woman of average height and with short brunette hair stood up from behind her desk and extended her hand out to him. They exchanged pleasantries. Then she motioned with her right hand for him to sit.

"How can I be of service?" she said.

Garner glanced down before he answered her inquiry. But then she stopped him. "Wait a minute. You're the guy on Channel 6, aren't you?"

He nodded.

"My husband talks about you all of the time."

He chortled. "I hope that's a good thing, but if it isn't—"

She waved him off. "Don't worry about him. He's a sore loser, anyway." Her observation about him made for a helpful icebreaker.

"I'm here because I want to file for a divorce."

Ms. Mercer initially reclined back in her chair, but then she decided to take notes. "Go ahead."

"I almost feel like I'm the one being interviewed," Garner quipped. "That's a bit unusual."

"Well, it is sort of like that, Mr. Davis. I do need to understand what your reason is for seeking representation."

He nodded again. "To me, this is very simple. I would like to file for divorce citing irreconcilable difference. I just feel things have reached a point where they make no sense for me to continue."

"Mr. Davis, a lot of couples feel that way at some point in their marriage. What makes yours any different?" she responded, leaning back in her plush leather chair. "May I ask how long you two have been married?"

"Since April 2009."

She leaned forward, resting her chin in her hand. "I don't understand. You've been married for just two and a half years? Have you two sought counseling?" She placed her pen on the desk and listened intently for his answer.

Taking a deep breath, Garner answered, "I understand that a person really doesn't need a reason for a divorce."

"Okay, so are there any children involved?"

Shit.

He hunched his shoulders. "Sort of—"

"How can there be a 'sort of?'"

He placed a copy of his blood test results on her desk. "I guess you might say there aren't any children involved. I really didn't want this to be an issue, but maybe it is." She picked up the two-page letter and glanced over it. She paused and studied him again. Then she placed it on the desk.

"If I agree to take this case, may I keep this?"

"Of course!"

Mercer folded her hands on the desk and sat upright. "Well, that's definitely proof of something. But I must warn you that in the state of South Carolina, as in many states, that a judge may not see your argument the same way."

He returned an intense glare at her. "What do you mean?"

She assumed a more relaxed pose in her chair. There's a saying in the legal realm 'you can't un-ring a bell.'" He returned a puzzled look while she continued with her thought. "In other words, the legal term is presumption of paternity. The husband is presumed the father, no matter what. There are states like South Carolina that defines situations like yours as being what is born in a marriage is considered of a marriage. There is no statue of limitation, either."

"You've got to be kidding me?" he reacted, shaking his head.

She shook her head, too. "I'm not saying you don't have a case. But I feel that I should present to you all of the possibilities you face if I were to accept this case. Otherwise, I would be a disservice to you."

Garner exhaled, folded his arms and leaned back in his chair. He decided to divulge to Mercer that he suspected Levi Harriston of being the father, and that Kadrece and Levi had been engaged in some kind of an affair for at least a year.

"I don't have any proof of when and where they've seen each other, and really I don't care." He pointed at the blood test results on her desk. "That's enough proof for me. Now I want out of it. There's no way that I'm going to put up with her and another man's child. It's that simple."

Mercer nodded and explained to him that she would not charge him for his initial visit but he would be billed at $150 an hour, and that did not include costs for copying, mailing, and phone calls. She also explained to him that a case like this could be filed within a matter of days. She also brought to his attention under South Carolina's statute it does not recognize irreconcilable differences as grounds for divorce.

"You've been watching too much television. What you can file for is under grounds of adultery." She then advised him that a divorce decree would not likely to be granted and finalized by the court for at least six months. During that time, he could not have any form of cohabitation with her, or for that matter any sexual relations.

He smirked. "She has a place in Spartanburg, and I've got a place in Columbia. There's no way I'm going there for any reason."

Chapter 51

The toys in his playpen became too boring. Looking for more adventure, LeKendrick pulled himself up by the railing and began surveying the living room area. Kadrece was busy washing dishes and clothes. Suddenly, there was a loud thud which startled her. She looked over her shoulder. She rushed over to check on LeKendrick, who was sprawled out next to the playpen. Only then, he began crying as she inspected him for any bumps or bruises.

"Ah-ha, I told you about trying to climb out of your playpen," she said, cradling him. "You're going to learn yet at your age that a hard head makes a soft behind." She then patted him there and placed him back inside his playpen.

As she headed back towards the kitchen, she reacted, "Now what?" She did not expect anyone to be calling her.

"Hello?" she answered, sounding preoccupied.

"Is that the way you talk to everyone?"

LeKendrick began making noise again. Kadrece felt she had no choice but to scoop him out of the playpen and hold him while she tried chatting with Kamryn, whom she had not spoken to in nearly a month.

"How is everything?" her sister inquired. "Sounds like you've got your hands full."

"That's an understatement."

Kadrece glanced down at her son and allowed herself to digress in thought for a moment. She had not heard from nor seen Garner in more than two months. It was increasingly apparent to her that he would not be around for the child's first Christmas holiday.

"Well, I'll have you to know that I'm thinking about leaving my job and starting my own business," noted Kamryn, an eighteen-year DeKalb County employee. "But I'm just waiting my time."

"What do you have in mind doing?"

"I don't know just yet. But you can best be sure that I'm sick and tired of being sick and tired of going to where I work. That's for sure. The only thing that I'm grateful about is that I still have a job for now."

Kamryn heard LeKendrick blurt out something in the background. It dawned on her that she had not seen her nephew since the summer. "Doesn't he have a birthday coming up soon?" she asked.

"Sure do. Next month on the twenty-sixth."

"He should be walking, if not pretty close?"

"He's been walking pretty much on his own for almost two months, but right now he likes to pull on things and try climbing over playpen railings like just before you called."

"Are you sure that I didn't catch you at a bad time?" Kamryn inquired.

Sucking her teeth, Kadrece answered, "These days, any time is a busy time for me."

The burden of dealing with Garner's estrangement from her had been bothersome. She had managed to keep the nosey ones at Mission Grove at a distance because she had a built-in excuse that Garner often worked weekends in Columbia this time of the year. But she wondered how much longer could she withhold information from her family?

"I don't want you to think that I'm trying to meddle in your business, but is everything all right?" Kamryn asked. "You just don't sound like yourself."

Kadrece remained quiet for several seconds. "It's about as good as it's going to get. I mean—"

"Are you and Garner getting along?"

She reacted with a long sigh. "Everything is fine if you allow for the fact that Garner's in Columbia doing whatever he pleases while I'm here in Spartanburg working and taking care of his child."

Kamryn reminded Kadrece that maintaining a long-distance marriage was a choice she made. "Has he been busy with work?" she inquired.

"I don't know what he's doing right now," Kadrece answered. "And I really don't care any more. But I've got something in store for him real soon."

"I really can't believe Garner is acting this way as you say he is. Don't tell me. You think he's messing around?"

Kadrece hissed. "I thought I married someone who wanted to spend the rest of his life with me, and that apparently isn't the way he wants things to be." She paused to instruct LeKendrick to be quiet.

"What happened? I thought you two were doing well," Kamryn reacted, closing her eyes.

"All I will say is that if he thinks that he can do whatever he pleases, and then come back here and think that I'm going to go along with it, he's got another thing to deal with."

"Have y'all tried counseling?"

Kadrece reacted with a sarcastic laugh. "Garner doesn't listen to anybody. So how would you expect for him to listen to somebody with a godly perspective?" She went on to explain that she once brought up McBride's name and Garner had a fit, and that he wanted no part with the pastor.

"No he didn't?"

"That's not even half of it."

"I'd rather not hear about it," Kamryn reacted. She then related to her sister that she and Mitchell constantly fought for much of the first five years they were married. "You know how upset I used to be. You know I also said all along that there's always going to be ups and downs in any marriage, but the important thing is that both want to make things work."

Nodding her head, Kadrece shifted LeKendrick from lying on his back to stomach. She stroked his head. Sighing, she answered, "Kamryn, I feel like that I've already cried myself out with Garner. I'm just hoping and praying that he'll come to his senses but . . ."

"What?"

Kadrece described to Kamryn that Garner had all of a sudden become withdrawn, but that she didn't make any issue out of it because she understood men liked having time to themselves. She sighed again. There was exasperation in her voice.

"At first I was upset. I tried calling him at home and at work, but he'd yell at me and hang up. I begged him not to do this to his family. All he'd say is 'I'm a grown man and I can do what I damn well please.' Then he'd hang up on me."

Sensing her sister's displeasure, Kadrece implored Kamryn not to mention anything to her parents or the rest of her siblings.

"Look, I can't tell you what to do," Kamryn said, "but I do hope that you two will work things out."

When Kadrece returned from spending the holidays with her family in Atlanta, she felt things had gone too far with Garner's self-imposed exile from her. She was aware, at least publicly, what he was doing by virtue of keeping up with him on the station's website. Beyond that, she was not convinced that he had kept his dick inside his pants during this separation.

Yet in a gesture of goodwill, she felt he deserved a final opportunity, and for LeKendrick's sake. She breathed a sigh of relief that she was able to catch him at the station.

"Hello, Garner?"

He initially froze at recognizing Kadrece's voice. He remained silent for several moments. "What is it you want?" he finally answered, speaking in a slow and agitated tone.

"Look, sweetheart, neither of us is perfect. We've both made mistakes in this marriage. Let's try reconciling."

Leaning back in his office chair, Garner reacted with raised eyebrows. "Mistakes? I know you didn't say that." He exhaled loudly through his nostrils. "Hold on. Where are you?"

"At my office," she answered. "You do still know that number?"

Garner stared at his computer terminal contemplating whether he should keep his word with her. His initial thought was to rip into her again and tell her not to call him at his job ever again, and if she had anything else to tell him let it be through his attorney.

For a moment, too, he allowed himself to think of the better times that once existed between them leading up to them marrying. Those were rather faint and distorted.

"Garner, you are there?"

"I'll call you right back."

Humph.

No fucking way that I'm calling her. That was my mistake three years ago. I never should have returned her e-mail.

Garner got up from his desk and visited the bathroom. On several occasions whenever he'd pass by a bathroom mirror he would stop and just stare into it. He'd question himself as to how he could be so damned stupid for allowing Kadrece back into the picture. Forget the fact that she had cheated on him with Levi Harriston. He figured the legal system should vindicate him for that.

Maybe it's time that I start seeing somebody new. I deserve something better after this. But what would I accomplish? Chances are that I'll end up doing something again that I'll regret like with this bitch Kadrece.

Sighing, he closed his eyes and wished that everything would change ever so seamless once he opened them again. Maybe that might work in a cartoon. Moments later, he returned to his desk.

Kadrece did not take too well that Garner brushed her off. It was now 4:45 p.m. She was barely able to concentrate on her work because she brooded and fumed over him for much of the afternoon. If this marriage were to end, she wanted it to be on her terms rather than his. Then all of her actions would be justified.

So she jerked her phone from the receiver. She took a deep breath before dialing. The phone picked up on the third ring.

"Garner, you said that you would get back with me. My work day is almost over, and I've got to go pick up LeKendrick from day care in a few minutes."

There was no response.

"You are listening to me, aren't you?"

Exhaling loudly, Garner finally replied, "Why should I? It should be obvious to you that I don't want to have anything to do with you. So why don't you just do the same thing."

"I call myself swallowing my pride by getting in contact with you to say that I apologize for whatever has pissed you off, and maybe you might find it within yourself to forgive and forget and we'd try making this marriage work once again."

"Hah!"

She rubbed her temple and leaned back in her office chair. "You know what, Garner? I think everyone was right. You were never husband material, let alone father material in the first place. LeKendrick may not be able to talk just yet, but his actions say that he misses you. I hope that means something—"

Glancing up towards the ceiling, Garner began to playfully bob his head. He then glanced down at his computer screen. It was 4:50 p.m.; he still had a five o'clock staff meeting to attend.

"Well, Kadrece, you caught me at a bad time," he replied. "I really don't have anything to say."

The phone clicked.

There was no reaction. Kadrece calmly nodded and placed the phone back on the hook. She gathered her purse, logged off the computer, and turned off the lights before she exited her office. Once she reached her car, she removed her wedding and engagement rings and stuffed them inside her purse. Then, on her drive over to the day care facility, she contacted Levi and invited him over to her place for the evening. The following morning, she stopped by Spartanburg County's courthouse on Magnolia Street in Spartanburg.

Chapter 52

Three weeks later

Y*ou've got to be fucking kidding me?* Garner exclaimed on his way back from the mailbox. He held the envelope closer to his face, making sure that his eyes had not deceived him. "I know this bitch didn't do this!" He looked both to his right and left hoping that nobody saw him before he entered his car.

With each breath he felt even more dazed by the realization that Kadrece had filed child support on him. The letter summoned him to attend a meeting in three weeks and he was to bring his most recent pay information.

This bitch is trying to cover up her tracks by painting me as the irresponsible party!

Still stunned by what he'd just opened, he contemplated tossing aside the letter from Spartanburg County's Family Court office for child support enforcement, but then raised it back up at eye level. He shook his head and scrambled for his cell phone. He dialed Candace Mercer's number, but cursed after it went to her message system. He did not leave one for her.

He put his car into gear and coasted back to his condominium. Hell, he probably could have run there faster than he drove. After setting the parking break and turning off the engine, he searched for Kadrece's entry in his cell phone. Thoughts of Levi and Kadrece, Kadrece and Levi, and then Levi, Kadrece, and LeKendrick fueled the inferno in his mind.

When Kadrece answered, Garner yelled, "Just what in the fuck you think you're doing?"

She nodded as though she had gained the upper hand. It was a moment worth savoring. "Oh, yes, by the way, I did get your certified package from Richland County . . . But to answer your question, I have every right to do what I did. You left me and your son, and now I'm seeing to it that you take care of him. I could care less if you ever do anything for me." She looked over her right shoulder and monitored LeKendrick's playfulness in his car seat.

"So, this is your idea of retaliating?" Garner retorted. He shook his head in bewilderment. *Just how in the hell could she be so fucking delusional to think she can get over on me?* he thought.

Sighing, he composed himself to say, "You won't get away with this. I promise you!"

"Well, I'll let a judge decide on that."

"Go fuck yourself!" he yelled, before hanging up.

Kadrece remarked in a deliberate tone to herself. "I . . . don't . . . think . . . so, asshole." Then she placed her phone back in her purse and carried LeKendrick inside her place.

Chapter 53

The customer is always right. No, the only thing that matters is money in the cash register. This is what Levi kept reminding himself as he dealt with a middle-aged woman, who struggled between buying a bedroom set or living room set, or both. While he awaited her decision, he noticed a buzzing going off on his hip. He always made it a practice never to stop to answer his cell phone while he was with a customer.

"I think I'm just going to talk it over with my husband before I decide," she said.

"Well, bring him by, as well. You have my card and you know when I'm here," Levi responded. "All we want is an opportunity to earn your business."

After she left the store, Levi breathed a sigh of relief and immediately reached for his hip holster. He walked towards the back of the store, ensuring that he was not in view.

The text message read,

> **Need to talk to you TODAY. Call me when you get this.**

At first, Levi smiled because Kadrece had sent him the message. Then he brooded for a moment. That had not been like her to send him a message in the early afternoon. There had not been any disagreements between them, he thought. Nor she had any reason to complain that him paying her $250 a month in cash towards LeKendrick. So he informed Patrick McShane, one of the salesmen whom he supervised, that he was taking a fifteen-minute break.

"Attorney Kendr ... I mean, Attorney Davis. May I help you?"

Leaning back in his driver's seat, Levi answered, "I called you as soon as I could. What's going on?"

"Your timing's good. You caught me as I was heading out to an appointment," she answered, stopping to check her watch. "The reason why I'm calling you is that I received a certified package from Garner. He's filed for divorce in Richland County."

Levi's eyes widened. He stopped short of grinning. "Are you all right with that?" he queried her.

"Oh, I'm fine with that. I sort of figured that he was up to something since he refused to talk to me whenever I'd try calling him." The door chime went off in the background. "I'm supposed to respond to this petition for divorce. But before that happens, I need to see what's going to happen with the child support order that I filed on him." She took off driving in the direction of downtown Greenville.

"Wait a minute, why are you filing child support when I'm already giving you money?"

"Would you rather that I had filed those papers on you?" She paused, allowing her words to sink in. When he did not respond, she continued, "I thought you'd see it my way."

Levi still was not sure what to make of Kadrece. It still seemed odd that she would be so bold as to have two men paying her. "He really must have pissed you off. That's all I can think of—"

Kadrece shook her head. "You're missing the point. Entirely." She paused to make a lane change. "I'm back ... Levi, I don't regret marrying Garner. What I regret is that we just never understood each other in what we wanted out of this marriage. There were things that I wanted that he didn't, and there were things that he wanted that I didn't—like this divorce."

Her words left Levi pondering just how their own relationship had developed to where it was. Early in her pregnancy, she encouraged him to remain involved with Carnette. She even went as far as to suggest him that he try convincing Carnette into having sex with him, but with some stipulations: He could not indulge into any oral sex, anal sex, nor could he ejaculate inside of her.

After some intense lobbying, Carnette actually gave in to his desires. She thought having sex with him might lead to them getting married. She broached the topic with Levi on a couple of occasions but he evaded her. Then she noticed the way Levi looked so different whenever she saw him around Kadrece and LeKendrick at church. One week she said, "Been taking care of business?"

"I'm always taking business," he retorted.

The following week, Carnette appeared with one of Mission Grove's ministers, Frank Chandler. It was not long before her relationship with Levi fizzled out. She and Chandler now attend another church in Greer.

"Sometimes, I don't know how I got caught up into all this with you," Levi said, laughing.

"Because you love eating and fucking this sweet chocolate pussy. That's why."

"You've got a point," he said. "But you know what I'd like to know?"

"What's that?"

"Do you think hubby knows anything about us?"

Kadrece first warned Levi that she was not far from her appointment. Then she said, "I'm not sure what he knows. But that might explain why he's not been around for the past three months."

"Well, I've not had any strange phone calls or somebody following me like a lunatic," Levi said, stopping to yawn. He also broke out into laughter.

"Why are you laughing?"

"I can't help it," he said. "It's like he's never had a clue all of this time. I find it amazing . . . well, maybe not."

Kadrece reminded Levi that she was the one who allowed him to fuck her. "I'm going to say this before I get off the phone, Levi. I don't have any regrets about being involved with you, and I definitely don't have any regrets about having LeKendrick. I hope you feel the same way."

When Garner entered Spartanburg County's Family Court for his eleven o'clock interview, he hoped that Kadrece might not show up and there would be no support order to be enforced.

Shit, I can't believe she's actually going through with this lie . . .

Dressed in a navy blue business suit, the court was very much her element; she showed no contrition towards him. It incensed him even more when he happened to catch a glimpse of LeKendrick. He snorted and stared at the carpet. There was no way in hell that child could have ever bore any traits similar to him, he thought. He made every effort not to acknowledge her while they waited.

Forty minutes passed before he and Kadrece heard their names. Reluctantly, he stood and began a slow procession towards the corridor that led to the office cubicles in back while Kadrece was quick to gather LeKendrick and their belongings. By the time they reached the door, she looked back at him.

"You know this didn't have to happen," she said.

He balled his fists, thinking to himself, *I'm going to do everything I can to make this not happen.*

"You're right. This didn't have to happen," he retorted in a tone that only she could hear him. "This is a waste of my fucking time."

With each step, the rage and anxiety grew within Garner. He was on the brink of going ballistic having to sit next to her in the caseworker's cubicle.

"Mr. Davis, I'm Trace Chaffee," he said. "I need your pay information, and yours, too, Mrs. Davis."

Garner was agape. This had to be a fucking nightmare. Slowly, he glanced over at Kadrece who searched through her folder for her information. Then LeKendrick began smiling at Garner. It took all of him not to slap her.

"Mr. Davis, I'll need your pay information," Chaffee reminded him.

"Why do you need pay information from somebody who is not this child's father?" Garner responded; his voice was more than agitated.

Kadrece snapped her head in his direction, looking intently at him. He caught a glimpse of her staring at him. He turned to her then at Chaffee. "I said it. This child is not mine. And I do have proof."

Chaffee folded his hands, responding, "Mr. Davis, my job is to determine the correct amount of child support you will be ordered to pay unless told otherwise. The 'otherwise', in this case, is the judge, and I'm not a judge.

"Now, Mr. Davis, do you have any proof of income?"

"What I've got is proof this child isn't mine!" Garner retorted, flipping a copy of his DNA test at Chaffee.

Chaffee did not bother to look at it, but slid the papers back towards Garner.

"Wait a minute, so I'm being drug in here by this . . . bitch," Garner reacted, looking at Kadrece, "so that you people can take money out of my goddamn paycheck for another man's child?"

Chaffee exhaled deeply. "You can either provide me the information that I've requested for today, or we can find it through our system. It's your choice." He returned to sifting through Kadrece's information.

"I can't believe this. I'm being summoned here because *she files* for child support. Essentially, you don't bother to ask whether the child is mine or not." Garner paused and snorted. "And I bet this goes on everyday with others."

He stood up, yelling, "Fuck this. And fuck both of you!" He then pointed in Kadrece's direction. "You know what you're doing is wrong, and you're just sitting there like you're some fucking victim!"

She offered no response to his outburst.

"Mr. Davis, I'm going to have to call security if you keep on like this," Chaffee warned him.

"You might as well call them because I refuse to give you any fucking information!"

LeKendrick began crying. Meanwhile, Chaffee scribbled a court date and time on a card and handed it to Garner. "You'll just have to find out what you'll be paying Mrs. Davis at your court hearing." Kadrece scrambled to hand LeKendrick his drink cup. She then looked up, glaring at Garner.

"Why don't you shove that card up her ass," Garner said before he stormed out of the cubicle, "before I put my foot up it instead!"

Chaffee moved to pick up the phone.

"You don't have to. I'm out of here!" Garner snapped.

As an attorney, Kadrece reasoned that her job has always been to present as compelling and convincing of an argument as possible before a judge. Along the way, she's to use the legal system to her advantage. And if it meant finding the loopholes or distorting legal precedent, so be it.

Shrugging off her guilt, she got up from her sofa and headed towards the kitchen for a glass of wine. On her way back she stopped off in LeKendrick's room. He was fast asleep. She paused to take a sip from her Pinot Noir. Placing it on the dresser nearby, she returned to her son's bed, bent over, and kissed him on the forehead. A tear slipped from her eye. All that mattered at that moment was she would have done it all over again the same way if it resulted in her sharing her love and affection with someone whom she birthed.

Well, maybe not the exact way, but close. She thought Garner could have made her choice easier had he been a more willing participant.

After leaving LeKendrick's room, she deduced that Levi wasn't a bad person for companionship. With Garner's divorce hearing slated in about four weeks, she figured there was still hope that she could cover her tracks.

"Levi, how was your day?" she asked as soon as he answered.

"I'm glad you called. You know I'm always better when I hear your voice."

She took a sip from her glass. "I had an interesting day. Garner showed up for the meeting," she said, pausing to chortle. "I was not surprised at the way he acted."

Levi raised his eyebrows. "How was that?"

"What do you think?" she answered. "He called me every bitch that he could think of. Oh, by the way, to answer your question he knows that you and I have been seeing each other."

"Did he really say that to you?" Levi reacted; his heart began beating faster.

"Well, not exactly in those words, but he made it known that Le-Kendrick isn't his son."

"How does he know?"

"Apparently, he managed to get a DNA test. I don't know how or where he did it. But the man at the courthouse didn't even look at the results."

"Do you really think he knows anything about us?"

"That, I don't know—"

"That's all right. You don't have to tell me anything else. I guess I'd be the same way if it had happened to me."

"Levi, I've spent many sleepless nights thinking about the way I've done things in my life. I'm no saint. Not by a long shot."

She had a flashback to the courthouse when Garner's eyes bulged, his face reddened, and the rage resonated from his voice.

"I still think he's a whore," she hissed. "I just stopped worrying about it."

"So are you saying that you're kicking me to the curb?" An intercom went off in the background.

"Are you at the store?" Kadrece asked.

"Yeah, a grocery store."

"To answer your question, Levi, I'm not kicking you to the curb," she said. "I wish you would stop asking me that."

She took another sip from her wine glass. Sighing, she went on to say, "Levi, I need to get some casework done. But I just wanted to let you know what happened today."

He was now at the cash register. "If you need any company, you know where to call."

Chapter 54

Thoughts of vindication were what Garner concentrated on when he woke up on an unseasonably cold April morning. This was better than just saying it was a day that the Lord had made. His reason for rejoicing would be that it was his day in court.

He had already primed himself that if Kadrece showed up he would not react the same way that he did in Spartanburg. The court's recognition that his marriage was over and it nullifying Kadrece's request for child support based on the adultery that he could prove made for a tidy daily double in the making.

When he met with Candace Mercer at Richland County's courthouse on Assembly Street, even she seemed confident. Thanks to a favor owed by a private investigator, she managed to gain access to Kadrece's cell phone records. The same private eye also provided her with photos of Kadrece, Levi, and LeKendrick spending time together on several occasions in Greenville.

"I can't see her coming up with a reasonable defense today," Candace told Garner as they waited for their case on the docket.

"She's a smart attorney," Garner responded. "I wouldn't be surprised if she had maybe one trick up her sleeve."

He reminded Mercer about the $1,265 a month that Spartanburg County's family court ordered him to pay Kadrece starting in two weeks. She told him not to worry about it.

He shook his head, lamenting, "A woman can claim anyone to be the father of her child, and the child support system appears to go along with it. Then it's up to the man to prove otherwise—"

"There is some truth to that, Garner, but this is not the time to discuss that," Mercer said.

Moments later, a relatively short man wearing a dark gray suit walked into the waiting area and announced Garner's name. He looked around, but he was stunned that Kadrece had not showed up. He looked over at Candace and queried, "Is that good? Like when the policeman doesn't show up when you're fighting a ticket?"

She exhaled loudly. "All I will say is that the papers were properly served. I made sure of that." They then walked together into the courtroom.

Within five minutes of presenting information before Stroman F. Winchester, Garner noticed the judge was ostensibly critical of everything that Mercer mentioned when she argued for his child support order be dropped since Kadrece's adultery was proven.

Winchester asked, "Is not Mr. Davis' name on the child's birth certificate?"

"It is, your Honor. But that was under the presumption the child was his."

"As you know, the Court recognizes that you can't un-ring a bell."

Mercer did her best to remain composed. "Your Honor, we also cannot perpetuate a lie, which is not in the best interests of anyone. Mr. Davis has clearly demonstrated he is not the child's father." She glanced down at Garner, who clenched his teeth.

Winchester scribbled on his note pad, and then he glanced at something from his computer screen just off to his right. He returned his attention to Mercer. "Counselor, it is not the Court's role to legislate society's ills. The Court must act in what is in the child's best interests." He leaned back in his chair.

"Your Honor, while there is no statue of limitations when paternity is questioned," Mercer insisted, "we feel we are reasonably within bounds."

"Counselor, you are familiar with presumption of paternity?"

"I am."

"And in the state of South Carolina there is no recourse."

"Your Honor," she pleaded. "We're talking about paternity fraud here. If this were fraud committed in any other context, there would be recourse!"

"The Court finds that adultery was established in this marriage; therefore, the petition for divorce is granted. The Court finds that there was a presumption of paternity; the Court also upholds the motion for child support filed in Spartanburg County. You must pay $1,265 starting on the first of the month."

Garner's eyes bulged. "Say what?"

Winchester cast a rigid glare at Garner, pointing his pen at him. "Your request for nullifying child support has been denied."

"That's not right!" Garner yelled.

"Mr. Davis, I have made my decision."

"Your decision is wrong!" Garner yelled again, pounding his fist on the desk; he then stood up, prompting the court's bailiff to be on alert. He pointed in Winchester's direction. "You'd rather support a lie than to adjudicate the truth, huh?"

"This is nothing but extortion!"

The bailiff walked over to Garner's table; his hands were at his gun holster. "Sir, please vacate the court or I'll have to arrest you."

"Come on, Garner," Mercer said.

Outside the courtroom, Garner felt like kicking the nearest trash can, and more. Mercer tried calming him. "I'm sorry that we had to run into an asshole of a judge. But I hope you do remember me telling you what you might be up against?"

He shook his head in disgust. "Un-ringing a fucking bell, hmmm?" He balled his fist. Thoughts of driving to Spartanburg and exacting justice vigilante style was a suitable consolation.

She shifted her case folder from her right hand to her left. "Garner, you can appeal this, but I must tell you that it's going to be very difficult. There's nothing within South Carolina's statutes that really allows a husband or ex-husband any chance at having a case like this overturned." She advised him that he had ten days to file his appeal.

He walked off, mumbling, "Fuck!"

Within seconds of exiting the courthouse, Garner took a deep breath and exhaled loudly. Then he reached for his cellular phone, punching in a number. The caller answered on the fourth ring.

"You fucking bitch! I should bash your fucking head in with one of my baseball bats if I ever see your corrupt ass, or that ape looking bald-headed motherfucker who's really that child's father!"

Kadrece blinked her eyes before she responded in a calm, deliberate tone. "I take it your plea for divorce was granted." She began shuffling through her paperwork seemingly unaffected by Garner's rage.

"You goddamn right it was. But you know why I'm calling!"

"I might, but that doesn't really matter. Right now, I would advise you to be responsible for the first time in your life." She then hung up on him.

Enraged, Garner dialed Kadrece's number again. She answered on the second ring.

"Attorney Kendricks-Davis . . ."

"I hope God strikes your ass dead!"

Sucking her teeth, she felt embolden to say, "If I were you, I'd stop before you regret saying anything else. Now have a good life!"

Garner's head pulsated as if it would erupt like a volcano. He vented some of his rage by hurling his cell phone against the wall inside the city's parking garage. It was of little satisfaction that it disintegrated upon impact.

Chapter 55

D *id I ever really have a marriage?* Garner asked himself.

The answer was a thousand times no. He had long since determined that allowing Kadrece back into his life had gotten him into this pile of shit, which could have been avoided had he not been so damned smitten by her sexually.

He realized that Miriam saw more than what he was too enraptured to recognize for himself. But that's what happens when pussy was freely thrown in his direction and it was too good beyond description.

Even worse, he never would have fathomed the woman he'd known longer than any of the rest was so ruthless. Now of all the cruelest ironies, he surmised to himself that a person who was born out of similar circumstances was an obligator of it according to the legal system.

It infuriated him each time that he expended any mental energy about being shammed, and a reminder of it occurred every two weeks when he saw more than six hundred dollars taken out of his paycheck before he saw it. For all his research in the ensuing weeks following his divorce hearing about paternity fraud, there was little hope for his situation. He lived in the wrong state and his timing was horrible. South Carolina's still among thirty states that had yet to enact any changes to the archaic assumption that what is born in a marriage is considered of a marriage.

The presumption of fucking paternity . . . you can't un-ring a goddamned bell . . . Son of a bitch!

The spring sports season was nearing its conclusion. The only local team that was still active was the nationally-ranked Chanticleers baseball program, which was poised to compete in the College World Series in Nebraska.

Garner had planned a meeting with Chuck Redfearn to discuss the logistics of traveling to Omaha.

"Close the door behind you, please," Redfearn requested, motioning him inside.

"Sure." Garner then sat in the chair directly in front of Redfearn's desk. "Did we get the approval to travel with the baseball team? I've got to put in our request for credentials no later than tomorrow afternoon."

Redfearn fold his hands, placing them on the desk. He glanced down at the paper given to him by the station's corporate management. "The fact that we're doing quite well in our ratings is a good selling point, but I'm sure you know there is more to getting people to approve travel money these days."

"I see. But we're talking about a program that's won back-to-back national titles within the past five years. This should be a no-brainer."

After he changed his posture in his office chair, Redfearn also picked up a pen on his desk and began toying with it.

"Garner," he said, pausing. "The station's not doing as well with its advertising revenue."

"Okay, but there's a lot of places saying that."

"I know. We've managed to bear much of the economy's impact over the past couple of years, and I've managed to shield the newsroom from many of corporate's decisions involving staffing."

"That's true, but we've been affected other ways. We've not been able to travel like in the past," Garner responded. "I also know we've

able to order any new equipment, but I figure that as long as it gets the job done why argue?"

Redfearn pursed his lips before commenting, "Garner, I'm letting you know that we've already decided not to renew your contract. This is purely a business decision."

He swallowed hard. His contract was due for renegotiation in six months. Coupled with having to pay Kadrece in what he had dubbed as legalized extortion money, this was not the news that he expected to hear.

"How does a station decide to get rid of someone who's giving them number one ratings?" Garner asked.

"I come in here expecting to receive word that we're traveling to Omaha, only to find out that . . . Humph, nothing surprises me with the way things been going on in my life lately."

"I'm sorry, Garner. It was out of my hands."

Garner glanced off to his left before he resumed eye contact with Redfearn. "So how long do I have here?"

"We'd love for you to finish out your contract, but we think it would be in everyone's best interests if we just buy you out of your remaining months."

Mentally, he calculated that six month's pay meant that he'd probably receive a check for roughly $27,500 after taxes, including unused leave time that was due to him.

"Shit, in everyone's best interests. I've heard that term," he scoffed, shaking his head. "So we're talking like today, huh?"

Redfearn nodded his head. "I see—"

Garner stood up and extended his hand out to Redfearn, who nervously shook it.

"You know what?" he said, looking Redfearn directly in his eyes. "I remember my mother once telling someone she worked for that she came there looking for a job, and she'd leave looking for one." He turned and began walking out of Redfearn's office.

"Garner—"

He looked over his shoulder.

"I'll allow you all the time you need to gather your personal items after you've gone over to personnel, okay?"

Garner did not bother to speak with anyone on his way out of WCAE, nor did he bother to take anything with him. Not even the certificates of recognition, award plaques that he'd earned, or photos that he'd taken during his five-plus years at the station.

On his way home, Garner pulled his car over in a Hardee's parking lot just before the Garner's Ferry Road and I-77 intersection.

"Attorney Kadrece Davis—"

"We don't have an Attorney Davis," the receptionist answered. "We have an attorney Kadrece Kendricks."

"Yes, may I speak with her?"

"Is she expecting your call?"

Humph, she's already changed her name.

A surge of rage began to overtake him. As a canine with his ears pinned back, Garner was more than eager to tear away at his ex.

"Attorney Kendricks, may I help you?"

"Yes, you can," he answered, angrily.

Kadrece easily recognized his voice. "Listen, Garner, I didn't stand in the way of you getting a divorce. You need to go on with your life."

He reacted with bugged eyes. "How in the hell can you tell someone to go on with their life when you've tried ruining it?" He waited for her to respond, but she didn't. "You never changed. You fucked around on me. Now I've gotta pay for your whoring around? That isn't right!" The thought of $1,265 a month was etched indelibly in his mind.

Exhaling in annoyance, Kadrece retorted, "Who's going to believe you? Life's not always fair. So deal with it."

"Go to hell!"

The phone clicked.

"Motherfucking bitch!"

Chapter 56

More than a year later

Life seemed to be worth a damn once again. Garner's new employer, WCLT Channel 47, an ABC affiliate in the Charlotte, North Carolina market, informed him that his contract with the station was renewed for another year with a mutual option for a second.

He had stability in his life once again even if it meant making less money as a weekend sports anchor, a back-up role to the lead sports anchor position.

Hell, for the first time in his adult life, he was even content being alone and not pursuing any women. Besides, he needed all of his spare money to survive after child support was taken from his paycheck.

His attempts at seeking redemption and relief from the legal system—appealing the initial support order and for a reduction in payments—were summarily denied by the presiding judges. It cost him roughly $4,500 in legal fees during his futile battle on top of the nearly $20,000 that he'd already paid to Kadrece.

Out of extreme bitterness and indignation, Garner decided to do something that he had resisted doing. He drove over to Spartanburg from his Gastonia, North Carolina apartment and spied out the Mission Grove parking lot for any sighting of Kadrece and Levi. He spent about a half-hour observing people entering the church building before he noticed Kadrece walking side-by-side with Levi, who held LeKendrick's hand. He was tempted confront them, but he drove off.

During the week, Garner drafted a three-page exposé that detailed Kadrece's adultery and her unscrupulous act of exploiting him through the legal system. He also enclosed a copy of his blood test and pictures of Kadrece and Levi that was used as evidence in his divorce hearing.

That next Sunday morning, he donned an olive colored Italian suit with matching alligator shoes that he had not worn since he was dating Kadrece. Prior to leaving Gastonia, he stopped off at the city's main post office and mailed three manila envelopes.

When he arrived at Mission Grove, gone were the bitter thoughts of him marrying Kadrece in the same place, the memories of that church serving as the impetus of him pursuing DNA testing, and later his divorcing her.

He waited until about 11:20 before he entered the church service. He figured they would be at least halfway through another of Mc-Bride's pitiful sermons. He found an empty space among the dark burgundy seat pews in the back near the double doors. Nobody seemed to recognize him.

As McBride rambled through his message titled *Don't Keep Your Frog Another Day*, Garner spotted Levi and Kadrece, in a stylish black pants suit with a leopard print blouse that she once wore when they were married, sitting near the front.

What a fucking joke, he mused.

When the service ended, Garner waited for the parishioners to file out. Only one person stopped to greet him. They exchanged pleasantries—neither he nor Garner knew each other.

He noticed that Kadrece had already exited through the sanctuary's side door. He presumed that LeKendrick might have been in the church nursery. So, he kept his eyes fixated upon Levi, who wore a burgundy suit with a gray shirt and tie that included both colors as an accent, as he worked his way towards the front. His timing was great.

While Levi chatted with McBride, he took a seat on the front row not far from where they stood.

"Well Pastor, I just praise the Lord for you," Levi said. "I really feel your message was for me."

"Bless you, brother. Bless you."

Garner smirked rather audibly.

When Levi later turned to his right, his heart began racing when he recognized Garner glaring at him. He managed a weak smile as Garner stood up.

"So you decided to join us today?" Levi calmly said.

Garner spoke in a tone that only Levi could hear. "Don't give me that brother-in-the-Lord shit, you sorry chicken shit hypocrite bastard!" Countless of times he had rehearsed a moment as similar as this, but would it unfold the way he had longed for it?

Levi's eyes widened and his mouth was agape, an obvious *how could you say that inside the Lord's place* reaction.

"Yeah, that's right. I said it," Garner sneered. He then pressed a manila envelope into Levi's chest, causing him to take a step back. He also pointed at him. "I hope your dumb ass knows how to read."

Levi attempted to walk past him, but Garner grabbed him by his right bicep; the tightness of Garner's grasp halted him in mid-stride. He spoke into Levi's ear, "I also have one for your bitch, too."

At that moment, Kadrece spotted them. She told LeKendrick to sit down on one of the seat pews.

"Garner, what are you doing here?" Her shriek caught McBride's attention. A few other after-church stragglers observed with gaped mouths as the drama unfolded. Nobody left the sanctuary.

"What am I doing here?" he repeated her remark. He tossed the other manila envelope at her feet. "I'm here to share the truth. Now, both of you deal with it!" He then glanced over in McBride's direction, pointing down at Kadrece's feet.

"There's one coming in the mail for you."

Next, he cut a glaring eye at Kadrece. "And there's one for your parents, and one for your law partners."

Annoyed, Levi shook loose from Garner, curling his upper lip at him.

"Like, what you're going to do?" Garner challenged him.

"Garner, Levi!" Kadrece screamed.

"What is going on here?" McBride also yelled.

"Why don't you shut the fuck up," Garner yelled back at McBride. "Let them tell you!"

Levi looked over at Kadrece and then at Garner, waving him off. Then he mumbled, "I don't know what your problem is. That child is your spitting image. You just can't accept the truth—"

He managed taking only a step when Garner cold-cocked him with crushing right to his temple that sent him crumbling forward onto the carpet. A loud ringing went off in Levi's head. He was not fully cogent of Kadrece's screaming.

"You're not only a stupid, ignorant motherfucker; you're fucking blind!" Garner said, standing over him.

"Garner, stop it," she cried. "Leave us alone!"

Meanwhile, McBride patted his suit pocket for his cell phone. "I need to call 9-1-1. I'm not putting up with any of this in my church!" Then he rushed to Levi's side.

Garner reacted, "Is that right?"

He took a couple of steps towards Kadrece. Her eyes widened as she remarked, "I know you're not going to—"

Stopping just shy of her, Garner gestured towards her with his index finger. "You're right. I'm not going to knock the living shit out of you like I promised you that I would after the last time in court. But one thing I will do today is this." He paused and glanced down at Levi, snarling at him. "I'll kick you in the fucking mouth if you even as much as flinch."

"You better leave this church—now!" McBride reacted.

Garner scoffed at McBride. "I told you to shut the fuck up!" Then he turned his attention back to Kadrece.

"Some things never change. You were a conniving whore when I met you, and you'll always be a conniving whore . . . What bothers me is not that you were fucking around with this stupid, ignorant motherfucker," he said, pointing down at Levi. "It's the legal system that allows you and others to get off with committing paternity fraud, and that same system merely tells people like me, tough shit, and pay up . . . Nobody wants to deal with that. Nobody. The judges, the politicians, and to some extent, not even the lawyers. But it's more politically sexy to build a multi-billion dollar enterprise that forces people to pay, and continue to pay, for the other person's wrong doing."

He paused, shook his head, and smirked. "But you know what? What goes around comes around, baby, because all of you motherfuckers in here deserve each other!"

"Just leave, Garner," Kadrece screamed at him. "Just leave us alone!"

"Whatever, bitch."

He snapped his finger as he began walking away from Kadrece. Those that remained inside Mission Grove were quick to avoid him while he left the property. He purposefully drove away without even looking into his rear-view mirror.

Minutes later, Garner was northbound on I-85 heading back to Gastonia. A smile enlivened his countenance once Miriam answered the phone.

"We've got a lot of catching up to do," he said, acknowledging it had been several months since she heard from him. "I've got a few days off coming up. I'll see you then."

"You know my door's always open, little boy." She took a seat at her breakfast bar and began updating him on what had been going on with her business and with his siblings and their families.

Chapter 57

Later that summer

The trip to Kansas was more than worth his while. Garner met relatives from Garrett Chaney's side of the family for the first time. The only thing missing during the trip was Miriam accompanying him. She insisted that this was something he needed to do on his own. She did contact Garrett's brother, Preston, whom she had not spoken to in nearly twenty years. It was a pleasant conversation, and it made Garner's trip much easier. Preston went out of his way to make Garner feel welcomed.

"I haven't told many people about you because I wasn't sure if your mother ever wanted that information to ever get out," noted Preston, a widower with two sons and a daughter. "You've got a lot of family who will be really glad to know who you are."

At a family barbecue in Hutchinson, a community about forty-five minutes away from Wichita, Garner heard for himself just how great of a man his father really was, and several of Garrett's surviving relatives all mentioned that he reminded them so much of his father in stature and personality.

Among his many memories from Hutchinson were those damn railroad tracks and trains that rocked his downtown hotel room each time they passed by, as well as the tumbleweeds that rolled across the streets.

As he browsed through his mail upon his return, he noticed a letter from Spartanburg County's family court. He wondered if they were after him for any arrearage. That would be shocking, he thought, considering these were same motherfuckers that took an additional five percent of his ordered amount in court costs.

He carefully opened the two-page letter dated for August 21. It stated,

> Dear Mr. Garner Davis:
>
> Enclosed is a copy of the Court Order.
>
> State Of South Carolina, Spartanburg County, Division of Child Support; Kadrece Kendricks, Plaintiff vs. Garner Davis, Defendant . . . In The Family Court Motion For Order Dismissal . . . Docket No. 07SC54-8983.
> Attorney for Plaintiff moves for dismissal based on the following reason or reasons:
> The custodial parent has requested that the defendant is no longer asked to make support payments by a statement in writing acknowledging that he is not the non-custodial parent.
> ORDER . . . There being sufficient cause shown in motion, IT IS THEREFORE ORDERED that the above case be, and hereby is, dismissed without prejudice to the rights of either party. AND SO IT IS ORDERED . . . L. Henry Beck, Presiding Judge, Judge of the Family Court, Fourth Judicial District."

Garner stared at the letter for several moments. He even checked if the document's seal was legitimate. Then he read it again. He walked over to the kitchen table, sat down, and tossed the letter to the side. Sobriety was the dominant emotion. There was no cause for celebration. Perhaps the truth did prevail, he thought; it just took longer than expected.

The experience left him wondering just how many other men never were as fortunate. According to the information he researched, the numbers were into the tens of thousands each year, and a disproportionate number of them were black males.

He closed his eyes, clasped his hands behind his head, and reclined back in his chair. It dawned upon him that Kadrece's withdrawal of child support was his only chance at freedom from a system that legally extort men in situations like his.

A Bible passage came to his memory. At the end of Job's trial, he recalled that God restored Job with twice as much as what he had before, but only after he repented and prayed for his friends.

Without any further contemplation, he prayed that there might be a change every state's legal system that might protect husbands from their wives and ex-wives that have children for men outside their marriage and the inevitably potential abuse of the system. He also prayed for Kadrece and Levi they might repent for their detestable actions.

Suggested Group Reading
Guide Questions

1. Has your impression of Garner changed or not changed after reading both *Warped Intentions* and *Presumption of Paternity*?
2. Has your impression of Miriam changed or not changed after reading both *Warped Intentions* and *Presumption of Paternity*?
3. Has your impression of Kadrece changed or not changed after reading both *Warped Intentions* and *Presumption of Paternity*?
4. Do you feel it is necessary that both spouses attend the same church?
5. Was Kadrece's motives hidden or thinly veiled with Garner?
6. Was this book helpful in any way shedding light to paternity fraud? What is your opinion about paternity fraud? Should a man pay child support for another man's child?
7. Do you feel Garner was a victim or perpetrator? Or did he bring it on himself?
8. What was your favorite scene in *Presumption of Paternity*? What was your least favorite scene?
9. Garner was seemingly at odds with church and pastors in both *Warped Intentions* and *Presumption of Paternity*. Do you feel the institution of church (religion) still serves a noble purpose or selfish one?
10. What is your opinion about maintaining a long-distance relationship or marriage?
11. Were the characters believable? Was there a character who reminded you of somebody you already know?
12. Was the plot and subplots believable? Were they predictable?
13. What is your feeling about the ending to *Presumption of Paternity*?
14. Do you think Garner finally learned any life lessons about his choice of women?

Other Books from MavLit Publishing

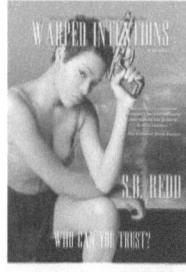

Warped Intentions
By S.B. Redd
978-1-9377051-2-1
$14.95

Temptation.com
By S.B. Redd
978-1-9377051-4-5
$14.95

Love, Song & Dance
By Jevon L. Mack
978-0-9831152-0-5
$14.95

The Shades of Passion
By S.B. Redd
978-1-9377051-5-2
$14.95

Thoughts of Life:
360 E. May St. B.H., Michigan
Birdman '313'
978-1-9377051-6-9
$14.95

www.maverick-books.com

www.ingramcontent.com/pod-product-compliance
Lightning Source LLC
Chambersburg PA
CBHW021208250626
47155CB00008B/2727